Colonel John Griffin Jr. had come to Far Hills for one reason.

To assure himself that Ellyn Sinclair and her two kids were okay.

But when he saw Ellyn up on the ridge, she looked like the sweet eighteen-year-old girl he'd never gotten out of his mind even as he'd remained friends with the woman she'd become.

With the wind whipping her hair into a froth, and that big shirt molding around her to hint at what lay beneath, Grif found himself praying.

Praying that he could check on Ellyn and the kids, find out everything was fine, then get himself away…from temptation.

He had to remember why he'd come here.

To help.

And nothing was going to stop him. Not the U.S. Army. Not Ellyn.

Not even himself…

Dear Reader,

Fall is upon us, and there's no better way to treat yourself to hours of autumn pleasure than by reading your way through these riveting romances in September's Special Edition books!

The lives and loves of the Bravo family continue with *The M.D. She Had To Marry,* in Christine Rimmer's popular CONVENIENTLY YOURS miniseries. In the page-turner *Father Most Wanted*, beloved writer Marie Ferrarella combines a witness protection program, a single dad with three daughters and an unsuspecting heroine to tell a love story you won't be able to put down. Bestselling author Peggy Webb deals with family matters of a different kind with yet another compelling Native American hero story. In *Gray Wolf's Woman* a loner finds the hearth and home he'd never realized he'd yearned for.

Lucy Gordon's poignant reunion romance, *For His Little Girl,* will sweep you away as an unexpected turn of events promises to reunite a family that was always meant to be. Janis Reams Hudson continues her Western family saga miniseries, WILDERS OF WYATT COUNTY, with *A Child on the Way,* a compelling amnesia story about a pregnant woman who ends up in the arms of another irresistible Wilder man. And Patricia McLinn's Wyoming miniseries, A PLACE CALLED HOME, continues with *At the Heart's Command,* a tale of a military hero who finally marches to the beat of his own heart as he woos his secret love.

We hope this month brings you many treasured moments of promise, hope and happy endings as Special Edition continues to celebrate Silhouette's yearlong 20th Anniversary!

All the best,

Karen Taylor Richman
Senior Editor

Please address questions and book requests to:
Silhouette Reader Service
U.S.: 3010 Walden Ave., P.O. Box 1325, Buffalo, NY 14269
Canadian: P.O. Box 609, Fort Erie, Ont. L2A 5X3

PATRICIA McLINN
AT THE HEART'S COMMAND

Published by Silhouette Books
America's Publisher of Contemporary Romance

To Carolyn, Cheryl, Kathy, Leigh, Mary Ann—true pals. And thanks, again and always, to another pal— Bill White, consultant extraordinaire on all things Wyoming.

 SILHOUETTE BOOKS

ISBN 0-373-24350-2

AT THE HEART'S COMMAND

Visit Silhouette at www.eHarlequin.com

Printed in U.S.A.

Books by Patricia McLinn

Silhouette Special Edition

Hoops #587
A New World #641
*Prelude to a Wedding #712
*Wedding Party #718
*Grady's Wedding #813
Not a Family Man #864
Rodeo Nights #904
A Stranger in the Family #959
A Stranger To Love #1098
The Rancher Meets His Match #1164
†*Lost-and-Found Groom* #1344
†*At the Heart's Command* #1350

*Wedding Series
†A Place Called Home

Harlequin Historicals

Widow Woman #417

PATRICIA McLINN

says she has been spinning stories in her head since childhood, when her mother insisted she stop reading at the dinner table. As the time came for her to earn a living, Patricia shifted her stories from fiction to fact—she became a sportswriter and editor for newspapers in Illinois, North Carolina and the District of Columbia. Now living outside Washington, D.C., she enjoys traveling, history and sports but is happiest indulging her passion for storytelling.

Chapter One

"What the hell is this, Grif?"

Colonel John Griffin Junior looked up just in time to see the bearlike figure of Brigadier General William Pulaski slap a sheaf of papers on the desk of his Pentagon office.

"That appears to be my request to take my accumulated leave, starting as soon as possible, sir."

"You're damned right that's what it is! What I want to know is *why?* Why in Sam Hill would an officer who's pegged to join the White House liaison team next month request this leave?"

A rumbling bass would have fit Pulaski's build. Instead nature had doled out a high, light voice. He made up for the lack of lower notes with volume. Plenty of volume.

"And not just a regular leave—an *extended* leave since we both know you've been storing up time like a squirrel expectin' winter!"

Grif could try to tell the general his reasons, but he hadn't reached the rank of colonel by being suicidal.

"I have the time, sir," he said without emotion. "I'd like to take it now."

General Pulaski gave him a long look that Grif returned. The older man broke the stare, sighed, then dragged the visitor's chair close, so the desk seemed as much his as Grif's, and spoke in—for him—a softer voice.

"As long as I've known you, Grif, you've taken tough assignments, but *smart* tough assignments. Always advancing. No ties, no entanglements. Just like your father."

Grif's hold tightened on the pen he'd been using to sign letters. He said nothing.

"You have a promising future—hell, more than promising." The general rubbed both hands across his bald skull. "But with this leave... What about after you've used up this time? White House liaison isn't going to stay open waiting for you, you know."

Grif met the dark eyes boring into him. "Then I'll take the next tough assignment available."

"If time to think this over might make you change your mind..."

"I'm not going to change my mind, sir."

Grif accepted that this might not be the right decision—certainly it wasn't for his Army career, but it also might not be right for reasons that had nothing to do with the Army—but he was sticking to it.

Pulaski glared. "Take your damned leave, then. I hope there's plenty of wine, women and song every damned night, because you might as well have a good time before you put your career in the—"

"Thank you, sir."

The general abruptly rose and strode out, followed by a fading trail of profanities.

Grif wondered idly how many degrees hotter those profanities would have turned if the general had known that instead of wine, women and song, there would be an eight-year-old boy, a ten-year-old girl and one woman.

None of whom could ever be his.

"Lieutenant Shaw," Grif called out the door Pulaski hadn't bothered to close. "The general forgot some papers on my desk. Take them to him. And be sure they don't go astray."

Ellyn Sinclair straightened the final pillowcase, took a clothespin out of her mouth, clipped it over fabric and line, then bent for the emptied basket. The Wyoming breeze would dry this laundry fast and for free. And up here behind Ridge House the breeze didn't stir dust; that made the climb worthwhile. She scanned the sheets flapping peacefully.

Even if her dryer fund wasn't needed to fix the car, she wouldn't have used a dryer on such a perfect day, an oasis of warmth in Wyoming's unpredictable April. Although it *would* be nice to have the option. Of course it would be nice to have a number of other things, too.

Ellyn raised her free hand and let the breeze float clean, crisp cloth against her palm. That was one worry she didn't have—that she'd overcompensate for her children losing their father by spoiling them with material things. Although she *would* make it up to them. With the most secure, loving home she could fashion. Standing on her own two feet.

Sometimes in the gray hours before dawn, she had to admit she hadn't totally banished worries about such matters as Meg and Ben bearing permanent emotional scars. But more often she reminded herself of one particularly pithy lecture from Kendra, who as both neighbor and friend, had pointed out the danger of self-fulfilling prophecies, expounded on the resilience of the human spirit in general and of Ellyn's children in particular, and wrapped up by extolling the effective double-whammy of love and common sense.

That prescription had certainly seemed to work; these past six months had been so much better than the previous six. Although... *Had* Ben been subdued? That question had popped into her mind after the kids went to bed last night and had intruded several times this morning at work laying out advertising for *The Far Hills Banner*. Well, she'd be sure to find out tonight.

Ellyn pivoted to start down the deteriorating path that led from the height that gave Ridge House its name. But she paused at the sight below of an unfamiliar sedan stopped in the turnaround area beside the house. Now and then strangers left the highway thinking the ranch entrance was a county road. But they usually stopped at Kendra and Daniel's place, rarely getting this deep into Far Hills land before realizing their mistake.

She shaded her eyes, watching a man's erect figure emerge from the car, straighten and turn. The dark-haired man looked up toward her. She could almost imagine...

Her heart lurched against her ribs, hard enough, it seemed to her, to leave a bruise. At least on the inside.

"Grif?" It came out a whisper. She swallowed, and stared a moment longer, making sure with her eyes of what some other sense already knew, before calling, "Grif!"

He smiled and waved.

She started straight down the hillside, not bothering with the path, and letting the slope hurry her steps.

A scene from the library videotape of *Gone With the Wind* she and the kids had watched recently sprang into her mind. The moment when Melanie spots a tattered, injured soldier returning from war—*her* soldier—and, half stumbling, runs to him. Laughing and crying, she runs to meet her man.

The straight-backed figure before Ellyn was definitely a soldier—even in jeans and deep green knit shirt instead of a uniform, that was obvious in the way he held himself as he climbed toward her. But she wasn't Melanie, and Grif wasn't her man.

Of course not. Because you have never known how to make a man yours. Not even your husband.

Before the familiar voice in her head echoed to silence Ellyn leaned back, slowing her descent, although her heart still stumbled. Halfway down, she stopped as Grif closed the gap to arm's length.

"Hello, Ellyn."

"Grif. I can't—this is unbelievable. What are you... Marti and Kendra must be ecstatic. I just—"

Words weren't working. She automatically reached out to give him a hug the way she had a thousand times in the years he'd been such an important part of their family, when she and Meg and Ben and Dale had *been* a family. Only at the last second did she remember that the laundry basket, empty except for the bag of clothespins rattling at the bottom, was still tucked on her hip.

That must have been why their hug felt so awkward.

Or maybe what intruded on their friendly embrace was the separation of the past fifteen months after years of almost daily contact.

She stepped back. He gave her space, but his arms lingered around her. Then she gained a few more inches of height as she backed up the hill, and his arms dropped to his side.

"You look great, Ellyn."

She didn't look anywhere close to great. She wore a T-shirt that had shrunk, topped by one of Dale's old flannel shirts, which was big enough for the tail to flap around thighs covered in leggings bearing proof of painting Meg's room yellow. She had no makeup on and her hair was a curling mess, as usual. But she'd learned long ago not to dispute polite compliments like this—acknowledging them with a quick smile, then plowing ahead was her strategy.

"You, too. A bit of gray, I see. Very distinguished."

With teasing fingertips already touching the silver strands filtering into the thick, dark hair at his temple, she saw the lines around his eyes deepen, as if he'd tensed. She faltered, dropping her hand.

"It's longer than you used to let it get. Are you relaxing that military discipline these days?"

"Missed a trim getting things squared away to leave."

She nodded, as if any of this mattered.

In the past fifteen months, she'd wondered so many times why Grif had disappeared from their lives so abruptly, and she'd wondered when she would see him again, but she had never let herself think about what the reunion would be like. If she had, it would not have been anything like this. Where was their old, easy camaraderie? Could a year's absence kill a friendship that had survived decades?

She pushed out more words, hoping she would stumble across the right ones. "Grif, I can't believe this. After all the times Marti's said she's asked you to come visit, you're really here. What persuaded you to finally come back to Far Hills?"

"You."

She blinked. Her mind repeated the single word as if it didn't quite grasp what it meant. Because it couldn't mean what it sounded like. Grif didn't feel that way about her, never had. Before she could hope to form a response, he was continuing.

"You and the kids. I have some leave..." His voice, which nature had roughened with a slight raspiness, dropped to that register that said he was worried. His direct eyes searched her face. "I wish I could have been here for the funeral last year."

He might be ready to jump into those deep and murky waters, but she wasn't. She kept her answer as light as possible, considering the topic. "We understood, with you in the Middle East and all."

"I didn't get word of the accident until six hours before the funeral."

Single-car accident, one fatality. That was the official

description of Dale's death. To Ellyn it remained a blur—from the moment Dale had driven away from the house that night, to the early-morning arrival of the state troopers at the door, and through the funeral—a surreal blur of alternating waves of pain and numbness.

"Even if I'd been able to leave," Grif continued, "I couldn't have made it back in time."

"You wrote all that." In a letter that said all the right things except when he would come to see them, delivered in an envelope oddly absent a return address. "I know—we all know you would have been here for Dale if you could have."

"Are you okay—the three of you?"

"We're fine." *Now.*

"Marti wrote that you've decided to stay on here for good."

She heard something in his voice as he surveyed the unimposing two-story frame house with no visible neighbors, so different from the Sinclairs' brick Cape Cod in a neat Washington suburb teeming with kids and bicycles and car pools. That's where Grif had so often visited the kids and Dale and her. Where he'd been practically part of the family. Before...

She forced herself to finish the thought. Before the problems between her and Dale. Before Grif disappeared from their lives. Before Dale moved them all back here to Wyoming. Before Dale died.

"I considered returning to Washington, but uprooting the kids again in such a short time didn't seem fair."

There'd been a third option. "Under the circumstances," her mother had said, she and Ellyn's stepfather, although retired to Arizona, would "take you and the children into our home, until we can get you back on your feet. So you can meet a man who can take care of you and your children." Even as low as Ellyn had been then, she'd had the strength to know that option would have been the worst possible. She'd had a lifetime of her mother's ways; she wasn't about to accept that future for her children.

"Meg and Ben loved it here. They had settled in," she continued. "They had friends, and so did I. We needed friends."

Only a flicker of his eyes gave away how he took that, but it was enough.

"Oh, Grif, I'm sorry. I didn't mean—"

She broke off the apology because maybe she *had* meant to reproach him. That would be quite unlike the old Ellyn, but not out of the question for the new Ellyn she'd been forming from the ashes of her old life.

Grif shook his head, then said, "*I'm* sorry," but she didn't know if he meant for his disappearing act or about Dale's death.

She could keep apologizing. She could ask what he was sorry for. Those were things the old Ellyn would do. She could demand to know why he'd acted the way he had. Or why he'd shown up now. She could throw him off her property...except she was renting it, and come to think of it, he was part-owner of Far Hills Ranch, so she couldn't very well throw him off *his* property.

Especially when she didn't want him to go.

Suddenly aware they were staring at each other—and chances were fairly good that his shrewd eyes were seeing more than she meant to reveal—she turned away and shifted the basket.

"Would you like to come inside for a glass of lemonade?" She started toward the house and, after a moment's hesitation, he followed. "I know it's cool yet, spring comes slow here in Wyoming, not like Washington, but—"

Her offhand manner might have been more successful if he hadn't come alongside her and gripped the laundry basket, forcing her to stop and turn toward him.

"I'll carry that, Ellyn."

She didn't let go. "No need. I can manage fine."

His mouth tightened, but he said nothing more as he gave it too firm a pull to resist.

She resumed her route.

From behind her left shoulder, he said, "I know my showing up like this has to be a shock, since I haven't been in touch and—"

"You've been in touch. Cards every holiday. Presents for the kids at birthdays and Christmas." *And in those first months their tearful questions about why Grif didn't come.* "I would have thanked you—if I'd known where to write. I'm glad to be able to thank you now."

He stopped to face her. She kept going.

"Ellyn, you have reason to be angry—"

"Angry? I'm not angry," she said as she opened the back door. She wasn't sure exactly what she was, but it wasn't angry. At least not much of it. Maybe she'd simply grown smarter, not so trusting. That was definitely a part of the new Ellyn. "How long has it been since you've been here at Far Hills, Grif?"

"Ellyn—"

"It must be years and years."

Once inside, she reached for the basket, and he handed it over. She opened the closet doors hiding the aged washer now valiantly chugging through another load and the useless dryer.

"I'd say you hadn't been back since you were best man for Dale at our wedding, but of course that was in Washington, so that wouldn't count. So when was it? I remember the last summer you spent here was when you were fourteen, and Dale was thirteen, so that must be, what, twenty-three years ago?"

She was babbling. She knew it. He knew it. But she didn't want to talk about any of the things he'd been taking aim at.

She transferred three rolled towels from the top of the dryer to the bottom of the basket.

Raising her head, she found him looking at her, long and steady, his expression giving away nothing. When his lips parted she had no idea if he would pursue his topic or go along with hers.

"Last time I was back here was for Amy's funeral, ten years ago. The time before that was when I came through right after I finished at West Point. I had just turned twenty-one, so you must have been eighteen or nineteen."

Memories as clear and sharp as broken glass showered over her. And she couldn't move out of the way of the slicing shards.

A final whine and shudder signaled the end of the washer's cycle, breaking the spell.

"Eighteen," she said shortly, flipping the lid open and devoting all her attention to pulling out the wet tangle of dark clothes.

"This house was a wreck then," he said. He looked around and for the first time she had the impression that his focus softened and widened. "It looks great now. Lots of room for kids."

"Marti started fixing up the old houses on the property a few years back." He probably knew that, since he was Marti Susland's nephew as well as owning a share in the ranch Marti had run for thirty-odd years. But even the new Ellyn was not above stating the obvious to keep this conversation in safe waters. "She rents a few to people she likes—and you know how generous Marti is, so I can't beat the rent. Another reason to stay here."

"Dale didn't have insurance?" No softening of his focus in that question.

For an instant, his directness nearly triggered her into answering as openly as she would have a year ago.

"He had some," she said instead. Before he could dig more, she drew a red herring across his path by adding, "'Course, even with the low rent some folks would be reluctant to live out here, what with the ranch being cursed.''

He frowned. ''What do you mean, cursed?''

''What does a curse ever mean? Bad things happen, so—''

''You and the kids? Has something—''

''No, nothing.'' Soothing his worry was too old a habit to shed easily. ''We're not Suslands. And it's the *Susland* Legend. Remember Marti telling us about it as kids?''

''That nonsense hasn't died out?''

''Your family's had more than its share of tragedies, and to some folks that proves the curse is real.''

''I don't remember you taking the legend seriously.''

''That was before Marti did research and found out Annalee believed it,'' she said with a wave of a hand, not sure herself how seriously she took the legend. She looked up as she put a final handful of wet socks into the basket. ''Annalee was Charles Susland's second wife. Remember?''

''Charles founded Far Hills Ranch in the 1800s,'' he said as if answering a quiz.

''Founded it and got it cursed for cruelty to the Indian wife and children he deserted to take a rich, white wife— Annalee.''

He was watching her with an intensity that prompted her to concentrate on putting in the next load, while she kept the conversation safely on the Susland Legend. ''After what happened with Kendra—''

''Kendra? My cousin, Kendra Jenner?''

''Kendra Delligatti now.''

Of course he knew Kendra and Daniel had married in January. Ellyn had told herself she wasn't surprised—or disappointed—when Grif declined his invitation to the wedding, blaming the press of work in his Pentagon job.

''What has Kendra got to do with that legend?'' he demanded in his old Grif-the-protector voice.

"Daniel tracked down Kendra and their son Matthew, and they're a family, so people say that's made amends for Charles Susland turning his back on his children," said Ellyn. "Next, someone has to make amends for Charles turning his back on the Indians who'd befriended him. The third part—"

"But Kendra's okay?"

Oh, yes, Grif-the-protector was back in full force. As the oldest of the kids who had gathered each summer at Far Hills Ranch, he'd always taken on the burden of being the designated adult. As a quiet, skinny girl with a mop of wild hair who communicated better with horses than people, she'd benefited from his protection more than once.

"Better than okay. She's happy." She lifted the refilled basket. "I'm going to hang these clothes and I'll be right back. Help yourself to lemonade—it's in the refrigerator—and there are cookies in the glass jar on the counter." Another thought occurred to her. "But I suppose you have other people to visit. I'm sure you've been to the main house, but if you haven't—"

"No."

"—seen Kendra yet... No?" she repeated as his answer sank in. "You haven't been to the main ranch to see Marti?"

"Not yet."

"You *are* living on the edge. If she finds out you didn't go straight to the home ranch..." She shook her head, as if the consequences were too dire to spell out.

His grin flickered. "I wanted to see you first."

Why? The question roared in her head, but there was no risk that she'd voice it.

"Well, now you have, but I got a late start on the laundry and I need to get these things hung up so they'll dry, and it's not much fun for you to wait around. So, go see Marti. And I'll finish the laundry."

Looking a little grim, he moved ahead to open the back door for her. "I'll carry the basket."

"Grif, there's no need for that. And Marti..." He followed her out and took the basket from her, this time using enough strength on his first attempt to overcome her resistance. "Grif—"

"Go on up," he said, tilting his head in the direction of the path to the ridge. The railroad ties that had formed rough steps had rotted, but the path was still passable, at least on good days like this. "Unless you want to stay down here and I'll hang these myself."

She'd already started up the path, recognizing Grif's never-to-be-budged tone. But at the incongruous image, she chuckled and tossed over her shoulder, "How would it look to have a major in the United States Army hanging up laundry?"

"Colonel," he murmured absently from behind her.

"Colonel? You've made full colonel? That's quite a jump in a short time."

She looked back at him, but could read nothing in his face nor his response. "I suppose."

They climbed the rest of the way in silence, but at the top, she turned and faced him.

"That must have been some assignment you got—the one you left Washington for so suddenly right when..." She took a breath and finished in a different direction. "Before we moved back here."

"It was." His quiet answer both filled in the gap she'd left and cut off the subject like a concrete wall at the end of a one-way alley. "Where do you want this?"

She gave up any thoughts of trying to break through that concrete, and nodded to a stretch of unfilled clothesline. "Thanks, Grif. Now, why don't you go see Marti and—"

He was ignoring her, pulling out a pair of racing stripe pajama bottoms and shaking them out. "Ben's?"

"Yes, but—"

"He must have grown a foot."

His tone—a crust of sadness overlaying awe—clogged her throat. She nodded, and swallowed. "Meg, too."

He took a clothespin and jammed it over the waist of the pajamas and the line. He looked at the items she'd hung earlier, then at his handiwork, and frowned.

"That's not secure."

"It works better," she told him gently, "if you pin each cuff to the line—the material catches more breeze that way and dries faster. But, really, Grif, this isn't necessary."

As she took out another of Dale's old shirts that she wore around the house, she used her peripheral vision to watch Grif remove the clothespin, turn the pajamas upside down and pin one cuff. He recognized the new problem immediately. She caught the inside of her cheeks between her teeth to stifle a grin.

Trying to keep the unpinned pajama leg from flapping around, he stretched toward the basket for a second clothespin. He should have looked awkward, ludicrous, uncoordinated. Instead the twisting, reaching motion pulled the knit of his shirt taut across long, ropy muscles in his back, and molded the fabric of his pants around the powerful curve of his thigh and the even rounder curve of his—

No longer tempted to grin, Ellyn jerked her gaze and thoughts from where they didn't belong, grabbed a clothespin and moved in to help him.

He released the loose pajama leg to her hold, then reached over her shoulder to help keep it in place. With his other hand still on the first pin and with the pajamas in front of her, she was surrounded. She drove the pin home with more power than finesse, and quickly ducked under his extended arm.

"That's how you do it," she said once she'd gained some distance. "But, as I said, this isn't the kind of duty you're used to, Colonel Griffin."

"Even a colonel can learn."

As they both bent over the basket, she to retrieve the shirt she'd dropped there when she grabbed the clothespin, and he to pull out one of Meg's sweatshirts, she glanced at him, found his eyes on her and looked away.

"You never learned to do laundry? I thought the Army made men self-reliant."

"I've washed clothes now and then, but nobody ever taught me the finer points. Mom did the laundry when I was a kid. When she got sick…" After a brief silence, his next words were matter-of-fact. "My father could never be bothered with household stuff, so we sent everything out. I suppose my self-reliance comes in the form of finding the best laundry in the shortest amount of time in a new place. One good thing I learned from my father."

A year and a half ago, and anytime in the eight years before that, she would have said that John Griffin Junior was her best friend. Now it struck her that in all the years she'd known him, stretching back to spending most of her childhood summers on this very ranch with him and the others, she'd heard him mention his mother maybe a dozen times, and his father half that. So, how well *did* she know him?

Certainly not well enough to have avoided being blindsided by his absence these past fifteen months.

She didn't know how long she'd been mulling that over while she automatically hung clothes before Grif's voice cut into her thoughts.

"Why aren't you using the dryer?" he asked.

"What? Use a dryer on such a beautiful day? That would be a homemaker's sin," she said airily.

"I don't remember you caring much about homemaking sins."

He must have caught her reflexive wince, because he reached a hand toward her that she evaded by stretching up to secure the corner of one of Ben's shirts.

"I didn't mean anything critical by that, Ellyn," he said

with his voice dropping. "I just remember you not being the kind of woman who'd worry about such things, so—"

"Of course not. You're right," she said, pleased by the light tone she achieved. "I was never that kind of woman. A mouse to start, a bit of a tomboy later, then a haphazard housekeeper, and, as a wife—"

Grif's right hand on her arm drew her around.

"You're talking nonsense—you know that, don't you, Ellyn?"

"Just quoting Rose Neal Brindford." And Dale, but Grif didn't need to know that.

"Don't. Your mother's a—"

She watched him bite back the word she could almost hear on his tongue. He turned away, and his big hand settled on the inside seam of her freshly washed jeans hanging upside down. Even as kids, he'd always hated the way her mother criticized her. Hated it even worse if she criticized herself with her mother's words. But that was another hard habit to escape.

"Ellyn." She couldn't take her eyes off his hand. In a motion she was certain was unconscious, his hand slid slowly along the inside seam of her jeans. "There are some things we should talk about. Get clear."

The caressing touch of his hand dropped lower along that seam—nearly to the point where the left leg met the right, to the point where— *Oh, Lord.* She spun around, looking for something else, *anything* else to absorb her attention.

Marti and Kendra were right. She'd been alone too long. Living out here without any male companionship. Letting her libido get so desperate it rioted at the sight of a strong hand sliding down the seam of her jeans, toward— No!

"About why I'm here," Grif was saying, "and…other things."

This was *not* the time for her to try to talk to him about anything, not while images of a hand on a pair of jeans strobed through her brain and bloodstream. She needed something to keep him occupied while she got her mind on a different track…an *entirely* different track.

"Ellyn? Are you listening?"

She let out an audible *whoosh* of relief as she spotted exactly the distraction she needed.

Saved by the school bus.

"The kids just got off the bus down at the highway." She gave a nod toward two distant figures starting along the ranch road. "I'm going down to wait for them inside."

And to get away from the unexpected dangers of hanging laundry.

Grif had turned to see for himself, and now he remained looking that way as he spoke.

"Maybe you should tell Meg and Ben about my being here before they see me. It could be a shock."

"A shock?" Her own unsettled feelings sharpened her voice and words. "In the past year and half, we've become shock experts, and believe me, this doesn't count, Grif. Don't make a bigger deal of this than it is."

And if he didn't realize after that little speech that she'd changed, he never would. But somehow she didn't want to see his judgment of this new Ellyn right now. She started back to the house without looking at him.

If the Army had Ellyn Sinclair, it wouldn't need drill sergeants to cut recruits down to size.

Don't make a bigger deal of this than it is.

That put him in perspective, didn't it? Grif thought with a grimace as he followed Ellyn's straight back down the eroded steps.

Well, what had he expected? That she—*they*—would fall on him like a savior? Just because pulling out of their lives had been like pulling himself off life support didn't mean it had affected them the same way.

When the four Sinclairs left Washington fifteen months ago, he'd known they'd have support in Far Hills, led by his aunt, Marti Susland. Even when he'd heard about Dale's death, he'd been certain Ellyn and the kids would be looked after. Still, he'd planned eventually to come to Far Hills to assure himself they were okay, maybe try to pick up some of the threads that had once tied them…when the time was right, when he was sure he was ready.

But the time had never been quite right, and he hadn't been ready.

Then some phrases in Marti's letters started to nag at him. Subtle at first, but not for long. Increasingly more pointed phrases about tough times for Ellyn and the kids—tough times emotionally and practically. She'd eventually written it flat out: They needed help.

And it no longer mattered if he was ready.

When he'd first seen Ellyn up on the ridge, before she'd noticed him, she'd looked like the sweet eighteen-year-old girl whose image he'd never quite gotten out of his mind, even as he'd become friends with the woman she'd become. With the wind whipping her hair into a curly froth, the sun glinting on the lighter strands woven among the rich brown, and that big shirt alternately molded around her to hint at what lay below and swinging free to show the T-shirt that did a lot more than hint. Seeing her like that he'd found himself praying that Marti was wrong. That he could check on Ellyn and the kids, find out everything was fine, then get himself back to Washington and away from… temptation.

But Marti Susland was seldom wrong.

He'd always been good at reconnaissance. This wasn't even a challenge. The unused dryer, the washing machine that could drown out a tank, the path that needed rebuilding, the evasiveness about insurance, the uncertainty tempering Ellyn's warm smile, the shadows under her soft brown eyes and, worse, the shadows *in* them.

He'd been the one responsible for turning those shadows into flashes of pain. *Stupid*. Why had he brought up his visit to Far Hills after his West Point graduation? They'd never talked about that incident. Instead they'd gotten past all that a long time ago by ignoring it. So why had he stirred it up now?

To remind himself of the decision he'd made then—the *right* decision. Or maybe to remind her, because it cooled the warmth in her face when she'd first seen him. And he knew he couldn't hold up against that warmth.

He had to remember why he'd come here.

To help three people who needed his help. His heart wouldn't do Ellyn or the kids any good, but his head and his hands could—*would.*

And nothing was going to stop him. Not the U.S. Army. Not the pair of kids he was getting ready to face. Not Ellyn Neal Sinclair. Not even himself.

Chapter Two

Grif hadn't said a word as they'd taken the path down to the house, and she had no idea what he was thinking.

He'd never been easy to read, now he was impossible. An absolute stranger. They would never recapture the easy adult friendship they'd constructed in Washington, or even the companionship of their childhoods. She should tell him to let bygones be bygones and send him on his way. That would be easier for all of them. Him, her, the kids. And—

As always, noise heralded the impending arrival of her children. At least this was limited to voices and a few thuds rather than any of the crashes and ominous silences a mother dreaded. Plus, it had the added benefit of damming her stream of thoughts.

Grif turned toward the door, his jaw locked and his shoulders even tighter. He glanced back toward Ellyn, and she caught a flicker of worry. Once she would have laughed at the notion that the Iron Warrior might be scared of an eight- and ten-year-old.

"Are they... They're okay?"

She didn't pretend not to know what he meant. The kids had each shown effects from the emotional buffeting of Dale's death, as each had shown surprising strength. She focused on the strength. "Yes."

He nodded, accepting her assessment. "They probably won't remember me, so—"

"Of course they'll remember you." The rest of his face remained immobile, but she definitely saw worry in his eyes. Her next words came without thinking. "It'll be all right, Grif. They'll—"

The door swung open with a muffled crash, and Ellyn went to meet her children in the small back hall.

"Mom!"

"Ben, honey, I've told you, don't slam the door open that way. You're going to break the door. Is Meg—"

Ben had halted inside the door to drop his book bag on the floor and toe off his shoes, and Meg stepped past him.

"Hi, Mom."

"Hi, honey. Meg, Ben, there's someone here to see you. Someone you haven't seen in a while."

Before she could say more, they stepped past her into the main kitchen. Meg, who had adored Grif from babyhood, halted as soon as she saw who stood by the kitchen counter.

"Oh. It's you."

"Meg, don't be rude."

Ben's reaction was entirely different. Showing no sign of the uncharacteristic lethargy she'd noticed last night, he lit up and hurried across the slick floor in his stocking feet. Quick, hot tears pricked at the inside of Ellyn's eyelids.

"It's Grif! Hi, Grif!"

"Hey, partner." He extended his hand, and Ben grinned as he shook it, man to man. "You're packing more muscle in that pitching arm, these days, Ben."

"Aw, I play mostly shortstop now. And ride horses."

"That sounds great. I hope you'll tell me more about it before—"

"Before you leave?" interrupted Meg, still standing in the doorway. "How long are you staying before you take off this time?"

Beneath the defiance, Meg's vulnerability was so apparent to Ellyn that she had to stop herself from going and wrapping the girl in her arms.

Meg was still so angry at Dale for dying; Ellyn understood that feeling, even shared some of it. Maybe she even understood a little about it spilling over to Grif. So she didn't have the heart to reprimand her daughter for rudeness again. But she could try to blunt it.

"Meg, you know the Army decides where Grif goes and how long he can stay. But Far Hills is his home, and he should be welcomed—" she gave her daughter a stern look as she took four clean glasses from the cabinet "—whenever he can come here."

"Couldn't you stay for good?" Ben's voice skidded up in excitement.

"Not for good," Meg said before Grif could answer. "You heard Mom—guys in the Army don't stay anywhere for good. They get their clothes for free but they don't live anywhere long."

"How would you know, Maggot Meg?"

"I read about it, Ben-jam-head-in." She twisted his full name with relish. "You know, in books. Or you would know if you could read."

"Meg—" Ellyn tried.

"I can read, I just don't spend all day with my nose stuck in a book, like a Maggot brain."

"Ben—"

"Oh, yeah? Well—"

"Ben, Meg that's—"

"Meg's right, you know," Grif interrupted quietly. Both children turned to him. "We get uniforms to wear when we're on duty, but we do have to move around a lot. That's part of following orders. Like you follow your mother's orders.''

The faint rebuke in his tone stopped them. Great. Just great. Ellyn pivoted around and opened the refrigerator. Grif walks in after more than a year out of their lives and already has more success controlling her children than she did.

His habit of command—she used to tease him about that. She grabbed the pitcher of lemonade from the refrigerator and started filling the glasses.

''As for how long I'll be here. I'm on leave, and—''

''Leave?'' Ben echoed plaintively. ''But you just got here.''

''Leave's what the Army calls vacation, stupid,'' supplied Meg, ducking the frown Ellyn sent her.

''Oh.'' Ben considered that. ''How long a vacation? Like spring vacation—that one's pretty short. Or Christmas? That's a couple weeks. Or—'' his eyes brightened ''—like summer vacation? That's months and months.''

Grif smiled, and rested one large hand on his shoulder. ''Somewhere between Christmas and summer.''

''Great! We can—''

''What does it matter how long?'' Meg interrupted. ''He'll leave in the end anyway.''

Ellyn's lips parted, but no words came out as her gaze met Grif's. She couldn't have said how she knew he wanted to—maybe needed to—handle this, because neither his face nor his eyes held a readable expression. But she knew it. And that alone was enough to both silence and unsettle her.

She also knew that Meg had meant the words to hurt, and they had.

She pivoted to finish pouring the lemonade and to keep herself from interceding, leaving a silence at her back.

She'd filled the glasses, and had handed Ben his before

Grif cleared his throat and spoke. "You're right, Meggie, I—"

"Don't call me that. I'm not a baby anymore."

"Okay." His words were slow, precise, like the steps of someone traveling through a live minefield. "I will be leaving in the end. And I guess you could say everybody does leave eventually when they die." Meg flinched, then glared at him. He pretended not to notice either reaction. "But I don't think you mean that. I think you mean about me going back to duty. And you're right. I will go back. I will leave here. In the meantime, we can either worry about when I'll be leaving or we can have fun while I'm here."

"*Fun?*"

Ellyn let out a short sigh. She'd thought kids didn't get sarcastic until teenager-hood, but Meg had it down pat already.

"Some fun," Grif amended. He had always been truthful with the kids—and her. Even when it would have been easier not to be. "There are some…things I'll need to do, but I'm certain there'll be time for fun, too."

"Yeah, right."

Ellyn offered him a glass of lemonade. Hoping to catch his attention to give him a bit of encouragement, she held on to her side of the glass even after he'd taken hold of the other. But he never looked up. Instead his gaze seemed intent on the glass that for a moment rested in their mutual grasp, though their fingers did no more than brush.

The instant lengthened. Then she heard her son's next words, and she dropped her hand abruptly.

"Will you stay here with us?"

"Ben, that's not—"

"No."

Grif's answer came in the middle of her longer response. "Why not?"

"I'm sure Grif will be staying up at the main house, Ben." Ellyn explained. "Marti's his aunt, and it's natural for him to stay with his family. Besides, it's bigger, so he'll have more room to…ah, be comfortable.''

"Actually I'm staying at Fort Piney," he said, naming the small Army post on the other side of the town of Far Hills, then took a long drink of lemonade. "BOQ."

"BOQ?" Ben asked.

"Bachelor Officer Quarters, where officers who don't have families stay."

Bachelor. How many times had she confirmed that status for her female friends back in Washington who had just met Grif? They'd first be caught by his smile—that surprisingly sweet smile in a face some would call stern. A little rusty, even a little shy—and that, she'd always thought, was what got to women. The idea that beneath that severe exterior lived a heart waiting for them to rescue.

But none—not even the ones she'd been sure could have any man they wanted—had ever succeeded with Grif. At least not to her knowledge.

She'd known he was no monk—if she'd wondered, Dale had made it clear by recounting in envious tones how lucky Grif was to keep finding willing women as uninterested in *long-term* as he was. But when he was around their family he rarely brought a date. The ones he did bring were never back a second time.

He definitely qualified for the Bachelor Officers Quarters. But why stay there instead of here at Far Hills Ranch?

And why did she feel faintly chilled at his choice?

"I better get going now." He drained the glass with a long, efficient swallow, then set it on the counter. "As you said, I should let my aunt know I'm here. But I wanted to stop by to—"

"I'm glad you did, Grif. It's been great to see you." She had to make it clear to him and the kids that they had no expectations of him, that they knew they had no claim on him. "We hope you'll stop by again, but of course family comes first, and—"

"Do you want to go to dinner?" The surprise of his blunt words effectively cut through the flow of Ellyn's politeness. He added more smoothly, "I'd like to take you out to dinner tonight. All of you. You and Meg and Ben."

"That's very nice of you, but I'm sure Marti will want to give you dinner at the main house for your first evening at Far Hills."

"Marti will understand. I thought we'd go into Sheridan."

"But…" She found it hard to believe Marti would willingly relinquish the right of family to have him around, but his tone told her that arguing that point wouldn't sway him. "I have the laundry to finish. And the kids have homework, so—"

"So, I'll leave now, and be back around six. That should be enough time."

Her lips parted to protest again, but he was too quick. Calling in his reinforcements, he turned to her kids and asked, "Will that be enough time to do your homework?"

"Sure," Ben said without pause.

"Meg?"

Clear as words would have been written across her face, the girl was torn between wanting to give him a negative answer and wanting the promised dinner out. "I suppose."

"Where're you taking us?"

"Ben…" Ellyn appealed without much hope.

Grif grinned. Sure, he could be amused. To her it wasn't so funny. She'd once confided to Grif that she wondered if Ben's unabashed pursuit of feeding his appetite left people thinking she didn't feed her son enough. He'd joshed her out of that concern then. Now, he didn't even try.

"Anywhere you want, Ben. What do you want to eat tonight?"

"Steak!"

"Ben—" Ellyn used her most quelling voice.

"Steak it is. And whatever Meg and your mom want, too. We'll find someplace that serves a variety, okay?"

"Sure, as long as they have steak."

"Ben! That's—"

The blaring ring of the phone overrode Ellyn's remonstrations. She'd forgotten she'd turned it up loud enough to be heard outdoors while she was hanging laundry, and there was no ignoring it now.

With a look at Ben and Grif meant to warn them this discussion was not over, she picked up the receiver. "Ridge House."

"Ellyn? It's Fran. Have you heard Grif's in town?"

Fran Sinclair had become Dale's stepmother when he was seven years old. Fran and Dale hadn't always gotten along well, but Fran had been a terrific stepmother-in-law to Ellyn and, in her practical, no-nonsense way, she adored the kids. She also had the best connections to the area grapevine of anyone around.

"Yes. But this isn't a good time, Fran. I'll have to—"

But Grif was already taking advantage of the interruption to start backing toward the door, with an assumption that he'd be taking them all out to dinner in his pocket.

"So you two get going on that homework," he was saying to her kids. "And I'm going to the home ranch to see Marti."

Ellyn covered the mouthpiece. "Grif, we haven't—"

"No, no, don't interrupt your call. I'll see you at six."

And he was gone, leaving her to answer Fran's good-hearted questions. At least the ones she *could* answer.

"I don't understand you, Ellyn," said Fran after she'd been filled in. "Why aren't you jumping at the chance to go out for a nice dinner?"

"I don't want to impose on his generosity." Ellyn looked around, but both kids had disappeared toward their rooms as soon as Grif left.

Fran snorted. "You're telling me Grif made you feel that way."

"No," she admitted. "But doesn't it seem a little odd to you, his showing up out of the blue and—"

"Is it his showing up out of the blue that's bothering you or that you're scared he's going to disappear again?"

Count on Fran to hit a nail firmly on its head.

Grif had been such a part of their lives in Washington that his disappearance had left a huge hole, especially with all the upsets in their once-staid life, including a move three-quarters of the way across the continent and from one world to another. When Dale's death followed so quickly, the three of them could have crumbled completely. But they hadn't. They'd rebuilt. At least they'd started. Was she paranoid to feel that Grif might pose a risk to that progress?

"The kids and I—"

"Oh, now don't go fretting about the kids. They're doing fine. And the three of you will be all the better for being taken out to dinner. And have dessert!"

With that final order, Fran said goodbye and ended the call.

Ellyn could either disappoint her kids and be ungrateful at best and rude at worst by refusing to go out when Grif returned, or she could follow Fran's advice.

Really, she thought, as she headed back up the ridge with the final basket of laundry, how big a deal is one dinner?

She reached the top of the path and saw that even more of the line was filled.

Grif had obviously come back up here and hung up the hand-washed items she'd left wrapped in the towels. Including her underwear.

She stared at the bras, panties and one slip, none new, all in utilitarian beige so they could be worn under any color, but all also embellished with a self-indulgent flourish of lace, and she felt heat rising up her neck.

Worse than that, though, was the knowledge that the heat

originated much, much lower than her neck, as her imagination lingered on the image of Grif's big, competent hands on her underwear. Holding them up, securing them with pins, and reaching down for more with that same twisting motion that had riveted her not so many minutes ago.

Good heavens, what had gotten into her? This was Grif for heaven's sake. Her friend from childhood. Dale's best man at their wedding. The godfather of her children.

And an enigma who had evaporated from her life at the moment she had most wished she could lean on him.

"Grif! Welcome home!"

He hugged his aunt, her graying curls tickling across his wry grimace. *Home?* Closest thing he'd had to a home was using the same suitcase for a dozen years. Even at the house outside Washington where Ellyn, Meg, Ben and Dale had treated him like a member of the family, he'd known he was just visiting.

"This *is* your home, you know," Marti added, as if she'd seen his expression. She stepped back from the embrace gripping his forearms as if he were still a boy and she could give him a shake if she felt the need. "Far Hills Ranch always has been and always will be your home."

"Marti, I—"

"Even if you don't come back near often enough. I wish you'd take some more interest in running the ranch. It's your legacy, too, after all. At least now I can drag Kendra to business meetings and such. But sometimes, I swear, if it weren't for Luke, I'd despair of anyone in the next generation caring about running this ranch."

Grif grinned. "That's right—Luke's still here. Foreman now, isn't he? Does he talk any more than he used to?"

"He's no chatterbox," Marti acknowledged. "But as for still here—it's not *still*. All you kids left Far Hills—for a while." She gave the final three words an emphasis that indicated she thought their returns had somehow been preordained. "Luke's family moved to Colorado not long after you stopped coming for summers. But a few years back he showed up looking for a job as a hand. Didn't take long to see he was suited to a whole lot more. He ought to have a ranch of his own."

"Why doesn't he?"

"Says he can't afford it. I could help him, but he won't hear of that. I think he's got a fool notion that he can't leave me on my own—as if I hadn't run this ranch since I was twenty years old. Besides, he loves Far Hills Ranch, just like…" She hesitated, then added briskly, "Just like he was a Susland. So, now that you're here, how long can you stay?"

"I've got a few weeks leave."

"Wonderful! Get your gear and put it in the—"

"No, no, Marti. There's no need. I have a room at the—"

"—room behind the kitchen. Of course there's need—this is your home. You are *not* staying at the motel. Besides, room's all ready. You'll have your own door to the outside, in case you're worried about having your old aunt knowing about your comings and goings—"

"Old aunt?" he protested, but she paid no heed.

"And you'll have your own bathroom. The bed's made up. I'll get towels, and you'll be all set."

"Marti, those are the foreman's quarters. I wouldn't put Luke out, even if—"

"You're not putting anyone out. Foreman's house is separate nowadays. Men don't want to be living in the main house, especially not young, single men like you and Luke."

"Marti, I'm staying at Fort Piney—Bachelor Officer Quarters."

His aunt harrumphed, but didn't argue anymore. At least not about that. "Bachelor Officer Quarters. What kind of a place is that for you to live? I never have understood why you aren't married, Grif.''

''It's hard on a woman being married to an Army man.''

''That didn't stop your father.''

''No. It didn't.''

Her eyes narrowed as she stared at him. ''And it doesn't keep I-don't-know-how-many thousands of people from having families while the husband or wife—sometimes both—is in the Army.''

''I suppose not,'' he acknowledged, knowing that what some people did didn't necessarily apply to others.

''Well, you must be thirsty as all get-out. I swear flying on an airplane makes me drier than a three-day drought. 'Cept that little plane of Daniel's—that's Kendra's new husband, you know.'' She opened the refrigerator, and began moving containers. ''I don't suppose you'd want milk, and you never did like apple juice. Here we go—lemonade.''

''No, thanks, I just had some. I stopped at Ridge House.''

''Did you now?''

Her voice was even, so it must have been something in the way she looked at him that made him feel obliged to add, ''You know I spent time with them in Washington. All of them.''

''Of course I know. Grif this and Grif that—that was practically all those two kids could talk about when they first moved here, wanting to know what you did when you were at Far Hills as a kid growing up with their mom and dad—wanting to do exactly the same thing.''

''I hope you didn't let them,'' he said with grin.

''I tried my best, but I was about as successful as I used to be stopping you from doing harebrained stunts. Like using the top of the pole fence as a tightrope. You should have broken more than your arm.'' She shook her head in memory. "'Course, that hero worship of Meg and Ben's wore off, what with not hearing from you.''

His smile dried up. Too late he recognized how closely she was watching him, and guessed that her comment had been a deliberate attempt to gauge his reaction.

''So, are you passing through to give those kids ideas for more mischief to get into or are you—?''

The ringing of the phone interrupted.

''Far Hills Ranch… Fran, you'll never guess who I've got right here… Oh, you did… Yes, I knew that… Uh-huh… Uh-huh… What? A colonel? No, he hadn't told me that!''

Marti managed to frown and smile at him at the same time.

Grif decided he needed a good, long look out the window at the once familiar sweep of land that bubbled briefly into sage-covered foothills before rising abruptly into the Big Horn Mountains.

Once, coming here and seeing this land and those mountains *had* been like a homecoming for him. Once, the big, open sky above him had made him feel like any weight pressing on his shoulders had scattered and dissipated into all that blue space.

Maybe Ellyn had felt some of that same relief coming back last year. He hoped so.

He hadn't missed the faint shifting of her expression when she'd talked about weighing returning to Washington or staying here, and he'd known there'd been another choice. Her mother.

He remembered the woman's one visit from town to the ranch when he and Ellyn were kids, an excursion frequently punctuated by Rose Brindford's exasperated sighs over nearly everything Ellyn did and how she did it. That changed to a twittering coo whenever an adult male came within range. Grif could have happily throttled the woman.

For the first time he'd recognized an upside to his father's complete lack of interest in him.

Some instinct—or maybe a desire to get away from the past—made him tune into the one-sided phone conversation continuing behind him.

"Uh-huh… He did…? Interesting…"

Knowing that the string of "uh-huhs…" and "isn't that interestings…" being murmured into the phone had to do with him brought an unfamiliar sensation into his chest. Rather than even trying to identify it, he turned his back to the window and faced his aunt, making it clear he was listening.

He should have known better than to think that would intimidate her.

"Uh-huh, I agree. That is very interesting," she said into the mouthpiece in a decidedly provocative tone, her eyes leveled on him. "You're right, it *does* bear watching."

A moment later, she said goodbye to Fran Sinclair.

"I hear you've got some time before your dinner date, so—"

"It's not a date."

"—let's sit down and have a nice talk. I know you're not thirsty, but I have cookies in the freezer—"

"You don't have to—"

"Almond cookies. You always did like my almond cookies. And they'll defrost fast enough."

"Almond cookies?"

She chuckled and waved him to the table by the big window as she put a plate piled with cookies into the microwave.

"So, how did you find Ellyn?"

He'd expected that. "She and the kids look great. Ben seems his old self. Meg…it's hard to tell. Maybe at dinner… And Ellyn…"

Marti came back to the table with the plate, and he

reached for a cookie, fully aware the movement masked his face from Marti's view.

"What about Ellyn?"

The back door opened to a mismatched pair, and saved Grif from answering.

The man was above medium height, with the kind of understated, wiry toughness that Grif had observed during his years in the Army often matched an equally understated toughness inside.

His companion was a girl of about four years old, with shining dark hair and sparkling brown eyes. She wore a pink jacket with a denim skirt and white tights.

"Mama!" she called as she hurtled into the room. The girl threw her arms around Marti's neck and the two hugged.

Grif had never doubted that his aunt had an abundance of love to give to the orphan she'd adopted three years earlier from a storm-devastated island off South America, but seeing the child's expression as she hugged Marti eased a doubt he'd harbored about whether that love would be returned.

"Grif, this is my Emily," Marti said unnecessarily.

Grif shifted to meet the little girl's eyes. "Hi, Emily." Then he stood. "It's good to see you, Luke."

Grif extended his hand. Luke Chandler took off a work glove and shook hands firmly. "Hello, Grif. Or should I call you Major?"

"It's Colonel now," interposed Marti. "He got a promotion he didn't tell us about."

"Grif will do," he said mildly, earning a glance from Luke that blended amusement and empathy. Obviously Marti continued to treat Luke as a member of the family, as she always had, so the other man understood exactly what Grif was being subjected to.

"Emily, dear, you should say hello. Grif's family. He's your cousin," Marti prompted.

Emily shook her head decisively. "Matthew's my cousin."

"That's true. But so is Matthew's mommy, and so is Grif."

"It's okay, Marti. All those family relationships still confuse me," Grif offered.

"Not at all. In fact, I've been doing research into the Susland family tree, and I've found out things—"

"Oh, Lord, don't let her get started on that again," Luke groaned as he took a seat at the table and reached for a cookie.

Marti swatted at his noncookie-reaching arm without releasing Emily.

Grif also helped himself to a cookie and sat back to listen to the banter of old friends and family.

He'd been wondering about Emily and he'd always liked Luke, but that didn't explain why when they'd walked in, he had never been so happy to see two people in his life.

It wasn't Marti's questions that had worried Grif—it was his answers.

Chapter Three

Ellyn did something she hadn't done in years. She tried on three combinations of clothes before she settled on what she was going to wear.

Only because she wasn't certain where they were going to go, she told herself.

With money tight, she hadn't bought anything new except socks, a pair of jeans and some necessary winter outerwear since they'd moved to Wyoming. Her wardrobe's saving grace was that she'd bought classics since she was in college, where she was also introduced to the wonders of mix-and-match dressing using basic and classic items.

Continuing to mix and match in Wyoming what she'd brought from Washington had let her dress for work, school meetings, church and the few other occasions when she had to be presentable.

In the end, she settled on the black skirt with a hint of swirl to it, a black cotton shell and a red wool cardigan sweater. With the black, red and white scarf her children had given her for Christmas—with an assist from Fran, she suspected—at her throat and loafers with a chunky heel, she looked good, but without any expectations.

That's why she'd taken off her silk sheath dress—it had *expectations*. Now, as she considered her reflection in the mirror, she was satisfied. And that was all that could be expected, she told herself. After all, this was simply dinner with an old friend. An old *family* friend.

She gave an exaggerated smile, then stuck her tongue out at her image in the mirror. *Are we having fun yet?*

"What are you doing, Mom?"

"Oh! Ben, you startled me." She pressed her hand to her heart. "I didn't hear you come in." She considered that, then added, "I also didn't hear you knock."

"That's because you were making faces in the mirror," he assured her, before adding quickly, "Mom, Meg won't get ready."

She gave him a look meant to make it clear she had noticed the flaw in his logic, along with his infraction of house rules, but was letting it slide this time, then pursued the other topic. "What do mean she won't get ready? If she's doing homework…"

"Nah, she finished that a *long* time ago." Ben had finished his homework in record time, bringing her all the papers to prove it, without being asked. He'd also meekly accepted her instructions on what he should wear. The boy must really want that steak, Ellyn thought with an internal grin. Then it twisted a bit, because she suspected what her son wanted even more was Grif's attention. "She's just sitting in her room, reading. And she's got on those jeans you won't let her leave the house in. I *told* her she had to put something else on before Grif gets here, but she told me to go away."

Ellyn started down the short hallway from her bedroom at the back of the house toward the stairs that led to her two children's bedrooms, a bathroom, some closets and a "guest room" that was bare of everything except dust bunnies. Ben trailed right behind her, clearly intending to witness his sister's comeuppance. Ellyn stifled a sigh. Sometimes she thought her children's greatest joy in life consisted of seeing the other sibling get scolded.

"Ben, will you please go check that the front door is locked, so we'll be ready to go when Grif gets here."

The chances of the rarely used front door being unlocked were nil, but the possibility that it might delay their departure for dinner got Ben moving.

"Meg?" Ellyn knocked on the halfway-open door to her daughter's room.

"What?"

Ellyn ducked her head through the small doorway of the room tacked on by some past generation of Suslands.

Meg was curled up on the upholstered chair that had once sat in the Sinclair family room in Washington. Ridge House had no family room, so Ellyn had been happy to agree to Meg's plea that it be in her room. She'd recognized her daughter's need to have tangible reminders of that earlier period of her life. Especially because in selecting what to sell before they came West, Meg's little-girl bedroom set of white and rose had been one of the items to go.

"Meg, Grif's going to be here in a few minutes. You need to get changed."

Meg slowly lifted her head from her open book, and gave her mother a look that it took Ellyn a moment to interpret. When she did, it gave her a jolt. Her daughter's look was almost pitying.

Meg didn't believe Grif would come. She didn't believe he would live up to his word. He would disappoint them all—except Meg, because she was too smart to believe in him.

Grif's not like your father.

The thought came too quickly to be blocked, but Ellyn had no temptation to speak it.

Their first months at Far Hills, the final months with Dale, had revealed what their network of friends and neighbors back East—especially Grif—had masked. Dale hadn't been much of a father to his kids for quite a while.

Meg had learned not to trust Dale over a longer period of time and with harder lessons of events missed, plans canceled, promises forgotten. But Grif, too, had disappointed her. He had failed to be there…not breaking a promise, because he'd made none, but breaking an expectation he had built by being there time after time.

"Meg, honey… I know it's hard, but…"

"Grif's here!" Ben called from downstairs. "I'll let him in."

Meg glanced toward her window that overlooked the driveway, but didn't move.

Ellyn walked across the room and looked out in time to see Grif's familiar figure emerge from the car with equally familiar ease. Right on time.

"It's Grif," Ellyn confirmed, then added firmly, "You need to change, and quickly."

She headed out of the room, as if in no doubt that Meg would follow that order, but felt tension ease from her shoulders as she heard Meg moving around in the room behind her.

With her mind less occupied by her daughter, she spared her son's room a glance in passing—a glance was all she could take.

Downstairs, she found Ben regaling Grif with tales of both Meg's behavior and his own triumphs in rodeo—simultaneously and very confusingly.

"Benjamin Madison Sinclair," Ellyn intoned, stopping Ben in midword. "You will not be going anywhere tonight if you don't get upstairs and deal with your room. The wet towels now residing on the floor and furniture are to be folded neatly over the towel bar in the bathroom. The clothes you were wearing are to be put in the hamper, or folded neatly and put neatly in the dresser or hung up neatly in the closet. Have you recognized the important word in all this?''

''Yes'm. Neatly.''

''That's right. Now get to it. You don't want to keep Grif waiting, when he's so kindly offered to take us to dinner.''

''Yes'm,'' Ben repeated with an anguished look toward Grif. ''I'll hurry, Grif. Honest.''

Then he was gone. But Ellyn could almost imagine she heard the word *steak* floating in the air behind him like a prayer.

''I'm sorry we're not ready, Grif.''

He smiled faintly. ''You're ready, Ellyn, aren't you? You look very nice.''

''Thank you.'' She must have had a dearth of compliments in her life lately to have such a standard one from an old friend threaten to jumble her thinking. ''Yes, I'm ready. But with Ben on cleanup duty and Meg, uh, delayed, we won't be getting out of here on time. If you made a reservation for six-thirty—''

''I didn't. Seven, with a request for salads to be served immediately in case the kids were starving.''

''That's very thoughtful of you—and wise.''

He handled compliments even worse than she did—he simply ignored them.

''Ben said Meg didn't think I was coming back.''

''It's nothing personal, Grif, it's—''

''Of course it's personal. I disappeared on her—on all of you. She's got a right to be angry. And to be cautious. It'll take a lot more instances of being on time to get her faith back than it took to lose it.''

His gaze dropped from her eyes, seemed to touch on her mouth, then lower, to the moon of skin between the scoop neck of her shell and the silk of the scarf.

She managed a smile. "How'd you get so wise about children?"

"I was one, remember?" His lips curled in a semblance of a smile. With his head still slightly dipped, a shadow prevented her from telling if it reached his eyes. "Besides, I had a wise mother."

She wasn't sure he'd ever truly been a child. From the time she'd known him he'd been reliable, steady, serious. Intent on doing the right thing when it came to important issues. Perhaps it had been the effect of his mother's long battle with cancer.

"Your mother..." She tried to call up an image, but failed. "I don't remember her. I know all the Suslands came back every summer when you and Kendra were babies, but by the time I started coming out to the ranch, it was just you and Kendra."

"I wish you'd known my mother," he said in a deep, low voice. "You'd have liked her. She'd have loved you."

Ellyn became aware of her heartbeat in a way she hadn't been even an instant earlier, not only the fact of it, but hearing the sound of it, feeling the warmth of the blood it pulsed through her.

"I wish I had, too." The words came out a throaty whisper, as warm and hazy as the sudden atmosphere between them. She cleared her throat, trying to grab back normalcy. "It must have been hard for you—"

"We're ready! We're ready!"

Ben's announcement preceded him like a trumpet call, ending the adult conversation. She could see Grif's relief, and understood it.

Where that moment of something else had come from, she didn't know—probably her imagination—and clearly Grif didn't want her imagining such things.

Hadn't she learned that lesson when she was eighteen?

Dinner was going better than Grif had feared, mostly because of Ben's enthusiastic anticipation of his steak. And to a small measure because of Grif's foresight in having the salads preordered.

It helped take the edge off their appetites, of course, but it also gave them each something to do during the silences. And with Meg's apparent vow of silence added to Ellyn's tendency to drift into unfocused abstractions, on top of his own lack of small talk and Ben's chatter being interrupted by the higher need to eat, there had been definite gaps in the conversation.

The waitress had cleared the salad dishes, and the main dishes hadn't arrived yet. Grif reached for the basket of rolls, intending to pass it around a second time.

"I heard it was true," came a female voice from behind him, "but I couldn't believe it until I saw it with my own eyes."

Grif was already rising from his seat and turning before the final phrase, a grin spreading across his face.

"Kendra." He wrapped the always-elegant figure of his cousin into an easy hug. "How are you?"

"I'm great, Grif. The question is, how are you? And why didn't you come see me? My cousin, whom I haven't seen in several years, drives right past my house and doesn't even stop to say hello."

"I was going to come by in the morning," he defended himself. "I wish I could have been at the wedding, Kendra."

"I do, too." She smiled and hugged him again. "Well, you're not getting out of it this time—you are going to meet the newest members of your family."

She gestured to a dark-haired man holding the toddler who looked like a miniature version of him with added hints of Kendra. She smiled at the man and boy in a way Grif had never seen his cautious, self-contained cousin smile.

"Grif, this is my husband, Daniel Delligatti, and our son,

Matthew. Daniel and Matthew, this is my cousin—Grif, to one and all, except the United States Army where he's now Colonel John Griffin Junior.''

"Congratulations, Colonel," said Daniel Delligatti, extending a hand with easy grace.

"I should be the one saying congratulations to you—for marrying Kendra." Delligatti's dark eyes warmed in a way that eased something inside Grif. "I've heard a lot about Daniel Delligatti from the family and…other sources."

Delligatti's eyebrows quirked up in immediate recognition of the "other sources" available to someone who'd worked at the Pentagon. "Other sources" could find out about someone who until recently had worked for the government, ostensibly strictly as a pilot. Delligatti's eyes revealed a shade of amusement.

"I'd be willing to bet that those sources found out no more than my brother wanted them to find out."

"Robert Delligatti Junior's not a bad man to have in the family tree," Grif acknowledged with a small smile.

"So you knew Daniel and Robert are brothers?" Kendra asked, as she reached over to adjust the collar of her son's jacket. Matthew had watched the entire proceedings in wide-eyed silence. "Wait a minute!" She turned and faced her cousin. "You had Daniel checked out? Grif, how could you do that? That's—"

The rest of what promised to be an indignant tirade evaporated under Daniel's laughter. "What are you griping about, Kendra? You had me checked out, too."

"That's different. It was my life—and Matthew's. I had every right."

"And if the situations had been reversed, you know darn right that you'd have checked out someone Grif was getting involved with," contributed Ellyn from her seat.

Grif immediately picked up that opening. "And would have been at the front of the line promising dire retribution if this someone ever hurt me."

"That was subtle, Grif." Judging from the twitches at the corners of her mouth Kendra was having a hard time keeping a grin under control.

"Sorry, Grif, but you'd have to get way back in a long line, anyhow," Daniel said cheerfully. "Behind Ellyn, here, and Marti and Luke Chandler and Fran and—"

"Me," Kendra inserted.

"And that's the most frightening of all."

The newly married husband and wife smiled at each other in a way that had nothing to do with fright.

"Why don't you sit down?" Grif offered, "We just ordered. I'll get more chairs and—"

"No, no, we can't stay," Kendra said. "Daniel's on call tonight with Search and Rescue and Matthew's tired out. He just had a shot, and I think it's made him particularly sleepy. Believe me, he's not usually this subdued."

"Yeah, Matthew's a chatterbox," contributed Ben, clearly repeating something he'd heard someone else say.

"He sure is," agreed Daniel. "Ben and I could hardly hold a conversation yesterday afternoon at the baby-sitting co-op. Hey, Ben, sorry again that I can't help you out with that project. Have you come up with another idea?"

The little boy seemed to droop. "Not yet."

Ellyn looked from boy to man and back. "What project's that?"

"Nothing, Mom." He pushed at the butter-smeared cracker on his bread plate with the tip of his knife.

"Daniel, I'd heard you were involved in coordinating and training regional search and rescue," Grif said, diverting attention from Ben. "I'd like to talk to you about that sometime."

"Anytime. I might pick your brain about how to get more cooperation from the folks at Fort Piney, too."

"Hey, we didn't come here to talk business," Kendra interrupted.

"You mean it's not lucky coincidence that you stopped by this restaurant?"

"My dear cousin, you have been away from Far Hills way too long if you have to ask. We were coming into Sheridan for Matthew's checkup, and I called Marti to see if she wanted me to pick up anything. She said you'd arrived this afternoon, and she said Fran said you were taking Ellyn and the kids here for dinner—so here we are, tracking you down to say hello, since you didn't bother to come see your poor old cousin." She looked at the Sinclairs. "You guys must have been more interesting."

"Grif's known me since I was a baby," explained Ben. "Littler even than Matthew."

"He's known me since I was littler than Matthew, too. That didn't seem to weigh very heavily with him." Kendra looked from Grif to Ellyn, speculation brightening her eyes. "Must have been something else that put your house on the top of his list."

The departure of Kendra, Daniel and Matthew coincided with the arrival of the main courses, producing a decided lull in the conversation. At least that was the reason for Meg and Ben's distraction.

Grif's face had stiffened into stern lines at Kendra's comment about the order of his visits. Ellyn felt a double dose of discomfort, on her own behalf and his, at the apparent misreading of the situation. Apparent, yet also awkward to rectify, because that would be making too big a deal of it.

So they ate in silence, a mocking parody of the companionable silences that had marked their friendship from the start.

As an only child of a widowed mother who had made a career of finding the right man to provide for her, Ellyn had been equally uncomfortable with people and words when she started spending most of each summer at Far Hills Ranch. Fran Sinclair, the Neals' new neighbor in town, had suggested Ellyn should go along with Dale to join the Susland descendants and the son of the foreman for the summers of ranch chores and ranch delights.

Dale had ignored her when he wasn't poking fun at her and the other girls. Kendra and Amy had been nice, but they had a special friendship that had made her feel left out. And Luke Chandler had tended to go his own way. So Grif had taken her under his protective wing. She had cherished their long, wordless rides.

Perhaps it had been inevitable that a girl like her would form a severe case of hero worship as they grew older.

After her blunder at eighteen, it had been the companionable silences of their childhood rides that had let them bridge that barrier and form the adult friendship they'd created.

And now that was gone, too…

Dismay washed over her—so much had changed. Too much. Why did this have to change, too?

Grif hasn't changed. He smells just the same. Like man and strength and integrity.

The thought popped out of a corner of her mind that Ellyn didn't even recognize, and it arrived so suddenly that her fork clattered to her plate dispersing its load of green beans.

"Are you okay?"

"Fine, fine." Aware of Grif studying her, she kept her head down as she scooped most of the beans off the tablecloth and deposited them at the edge of her plate.

"Don't you have to eat those in order to have dessert?" Ben asked, and Ellyn could practically hear the vegetable-hating gears in his brain whirring.

"No. I've already eaten most of my vegetables."

"But they didn't fall on the floor or anything," pointed out Meg.

"Yeah, so—"

Ellyn cut off this rare accord between siblings. "You

have to eat your vegetables, or you get no dessert. And if you have a staged accident with your vegetables, you still won't get dessert.''

There were no further accidents, staged or otherwise.

Over dessert—Ellyn ordered a white chocolate mousse, and simply shook her head when Grif asked why she was smiling—Meg dropped the next rock into the calm waters of the evening.

"I have to go to Buffalo to sign up for the select soccer league—you *promised* I could play this summer after we missed sign-ups last year.''

"I know I did. When are sign-ups? I didn't see it on the calendar.''

"I haven't put it up yet," Meg admitted. "It's Saturday. At nine.''

"Oh, Meg, I can't. I have to work that day. It's on the calendar. Did you check?''

"But it's a *Saturday!*'' That protest made it unnecessary to answer the question—Meg hadn't checked the family calendar because she'd assumed her mother would be free. As she used to be at all times before she'd had to go to work at the *Banner*.

"I know, but that's the day the special section Marti and Kendra and I have been working on since the fall comes out. There's a festival to celebrate Far Hills' history at the library and we all have to be there to help promote the special section.''

"Mom! You have to do this. You *have* to.''

"Meg, I'm sorry, honey, but I can't. Perhaps if you call, they can make other arrangements—''

"The notice said no special arrangements. This is the only time—*ever*.''

Her daughter's drama threatened to overflow into tears, but Ellyn knew she couldn't buckle on this.

Household rules had been looser in Washington. Now, sticking to the rules, whether they had to do with organization, economy or consideration of other members of the family, had become a necessity for keeping their lives in order.

"It's unfortunate, Meg, but—"

"I'll ask Luke. He'll—"

"You will *not* ask Luke. He's in the middle of calving season, and the poor man is getting very little sleep. I forbid you to ask him this, do you understand?"

"But *Moooom*…"

"I'll take you, Meg."

Grif's low voice brought Meg's head around, tears suspended on her eyelashes.

"You?"

"Me. I'm free Saturday morning."

Ellyn opened her mouth to protest, then closed it. True, Meg would be getting around household rules, but it was also true that if their family were still whole there would be a second adult available to fill in the inevitable gaps— as Grif was offering to do. Just like a father. She slanted him a look without turning her head. Did he realize the role he'd be filling?

No, of course not. He was just being a nice guy. Slipping into his role of family friend he'd held before. His life had been a clear path of opting for career over home and family. The idea that he'd been acting like a father would probably appall him.

"You'll forget."

Meg's harsh words snapped Ellyn's attention back to the moment. "Meg, you apologize. Grif's offered to do you a favor and you're being rude."

Meg stared at her, clearly startled at her vehemence.

"It's okay, Ellyn—"

"No, it's not okay. Margaret Ellyn, I'm waiting."

Meg's eyes had gone from one adult to the other, now her gaze dropped to her lap. "Sorry."

When Grif would have responded, Ellyn stilled him with

a gesture. Finally Meg glanced up, then down again. "I'm sorry for being rude, Grif. Thank you for offering to give me a ride."

The words were stiff, and she made no eye contact, but they did fit the requirements.

Grif waited until Ellyn gave a slight nod before saying, "You're welcome, Meg. I'll be at your house at eight-fifteen. And here—" he added as he jotted something on a napkin "—is the number you can call Saturday to make sure I haven't forgotten."

"Grif, that's not necessary," Ellyn protested.

He handed the slip to Meg anyway.

"I can understand Meg wanting to make sure. Just remember, Meg, you need to be ready so we can leave."

Meg mumbled an agreement, but Ellyn noticed she also folded the napkin and placed it in her sweater pocket.

The drive home was silent. A sated silence from Ben. A torn silence from Meg, who still didn't want to believe, but didn't want to refuse, either. A customary silence from Grif. And from her?

A busy silence. Busy sorting out what had happened since Grif emerged from his rental car this afternoon.

Busy sorting out how she felt about it.

She'd been thrilled to see him.

Well, why shouldn't she be? John Griffin Junior was one of her oldest friends. *Friend* being the operative word.

Okay, so she'd had a few stray thoughts of another kind about him this afternoon. She'd been caught off guard by Grif's appearing as abruptly as he'd departed fifteen months ago. The surprise had left her off balance, distorting her reactions.

That, and maybe a little bit of what Kendra and Marti and Fran kept saying about her spending too much time alone, isolated on the ranch. She *was* lonely. She would admit that. At least to herself.

Lonely for the kind of connection a man and a woman could have.

Although that hadn't prompted her at any point in the past year to look at Luke Chandler's rear end with anything but the technical recognition that it was a fine bit of anatomy. Not the way she'd looked at Grif's when he'd been bending—

Ellyn shifted against the seat belt so she was looking out the door window.

What was the matter with her? It was as if her libido had forgotten Grif was her friend. There'd never been the least confusion about that during their years in Washington. From the time she and Dale had married, her friendship with Grif had never felt anything but natural and comfortable. It shouldn't be hard to get back into that groove. Especially since she'd thought her libido had just about died, what with Dale—

She pulled her mind from that too-often traveled route and back to the matter at hand.

Getting back into the groove of friendship with Grif. Kendra—and anyone else who might have doubts—would soon recognize that Ellyn and Grif were strictly friends.

If he stays around long enough for it to become an issue.

Reflected in the car door window, she could see faint, wavering images of her daughter and son in the back seat. All her scattered, contradicting, unfocused reactions dissipated, as if she'd been in a fog and the sun had come out.

That was the real issue.

Meg and Ben.

If her reactions to Grif were this jumbled, what would theirs be? They might *hear* that he was only staying a short time, but would they understand it and believe it? Especially since he was already slipping back into the role he'd once played in their lives.

So it was time to ask some hard questions. For her kids, and for herself.

Grif braked to a smooth stop in the driveway behind a parked pickup. "Were you expecting someone?" he asked.

"Must be Luke. He said he might stop by, but I didn't think he'd have a chance."

"Stop by?"

She felt the probe behind that. "He fixes things for us."

"Like?"

"Things," she repeated as they got out of the car. "Kids, say thank you, then go in and get ready for bed. It's late."

Ben said a sleepy thanks and good-night. Meg's was mumbled, but passable.

"You're welcome. I'll see you both soon."

Ellyn slowed her steps even more, and Grif matched her, so the kids were inside before the adults had reached the bottom of the corner steps that opened to the porch both along this side of the house and across the back.

"Grif, I'd like to talk to you."

"Okay."

The words she'd carefully gathered during the drive scattered like dust motes in the Wyoming wind. How could she start this?

"Ellyn?"

"Grif, why did you come?" she asked in a rush.

"You don't think I should have? Everyone else seems glad I'm visiting Far Hills."

"Of course you should come back anytime you want. This is your home. I didn't mean— But you haven't come back before. Not for a long time."

He looked away. "It was time."

"Okay," she said slowly, accepting his right to not reveal his reason. She didn't need to know his reason to make her point. "I can understand that—because an adult knows friendships can be transitory, or relationships you once thought were forever can crumble, but kids think such things are forever. Maybe you've forgotten how Ben and Meg—"

"I haven't forgotten anything." His voice dropped lower. "Not about any of you."

"Then why did you leave like that? How could you, if you—" The words were out of her mouth before her mind could catch up with them and stop them. And then all she could do was try her best to patch up the hole in her pride. "No, don't answer. I shouldn't have asked. It's none of my business. I've thought about this, about how things were back then, and I know I made mistakes. I shouldn't have leaned on you so much when we were all in Washington. I had no right. I'm truly sorry for having burdened you that way—"

"You didn't—"

"—all those years. You had no obligations to us—no obligations to anyone except the Army, and I know that's how you like it, how you've arranged your life, so I shouldn't have been surprised…" Still, she had been. Surprised and hurt. That was her problem, though, not his. But she hadn't been alone in being hurt. "But Grif, Meg and Ben don't understand that. They only know that you were there for them all the time and then suddenly you weren't. And then Dale was gone, too, and…"

She straightened and raised her head. She had to tilt it back to look him in the eyes. "And now you're here, and doing things for them, and they'll think everything can be the way it was before. They don't understand… I don't want them to be hurt anymore."

"I'm not here to hurt anybody, Ellyn. I'm here to help."

"Help?"

"There's a lot I can do. Practical things."

"Practical things," she echoed again. Ellyn's thoughts immediately went to Marti. The older woman had a lot on her shoulders, with the ranch and Emily, and Marti wrote to Grif regularly. Could he have picked up on something all of them here who cared about Marti had missed? "Is Marti—?"

"I know things have been tough for you since Dale died. With taking care of the kids and working and the house, you've had—"

"Me? You're here to help *me?*" She saw the truth from his face, but she still waited for his nod to confirm it before she said baldly, "I don't want your help, Grif."

"Ellyn, there are a lot of things with the house and—"

"I am not a charity case who needs some man to rescue me."

"I'm not *some* man," he said with a hint of something under his reasonableness that she was too riled up to decipher. After more than a year, he'd come out of pity—not friendship, but *pity!* "I'm your oldest friend."

"You were." He winced, and she relented. "I'm sorry. I didn't mean… You know I'll always consider you my friend. Maybe we could get back to… No, that's just what I'm afraid the kids are thinking. I don't know what sort of friends we can be now, especially when you go back to Washington. But I *do* know I don't need your help, John Griffin Junior."

"Don't call me that."

Even riled up she recognized the edge in his voice this time. She supposed he didn't like the formality, being reminded that he couldn't simply slip back into the role of close family friend when and if it pleased him.

"I don't want your help, *Grif.* If that's why you came, you might as well just go away and drop out of our lives again."

Chapter Four

Ellyn's declaration was barely out of her mouth when she turned and started up the steps.

Grif reached for her, but he was too late.

He smacked the edge of his fist against the railing. *Real smooth, Griffin. You handled that just great.*

"Ellyn—"

He was following her, not sure what he'd say or do, when the back door opened and Luke appeared, drying his hands on a bandanna.

The foreman looked from one to the other before saying, "Sorry, Ellyn, no luck."

"Okay. Thanks for trying, Luke. I really appreciate it." She patted the foreman's arm affectionately, then turned to Grif with her hand extended for shaking and her voice distant. "And thank you, Grif, for the lovely dinner. I hope you have a wonderful time during your visit. We might run into each other while you're here, but in case we don't, I want to say I'm glad things are going so well for your career, and I wish you great continued success. Goodbye. Good night, Luke.''

''Night, Ellyn.''

''Ellyn—''

But she was gone before Grif's protest had echoed to a close. There was no sense chasing after her while she was in that mood. Or while he couldn't think of the words to make her see he was right.

Maybe words weren't the way to go anyway. If he just did what needed doing, she'd find out soon enough that she hadn't had the final word.

He turned to find Luke regarding him with a faint expression of sympathy. But the younger man said nothing as they fell into step heading down the driveway toward their vehicles.

''What were you working on?'' Grif asked

''Dryer.''

Grif muttered a curse. ''So that antique *is* broken. Why doesn't she get a new one?''

''Ask her.''

''Hasn't Marti—?''

''She's tried.''

Grif should have guessed that. And he should have known that Ellyn would think Marti had already done enough—too much—in renting her Ridge House.

''There's got to be a way...'' he muttered to himself.

''Good luck,'' Luke said with a skeptical shake of his head.

Grif faced Luke as they came even with the ranch pickup. ''How rough are they having it?'' he asked.

''Up and down.''

''Money's tight?''

Luke nodded. ''Nobody'd let them go without necessities. But things like a dryer... That's harder to slip in unnoticed.''

''This job of Ellyn's...?''

"It's their only regular income."

"But Dale had insurance—"

"He'd borrowed against it."

"What the hell was he thinking?"

Luke looked at him from the shadow of his hat's brim. "If anybody knew, I'd have thought it would be you."

"In that case, nobody knows, because I sure don't."

As he shook the other man's hand and climbed into his car to head for his temporary quarters at Fort Piney, he remembered the last time he'd talked to Dale Sinclair. A year ago January. Fifteen months ago.

"It's not turning out the way I thought it would."

Grif stared across the small table at the man whose agitated phone call had brought him to this smoky, dingy bar at 2:23 in the morning. "What does that mean?"

Dale made a familiar, futile gesture, then wrapped his hands around his beer bottle. "It's hard to explain."

"Try."

"Remember the day we got married, Ellyn and me?"

He remembered.

Grif saw only the woman dressed in white, with a sheer veil covering her curling hair. The bouquet shifted as if the hand holding it might be trembling slightly, as she came down the aisle toward where he stood at the front of the church. Even through the veil, her expression radiated excitement and hope and love.

The excitement and hope and love weren't for him. Could never be for him. She deserved more than he could ever give her. She deserved a home, a family, all that the right man could give her.

"I had dreams then. Now our life's all wrapped up with teacher days and doctors visits and—God! I mean, I love my kids. It's just... Hell, how could you understand? What do you know about marriage or family life? It's more than that, anyhow. It's everything. And Ellyn. She's changed or... I don't know, but... She's not what I expected and—''

"I'm not the one you should be saying this to."

His voice was strained enough to catch even Dale's self-absorbed attention. "Why not? You're my friend."

Ellyn and Dale apart... Ellyn free... Ellyn...

He took a slow pull on the bottle, forcing the liquid down his tight throat, down toward the sensation in his gut. Like something locked up for a long time was trying to get loose.

"It's like you said, Dale, what do I know about all this? Nothing. You should be talking to somebody—a therapist, a counselor—somebody who'll help you and Ellyn out."

"I don't know. I've got a bag in my car. A clean break—''

"*Clean break?* You think it'll feel like a *clean break* for Ellyn or the kids? You go back and try to work this out—''

"If it were right, it wouldn't be so much work."

Grif looked at the face he'd known most of his life.

"How would you know, Dale? You've never worked at anything. You've got charm, looks and some brains, and you've coasted, moving on anytime a job or situation or people got a little tough. But this time, you're going to go home—to your wife and your kids—and try like hell to work it out. You'd be an idiot to give up the family you have, a family men dream about."

Dale had spluttered and protested, but in the end he'd done what Grif had ordered. Except he hadn't really. He'd moved them two-thirds of the way across the country, then gotten himself killed.

Grif blinked back to the present. He'd pulled the car nearly off the road in the stretch between Ellyn's and Kendra's houses where he'd be out of sight. He found himself staring up at the jutting outcropping of rock well up Crooked Mountain, the spot they'd always called Leaping Star's overlook.

He didn't believe in this stuff Ellyn had been saying about a Susland Curse, but any way you looked at it, the legend was a damned sad story, especially for the Indian woman and her children, who'd never done anyone any harm yet still paid the price.

Just like Ellyn and her kids.

Maybe Dale hadn't asked to get killed, but he sure could have left his wife and kids better provided for.

And him? Grif couldn't feel blameless, either. Had his leaving done Ellyn and the kids more harm than good?

Maybe if he'd stayed around…

No, that was one decision he knew was right. No matter how Ellyn and the kids blamed him for disappearing, he couldn't have stuck around once Dale's confession had let Grif's feelings for Ellyn shoulder their way past all his barriers.

Those barriers were there for good reason.

He just hoped he'd done enough repairs to them over these past fifteen months to keep from doing any more damage while he was here.

The campfire burned for four days and four nights on the outcropping on Crooked Mountain before Charles Susland rode up the mountainside. He'd have ignored Annalee's carrying on about it, but she was expecting again and he wanted another son.

The Crow woman rose slowly when he rode into her camp.

"You have no place here, woman."

"This is my place, my only place, my people's place," she said. *"They brought you to it when you took me as wife. They helped you. And you took our place."*

"Far Hills is mine. I built it. Go back to the reservation, Leaping Star."

"Your children die there. Your son, your daughter. Runs

At Dawn will follow if you do not care for her. There is nothing left in me."

"I can't go running off leaving Far Hills. And I have a son to care for here. A white son, who'll carry on what I build." He would have ridden away then if he could have, but Leaping Star's will was still too strong for him.

"Charles Susland. You turn away from your children, so your blood will be alone. You turn away from my people, so your blood will have no home. You turn away from me, so your blood will be lost. Only when someone loves enough to undo your wrongs will the laughter of children live beyond its echo in Far Hills.

"If these wrongs are not righted in five generations of your blood, Far Hills will be ever silent."

One more night the fire burned on the outcropping. Then it went out.

A sound woke Grif to instant alertness.

The room was empty, still, safe. The unfamiliarity of the room didn't bother him; the unfamiliarity itself was familiar. It took him another moment to realize the sound was his own, harsh breathing. He was slicked in sweat, as if he'd been surrounded by the fire of his dream.

He forced himself to lie still, to breathe slowly and calmly.

He hadn't had the dream in a long time. He'd come to terms with it long ago. He'd heard of people dreaming of showing up in public without their clothes or arriving in a new class only to discover it was the day of the final exam. He accepted this dream as his personalized version of that. He'd had the dream sometimes as a kid. More recently a time or two right before he went into an action.

Why tonight? No mystery there. It was being back here at Far Hills and Ellyn's talk about the legend, triggering memories of a campfire story.

Had nothing to do with him. Or his mission.

* * *

Parking in front of the Far Hills Market, Grif spotted Ellyn in the open garage door of Mechanic Ed's shop kitty-corner from the Market. Beyond her, inside the garage bay, he recognized her aging Suburban.

Conscious thought wasn't necessary—he headed directly for her. Even when Grif was a kid, Ed Bressler had a reputation for running roughshod over his customers, especially women.

"…and any item that's not properly itemized, I won't be paying for."

"Ellyn, that's not hardly fair—"

"We've agreed. Here's the list. You sign both copies, then I'll sign them, too, and we'll be all set."

Ed grumbled, but signed the paper Ellyn placed on the bumper. As she added her signature, the gray-haired mechanic looked up and spotted Grif. "Well, if it ain't the general!"

Ellyn's pause as she folded one copy of the paper and slipped it into her purse was so slight that someone not watching her carefully would have missed it. Grif didn't miss it.

"You're a few promotions ahead of the Army, Ed. How are you doing? Hi, Ellyn."

"Can't complain. Except when this one comes around." The older man gestured toward Ellyn. "Orders me around something fierce, and cuts my profit to worse than nothing."

"Morning, Grif." Did Ellyn sound like her usual self? He hoped he was imagining the note that indicated she would have preferred to not see him. "Ed, you're not doing so bad. You got another brand new snowmobile this winter, didn't you?"

"Well, I gotta have some fun in life, don't I?"

"Of course," she agreed, then added dryly, "As long as it's not all at my expense."

Ed grinned, not the least abashed. "No, ma'am! Don't

you worry, Ellyn, your vehicle will be ready come three o'clock.''

"Good. Thank you, Ed.''

She gave Grif a slight smile as she started past him. He waved to Ed Bressler, and followed her.

"You need a ride, Ellyn?''

"Oh, no. Thank you. I'm just going to the *Banner*.''

"I could drive you—''

"That's not necessary. It's a few blocks and I have to stop at the post office on the way.''

"Mind if I walk with you?'' When she didn't answer right away, he added, "I'd like to say hello to Larry. He was in D.C. a few years back and we got together.''

"I'm sure he'll be glad to see you'' was her non-answer.

They had little need for conversation as they walked because they were kept busy answering greetings. Most of them for Ellyn, but a fair share for Grif.

"You're surprised so many people remember you, aren't you?'' she asked as they headed into the post office.

Almost as surprised as he was that she'd spotted and identified his reaction. He'd have said she wasn't paying any attention to him at all.

"I was a summer visitor for a few years, nothing more. And that was a long time ago.''

"A lot more than a casual summer visitor,'' she disputed. "You're a Susland. A Susland of Far Hills Ranch, and that counts for something around here.''

He shrugged. "I suspect it has more to do with the people doing the remembering than with me.''

"They *are* nice people around here, aren't they?''

Actually he'd been thinking they didn't have a lot to keep them occupied, otherwise they wouldn't have had the attention left over to remember from all those years ago. But that seemed damned churlish to say now. "I suppose so.''

She eyed him for a long moment, then turned to the racks

in the lobby filled with federal tax return forms and information.

What was with everyone acting like this was some emotional homecoming for him? How could someone who'd never had a home have a homecoming?

"What are you getting those for?" he asked, mostly to fill the silence with something other than his own thoughts.

She looked over her shoulder at him.

"If I wanted wallpaper, I'd go with something a little more decorative." He grinned at her sassy tone, and thought she fought to hold off an answering grin. "What do you think I'm getting these for? To do my taxes."

"Yourself?"

"Yes, myself."

"You didn't used to do your taxes."

"No, Dale had an accountant. But doing them myself is one more fee I can save. Besides, I already did a good portion of the work, gathering all the information. Actually, I had them all done, but a glass of orange juice somehow got spilled over them this morning, so I need clean forms to fill in before I can mail them."

"You never were much of a morning person. You should be more careful," he deadpanned as they headed out.

"Me!" she started indignantly, squaring off at him. Then she caught herself and smiled wryly. "You're right, I should have picked the papers up before they fell into harm's way, but…"

"But you'd washed Superwoman's cape and couldn't throw it in the dryer because that's broken."

She ignored both his poke at her tendency to take on responsibility for everything and the jab at her dryer situation. "But I was preoccupied this morning. Grif, I…"

"You what?"

"I don't want you to misunderstand this."

"There's nothing to misunderstand yet."

She gave him a surprisingly dirty look. Surprising because in the past she'd likely have apologized, and because he found he liked this new tartness in her.

"I don't want you to misunderstand that I meant what I said about the kids and about thinking you have to help me. But I am sorry if I made you feel unwelcomed. This is your home."

His mood sobered with her first words.

"Don't worry about me feeling unwelcomed. And I don't think I *have* to help you. But I'm going to." She opened her mouth, no doubt to argue, but he marched on. "I will make it as clear to the kids as I can that I'm here temporarily. But I'll also tell them that I'll be back again—because I will be.

"As for now, I've made promises to your children that I intend to keep—catch with Ben this afternoon, and driving Meg Saturday morning. I hope there will be more. And I can tell you this, Ellyn, I will keep any promise I make."

They'd stopped in front of the main door to the *Far Hills Banner* and were practically toe-to-toe, their gazes locked. Grif watched Ellyn's chest rise and fall at a stepped-up rate, and became aware of his own faster than normal breathing.

"Grif! I'd heard you were in town!"

The grip on his arm and the hand pumping his own jerked Grif's focus from Ellyn to Larry Orrin, editor/publisher/owner of the *Far Hills Banner*.

"Great to see you. I hear you've been promoted again. C'mon back and give me the details."

At the door to the glass-and-partition office with Larry's name on it, Grif glanced around, spotting Ellyn watching them from a doorway at the opposite side of the room.

Before he could read her expression, she went in an office and closed the door behind her.

When Ellyn emerged from her office three hours later, Grif was no longer in Larry's office.

I will keep any promise I make.

Grif keeping promises had never been the problem. The problem had been the promises other people—she—had wanted him to make that he didn't.

But that was a long, long time ago.

Suddenly restless, Ellyn decided to use her lunch break to walk across town to the church that housed the baby-sitting co-op Fran Sinclair ran. Sometimes Meg and Ben took advantage of the after-school program, so Ellyn filled her fair share of shifts. With work and her commitments to help in the kids' classrooms, Ellyn thought her pocket calendar often looked like computer code.

"So, how's Grif?" Fran asked once the scheduling was done.

"He seems fine." Ellyn tucked her calendar into her purse.

"I saw you walking with him this morning. I would have stopped, but you looked deep in conversation."

"He was walking with me," Ellyn corrected mildly, her thoughts on something Grif said yesterday. "Fran, do you remember Nancy Susland? I mean Nancy Griffin—Grif's mother?"

She looked up to see Fran's sharpened interest, and regretted her impulsive question.

Ever since Kendra and Daniel's wedding nearly three months ago, Fran and Marti had been egging her on to start dating. As if she didn't have enough to think about without a social life to factor in. She'd been turning a blind eye to their efforts, sidestepping when she needed to, and not making a big deal of it.

"Of course I remember her. When I was a kid, she and Wendy still lived on the ranch. And I remember summers when she'd come back to visit, first with her husband, then with him and Grif as a little one, then with Grif alone."

That sequence must have represented a great deal of significance in Nancy Griffin's life—leaving her home to marry a military man, and then returning without him.

Fran blinked once, then again. ''I know one thing, she loved her son more than anything else in the world. She'd hate to see him lonely.''

Lonely. Was *Grif* lonely? He always seemed so self-contained, his emotions so firmly under control.

''But at least he's come home to Far Hills again. Nancy would like that.''

''Damn, double damn.''

The afternoon had not gone well for Ellyn. A display ad from a dry cleaner's end-of-season special on winter uniforms for soldiers from Fort Piney had refused to go together. And for some reason her mind kept wandering from possible solutions.

That put her behind in getting out of the office, so she missed picking up Meg and Ben at school. By standing agreement, if she wasn't there to pick them up, they took the bus.

Taking the direct route home, she beat the school bus, allowing her to get the bedding she'd put in the washer before work, out on the line. She'd changed into leggings and another old shirt—she was not going to stay in her work clothes because Grif was coming to play catch with Ben—when two things happened simultaneously.

She heard a car stop near the back door and she saw a starburst splatter of an unexpected rain shower against the kitchen window.

Sprinting out the door, she barely gave the car a glance as she headed up the hill. Apparently she didn't give her footing as much attention as it needed, because three-quarters of the way up, her right foot went out from under her at a particularly eroded spot and she came down hard on her left knee.

Even then she didn't swear, but clambered up and kept going. She reached the mattress pad first, and was bundling it into the basket when Grif arrived at her side.

"More sheets?" he asked as they started pulling the pins that secured the bottom sheet.

"Yes," she said shortly. She wouldn't give away Ben's secret. Or her worry.

The wind caught the cupped interior of the elastic-rimmed sheet and puffed it up like a spinnaker. The end she held pulled out of her hand, and it collapsed as quickly as it had inflated, trailing the loose end into the dust that had absorbed just enough moisture to make it cling to the damp fabric. Mud.

That's when she swore.

"You get the basket," Grif instructed, as he reeled in the cloth to a dirt-smeared, damp lump against his chest. "I'll keep this one separate."

She didn't argue, grabbing the basket with the still wet, but at least clean mattress pad, and scrambled down the path to rush breathlessly into the back hall, with Grif on her heels to escape the big, hard raindrops that had kept battering them.

Not that a raindrop would have a chance against the Iron Warrior.

They stood there a moment, catching their breath. At least she did. He hardly looked affected at all.

The Iron Warrior. Ellyn had never cared for Dale's nickname for Grif, yet here she'd used it twice in two days in her own mind.

"Thanks for the help, Grif. And I'm sorry for the outburst."

"I'd say you had a right."

"It'll wash out." She dredged up a smile for Grif's benefit. "Besides, the cattle ranchers need the rain."

"What *you* need is a dryer."

"I'd like one, sure, but it's not in the budget right now."

"It *should* be. If Dale had—" He bit off his word, then muttered a curse under his breath. "You shouldn't have to struggle."

"We're fine, Grif. Compared to a lot of widows, I'm truly well off, especially with all the good friends around us here."

"You shouldn't have to struggle," he repeated stubbornly. "Ellyn, let me buy you—"

"No." The word hung there, solid and weighty, not a word to be easily swayed. "That's very sweet of you, but no. This is not your responsibility, and—"

"Maybe it is."

"What?" Her initial surprise quickly gave way to amusement. "How on earth could you figure it was *your* responsibility?"

He hesitated. The stark planes of his face revealed nothing—no ticking muscles, no clenching jaw—but shadows in his gray eyes gave her the impression he'd looked at a precipice, and backed away from it.

"If I'd been paying closer attention... I might have known," he said gruffly.

She tipped her head, trying to hold onto the amusement that had suddenly gone sour in her stomach. "You might have known Dale was going to be killed in an accident?"

"I should have known he was borrowing against his insurance, eating away at your savings."

She didn't bother to ask how he knew. Several people around Far Hills knew her financial situation, and its cause. She doubted any would think twice about filling Grif in.

"If I'd known," Grif was continuing, "if I'd paid attention—I could have talked to him. And then you would still be living your comfortable life in Washington—you and the kids."

She sat at the kitchen table, and he joined her.

"I don't think Dale was listening to anyone at that point, Grif. Besides," she added more briskly, evading the probing look he sent her, "what about me? I was his wife. *I* should have known. And looking back, there *were* indications. Things I should have picked up on. But I shut my eyes to the warning signs.''

And not just about Dale's irresponsible use of their savings cushion—never as thick as she would have liked it.

She'd shut her eyes to warning signs of all kinds.

So she'd been absolutely unprepared that night fifteen months ago when Dale came home, smelling of stale beer and staler cigarette smoke, and announced he'd been thinking about getting a divorce, but he had decided to "give her another chance."

Maybe now she'd react differently to such an announcement, but that night she'd been stunned, numbed. Barely able to respond as Dale talked. Near dawn, he'd decided they should return to Wyoming. Get back to where a man could breathe, where he wasn't hemmed in by suburban life, where he didn't have to mow the lawn every damned weekend.

Even at the time she'd known there was a flaw in his reasoning. But she had been too scared to acknowledge that he was feeling hemmed in by his family, not the lawn mower. And his wife and children were moving with him to Wyoming.

With full daylight, Dale had experienced a feverish burst of energy. He'd written a letter of resignation to the mortgage company where he worked and faxed it, despite her protests. As soon as she had the kids off to school, Dale had dragged her to a real estate agent, then on to a mover, and next to a woman who arranged sales of household goods. When Dale wound down enough to take a nap that afternoon, the first person she'd called was Grif.

He was gone.

No warning. No half-measures. His phone disconnected and the only explanation a message on her answering machine saying he'd been given an urgent assignment, and he would be in touch.

But he wasn't in touch. Not really. Not until now.

When he was blaming himself for her no longer having that comfortable life in Washington he thought she should have.

I don't want that life back.

The thought, clear and firm, came out of nowhere. As the words streamed through her mind, she knew they were absolutely, one-hundred percent true. She didn't want that old life back. Sure, a few of the conveniences wouldn't be bad. But not the whole thing.

And not the old Ellyn.

She sat up straighter, her mood considerably lightened from moments ago.

"Ellyn?"

She blinked away the past, and focused on the man before her.

"Grif, you have an overdeveloped sense of responsibility. It's one of the things I've always admired about you. Along with you being such a…an *honorable* man."

He made a sound less benign than a snort.

"Don't argue, Grif. You're the most honorable man I've met in my life, and I won't let anyone say otherwise—even you."

"There's a lot you don't know—"

Ben rushed in, moving fast enough to arrive at the same time as the noise that usually preceded him.

"Grif!" Without waiting for a response, he spun around to his trailing sister. "I told you he'd come. *Told*cha."

She shrugged with frigid lack of interest as she passed him and began undoing her shoes. "So what. It's raining."

"It's letting up," Ben declared as he tugged off his shoes.

"Is not."

"Is, too."

"Children!"

"Mom, it is letting up, honest. You *caaaaan't* say I can't

practice baseball with Grif because it's raining, because it's nearly not. Honest, Mom.''

''Even if it's dry as a bone, you're not going out in those clothes, so go change, and then we'll see what the weather is.''

''Okay. I'll be right back, Grif. I'll hurry.''

''Neatly!'' Ellyn called after him. Meg started after her brother at a more leisurely pace but without her usual detour to the refrigerator. ''Don't you want some milk or juice?''

''No, thank you.''

''Did you say hello to Grif?''

''Hello,'' the girl half mumbled without turning around.

Ellyn grimaced apologetically. Grif started to reach toward her, as if to pat her arm to say it was all right, then seemed to think better of it. Instead he went to the kitchen window, pushing back the curtain and looking outside.

''Ben might make a good weatherman. It *is* clearing up.''

''I wonder when things are going to clear up with Meg,'' she muttered. ''She's been as rude as humanly possible to you without overtly breaking any house rules.''

''I told you, she's got cause. Don't let it bother— What?''

She was shaking her head. ''You're not going to change the subject. I want to get back to what you said before the kids came in. That there was a lot I didn't know about something.''

''I don't remember.''

''Grif—''

''Sorry, I lost the train of thought.''

She didn't believe him, but what could she do? Call the man who truly was the most honorable person she'd met a liar?

Ben charged back down the hallway, panting, carrying his precious baseball glove. ''My ball and bat are on the back porch. I put them there so we wouldn't waste any time.''

"Okay, let's go. We'll loosen up, then you tell me what you want to work on."

Ben was already reeling off fielding techniques when Grif turned at the doorway and looked back at her. "When it comes to being honorable, you don't know me as well as you think you do, Ellyn."

Only with the greatest of willpower—and by finding things that needed doing at the other side of the house— did she overcome the temptation to watch them. She wouldn't allow Grif to make her the beneficiary of his compassion, but that didn't mean she could deny Ben what he so clearly needed. Ben needed time—on his own—with Grif.

In the usual way of things, it should have been Dale out there playing with his son. If she'd done things differently, maybe… But no amount of regrets could change that now.

And if Dale had continued being the sort of father he'd been, it still wouldn't have been Dale out there with Ben.

The slam of the back door startled her out of her dour thoughts. She rolled the last pair of Ben's socks together, and left the array of folded laundry on her bed to head for the kitchen.

She arrived to hear Ben offering, "You could stay for dinner."

It caught her by surprise—and it shouldn't have. The words to second the invitation, and the contradictory words to undermine it both rose to her lips, causing a gridlock that left her mute.

"Thanks, Ben, but I'm having dinner tonight up at the home ranch with Marti and Emily."

"Sometimes, we have pizza on Fridays."

She had to admire her son's ability to double-dip—both offering an invitation and lobbying for a treat.

"I'm going to Kendra and Daniel's Friday."

"Okay, then tomorrow night. We can play catch and—"

Finally Ellyn's mouth started working again. "Ben, you and Meg are going to the after-school program tomorrow because I work late."

"I forgot. But Grif could still come to dinner."

With a slightly apologetic look toward Grif, she added, "I won't have time to cook a special dinner for a guest."

"Regular dinner would be okay, wouldn't it, Grif? She always makes real good macaroni and cheese. Better even than the box."

"The kids like macaroni and cheese," she said defensively, torn between loyalty and embarrassment. Here she'd been telling Grif they were doing fine, and Ben made it sound as if they were destitute.

"So do I," Grif said. "But I don't want to make more work for you, so how about if I take you out to dinner tomorrow."

"Yeah!"

"No," Ellyn said—not as loudly as her son's agreement but just as firmly. "We are *not* going to take advantage of Grif's generosity by letting him take us to dinner twice in one week."

"But *Mo-oom*..."

"I could bring some fried chicken and you could provide the macaroni and cheese, and even a vegetable," Grif bargained.

"Grif, I don't—" But then Ellyn saw that her son had caught sight of the mattress pad, strung up to dry across the tops of the two partially opened doors used to mask the washer and dryer. And the look on his face was so glum that she nearly made the whole situation worse by wrapping him in her arms and cuddling him. "Is six-thirty too early to eat for you?"

He looked from her to Ben, then followed the direction of Ben's gaze to the mattress pad.

"I'll come around six. In case you need any help."

"That's not neces—"

But he wasn't listening to her protests. Did he ever?

"Ben, didn't you say you had math homework? Better get to it."

"Huh? Oh, yeah. Okay. See ya, Grif."

"Good night, Ben."

For a moment Ellyn thought he was going to say something. Instead he simply brushed his fingers across the back of her hand. She supposed this was compassion, too. But she didn't mind accepting this. All he said was, "I'll see you tomorrow."

Ellyn had poured the macaroni into the boiling water when she heard a vehicle pull up beside the house the next morning. A glance out the window revealed one of the battered ranch pickups. She'd gotten the impression that Luke had about given up on her dryer, but if he was willing to take another crack at it, she wouldn't say no.

She was cutting up cheese across the top layer of macaroni, so all she'd have to do was add the milk and put it in the oven when she got home, when it struck her that Luke had never come inside. Maybe it was another hand who'd parked here as the nearest spot for some work. But the regular hands usually checked in to say hello and let her know they'd be around. She went out to check.

She recognized the pungent smell as soon as she stepped out the back door. The back of the truck bed was half loaded with the used straw and manure from the barn where Luke sheltered any horses that were about to give birth, ailing or otherwise needing to be kept under supervision. The other half of the load was already piled beside the rectangle of earth where she'd grown vegetables and herbs last summer.

The compost made great fertilizer for the garden, but as aromatherapy it left something to be desired.

Movement from the corner of her eye made her turn. Grif had just driven a shovel into the firmed earth of last year's garden, where a segment was already turned over. He'd taken his shirt off, revealing to her an angle of a muscled back and a slice of a rib cage narrowing to his waist.

She was staring.

That realization finally jerked her out of her reverie, and she strode toward where he had been steadily shoveling.

"What are you doing?"

"Digging."

"I can see that. Why?"

"To turn the soil over."

"Grif, if you don't stop answering like Ben at his most frustrating, I'm going to give you a good whack on the behind."

He stopped and leaned on the shovel like a caricature of a farmer. "A whack on the behind? You never hit Ben."

Now why on earth had she said that? And why did she keep getting an image of that very part of his anatomy as he'd bent over the laundry basket?

"No, but you're even more frustrating than he is. And don't you dare tell him I said that, because he'll do his best to catch up!"

He grinned.

"So?" she prompted.

"So?" he parried.

"Grif!"

"All right, all right. Marti says you put in a garden last year and you've ordered seeds for one this year. She's already dug the compost into hers, and so has Kendra."

"I'll get to it, too. But I've been—"

"Busy. I know. And I know you'd get to it when you could. But Marti says it's best to let the ground sit after you've put the compost in, so you'd be late planting."

"Grif, I don't need your—"

"Help. Yeah, I know that, too. But it makes sense. You're short on time. I've got time on my hands, and I need to keep my training up, so…"

"Somehow I don't think digging horse manure into a garden is part of the Army's fitness program."

"The way they like to punish folks at boot camp, it would be if they thought of it."

She suppressed a smile, and made her voice as stern as she could. "Grif, I told you that I don't need your help. I can't deny that Ben is ecstatic to have you around, and I'm glad you're spending time with us during this visit. But I also expect you to respect me on this. If you can't do that…"

"Okay," he said slowly. "I can't very well load this back into the pickup and take it back to Luke. So I guess I'll put the rest of it here and leave it for you for when you can get to it."

A stinking reminder every time she walked out the door of one more chore she hadn't accomplished. And he was right about the timing. If she hoped to get a good crop of vegetables—and last year's had come in very handy this past winter—it was important to make the most of Wyoming's brief, intense growing season.

She crossed her arms under her breasts and frowned. "All right, Griffin, you win this one. But I'm going to get angry at you if you keep disregarding what I've said. I don't need your help, Grif, and I don't want it. And don't think that I'm going to accept any more of this sneaky, underhanded maneuvering to do things for me just because you think I'm some pathetic charity case. Do you understand?"

He met her frown with a direct, intense look. "As long as *you* understand that I don't think you're pathetic or a charity case, and never will."

"Okay."

"Okay."

Neither looked away.

"I…" Ellyn felt a tightening in her throat, spreading down to her chest, then lower, and lower, where the tightening curled in on itself in a knot of warmth. She turned her head. "I've got to get ready for work."

"Okay. I'll see you at dinner."

She nodded as she started to walk away, then heard the solid sound of the shovel digging into the earth before his voice came from behind her.

"By the way, Ellyn, in the Army, sneaky, underhanded maneuvering is called strategy."

She kept walking so he wouldn't see her grin.

Getting ready for work required no more than automatic pilot attention. And that left her mind free. Too free.

That summer she was eighteen… That night…

Grif so tall and straight and serious. So familiar and so foreign. The boy she'd idolized, now a man at twenty-one, and her feelings at eighteen too big to contain. Taking every ounce of courage she owned and then going into debt a pound or two for more. Taking the opportunity of the two of them alone in the lingering twilight after a swim. Putting her arms around his neck and her lips against his closed mouth. Telling him with her halting words and her awkward embrace how she felt.

And Grif firmly setting her away from him. His hold on her tight enough to bruise her for several days. The bruise from his words had lasted much, much longer.

"Don't, Ellyn. I can't feel that way about you. Do you understand? I can't—I *won't*. I'm never going to marry, and you should have a husband who loves you and a houseful of kids. So don't feel that way—not about me. Do you understand?"

Responding to the absolute certainty in his voice, she'd nodded numbly, although she hadn't understood anything except that he didn't feel about her the way she felt about him, leaving a void in her heart.

A void Dale had set about trying to fill. And gradually, over the next three years, he had. Until she'd loved him, married him, had Meg, then Ben and built what she'd felt was a good life.

During those same years she had happily received what Grif *had* offered. She'd let herself believe it was a permanent friendship, despite what her mother always said. *A woman's got to keep working all the time for a man to keep giving her anything.*

She met her own eyes in the mirror as she put on lipstick. Enough of this retrospective. Enough *brooding.*

She snatched up her purse, and headed out.

"Grif? I left the back door open, in case you want to get something. There are oatmeal raisin cookies in the cookie tin next to the fridge."

"Thanks."

"You're welcome. I'll see you tonight."

"Yep."

She turned and started away, feeling oddly warm. Then she thought of something else and turned back.

"Oh, Grif? One more thing."

"Yeah?"

"Don't forget to take a shower before tonight!"

His chuckle followed her into the car and seemed to stay in her head all afternoon.

Chapter Five

Dinner went together quickly with the kids doing their part—Ben without dragging his feet for once and Meg in absolute silence—and Grif helping.

When they'd all sat down and Ellyn suddenly realized she'd forgotten a serving spoon for the macaroni and cheese, Grif rose before she could get up, laid a restraining hand on her shoulder and said, "I'll get it."

The warmth and weight of his hand through the fabric of the blouse she still wore from work—she simply hadn't had time to change into her usual disreputable attire—was unexpected enough to draw her breath away for a second. He was back before she'd finished wondering at herself for being so easily...*startled.*

"You've organized the drawers the same as the other house," Griff commented.

"I hadn't realized that." For some reason she didn't like the idea.

"Mom, you remember I got baseball practice Saturday?"

"Yes, Ben. Mrs. Hamil will take you and Tommy, then drop you off at the library where I'll be at the history festival when practice ends. I'm sorry I have to miss your practice."

"That's okay. It's pretty boring unless you're a player—at least until we start games. That's in two weeks, Grif," Ben added in a hopeful tone.

"Almost three weeks. And that's provided it's decent weather. The first weekend in May can still be pretty co— Oh, no!" Ellyn recovered fast, but not fast enough.

"What?" Ben and Meg chorused.

"Nothing it's nothing. I remembered something. But talking about May in Wyoming, I remember one year when it snowed almost at the end of the month."

"What did you remember, Ellyn?" Grif pursued.

"Nothing catastrophic. I realized I forgot to drop those tax forms in the mail. As long as I put them in the box when I'm in town Saturday, they'll be fine."

"Give them to me, and I'll drop them in the box tonight. I go by the post office anyway. It makes sense, Ellyn."

Maybe, but it felt like a rescue. And she didn't like the feeling. She could stand on her own two feet.

She thanked him shortly. Then, not bothering with subtlety, she turned to her children and asked about their day. Meg shrugged in world-weary disinterest. Only Ben started prattling on about how his teacher, Mrs. Hammerschmidt, had dealt with a classmate of his who apparently had encountered some poison plant during recess.

"Ben, what's this project Daniel mentioned at the restaurant the other night?" Ellyn asked, reminded by talk of his teacher.

He pushed a stalk of broccoli from one side of his plate to the other. "Nothing."

"Ben, it can't be *nothing*. Is it something for school?"

"Yeah, just something for school," he agreed, before picking up a chicken leg from his plate and biting into it.

"What kind of project is it?" she persisted.

"Aww, Mom, you know—"

"*Eeew,* Mom! He's talking with his mouth full again!" protested Meg.

"Wait until you've finished chewing, Ben," Ellyn instructed. "But then I want to hear about this project."

But Meg, having broken her silence, apparently decided her brother had held the spotlight long enough, and began talking about one topic covered in her class today—the history of Far Hills and the Suslands.

"Vicki says her mother says that her family's been here nearly as long as the Suslands. And they've seen the whole thing, from the start. When the first Susland was so horrible and mean that he got the ranch cursed forever."

"The Suslands as well as the ranch," Grif corrected mildly.

Meg gaped at him. Ellyn supposed her daughter had expected him to object to this account of his family's perfidy, rather than fleshing it out. But she was not a quitter, and she recovered quickly.

"*And* Vicki's mother says the Suslands carry tragedy and bad luck in their back pockets, so it follows them everywhere they go. Her mother told Vicki all about it, and she told me—at least what she could remember. People killed each other and got murdered and got horribly sick until they died—"

"Meg—" Ellyn started to protest, remembering that Grif's mother had suffered a long, painful illness before she died, but Meg had already rolled on.

"—and some went crazy, and *then* they got sick and died. And I told Vicki, I thought *all* the Suslands must be crazy."

She shot Grif a look of smug triumph.

He met it blandly for a moment, then turned to Ellyn, a

frown drawing down his brows, but a glint in his gray eyes. "Has my Susland cousin Kendra been foaming at the mouth again?"

"Kendra? Kendra isn't—" Meg snapped her mouth shut as she realized that Kendra *was,* and that her triumph had evaporated.

She pushed back her chair, but before she could do more, Ellyn quietly reminded her, "You need to ask to be excused, and clear your place."

"May I *please* be excused," she enunciated with bitter emphasis.

"Yes, you may. And don't forget—"

"I know, I know."

Meg snatched up her plate and perched her glass at a precarious angle on top. Ellyn bit her lip to keep from issuing a warning. If there was an accident, Meg would have to deal with the consequences, but Ellyn had vowed from the time she knew she was pregnant that she would not be a mother who issued a constant stream of dire warnings and potential failings.

Meg kept the glass in place despite exaggerated flouncing as she went into the kitchen then returned, passing them without deigning to look at them.

"May I please be excused?"

"Yes, Ben."

After Ben cleared his place and disappeared toward his room, a silence fell.

Grif looked at her. "Sorry. That was childish with Meg."

"I can't blame you. She has been impossible, and you've been very patient. Besides, it's good for her to know she can push you only so far. Otherwise, my dear daughter will keep pushing."

He insisted on helping her clean up. In companionable silence, she washed and he dried the dishes. When she'd finished at the sink, she gathered the silverware to put away, sorting it into the drawer…in exactly the same place and pattern as in their home near Washington. Just as Grif had observed.

Had she brought other things with her from there without knowing it? Had she inadvertently brought the ghosts of old disappointments with her across the country?

After sliding the drawer closed with her hip, she turned for more items to dry, and ran hard into Grif. Her hands instinctively spread against his solid chest, and one foot shifted forward to help her balance. Except that movement brought her thigh high and snug between his legs, and that did nothing for her balance. He'd automatically caught her, a strong hand behind each of her shoulders, steadying her, keeping her from stumbling or toppling over.

A sudden fire burned in her chest, turning her throat to ashes. The slightest pressure against her back would bring them chest to chest, a drop of his chin and a lifting of hers would bring them mouth to mouth.

Without thought or intent, she raised her face to him. His legs seemed to tighten on either side of hers.

His eyes were closed. His lips pressed tight against each other. His expression impenetrable.

Then his lips moved, and she watched the motion so carefully that at first she didn't absorb the meaning of the words they produced.

"Do you ride?"

She cleared her throat trying to brush away the ashes. "What?"

"Since you've been back here, do you go riding?"

What path could his thoughts have taken to reach that destination? Not the same path hers had been following, that was for sure. Of course not. Grif didn't think of her that way.

"No." She stepped back, careful not to look at him. Gaining oxygen with a near hiccuping sigh. "I...I haven't had time."

"That's a shame. You were so good."

"No better than any of the rest of us."

"Yes, you were. It was like…like the horses wanted to carry you instead of it being a chore for them." That surprised a chuckle from her. "Didn't you notice you were always the first to catch your horse?"

"Not *always*—"

He shook his head. "Every time. Because the horse *wanted* to get caught. They'd all get up there and vie to be the one you were going to ride, and when you picked one the others would deflate."

She felt oddly flattered and flustered by this ridiculous notion. She laughed. "This is a side of you I've never seen before. I didn't know you could be so fanciful, Grif."

"It's not fanciful, it's the truth. I never said it then because it was part of how things were. And later…riding wasn't part of later."

"We had some great rides, didn't we?"

"Yes, we did."

His deep voice mellowed, drawing her. She risked a glance, then didn't look away.

His eyes were open now, focused on her, a faint softening around them not quite qualifying as a smile, a steady, familiar glow in them. A glow that brought such warmth. The comfortable, caring warmth of their past, and the warmth she'd enjoyed in their adult friendship.

Maybe they *could* rebuild. Maybe the past fifteen months, and all she'd gone through, wouldn't matter.

And then a flare flickered across, around, through the warmth. For an instant, before Grif blinked, and looked away.

Or perhaps she imagined that instant, because there was nothing like that as he said good-night and headed out. Imagining such things about Grif was not good. Definitely not good.

* * *

Ellyn's heart sank as Meg shuffled into the kitchen in her robe and slippers at 8:05 Saturday morning.

Ellyn had woken her up forty-five minutes ago, plenty of time for her to have gotten dressed and be ready for breakfast. But as she had that first night when Grif took them to dinner, Meg appeared to be unwilling to act on the assumption that he'd arrive as promised.

"Meg, you better get ready, or you'll be late for Grif."

"How do I know he's really coming?"

Because he told you he would.

If Ellyn gave that answer, her daughter would be fully justified in pointing out how many times Dale had said he'd do something—promised, sworn, pledged—and then had failed to follow through. Always with plenty of excuses of how it couldn't have been avoided and it most certainly was not his fault.

And Ellyn would be in the position of holding Grif up as a paragon in comparison to Dale. That wouldn't be fair to Grif. Or to Meg. Maybe not even to Dale.

"I can't tell you that, honey. Trusting that Grif will come because he said he would is something that has to come from inside you. Only you can decide if you believe he's coming."

Meg chewed on her bottom lip. She caught Ellyn watching her, gave her mother a faintly defiant look, then pulled an often-folded napkin from the robe pocket. Spreading it out, she lifted the phone receiver and punched in the numbers.

The phone must have rung enough times that Meg had started to believe, because she seemed to relax. That ended abruptly, her expression darkening. After a moment came a flash of relief, then a jumbled mix with uncertainty the dominant note.

Without having said a word, Meg hung up the phone. Ellyn bit her lip to keep from demanding what had happened.

"Grif left a message," Meg said at last. "For me." The bemusement of those last two words was fragile. "Mom? How'd he know I'd call?"

"I don't know. I guess you'll have to ask him if you want to know."

Meg looked at her, doubts and hopes swirling in her eyes, then spun around and could be heard clattering up the stairs.

Ellyn found herself staring at the telephone. She withstood temptation for another full minute, then she lifted the receiver and hit redial. After four rings, a voice answered at the other end—Grif's voice, but without a key element of vibrancy, telling her immediately that this was a recording.

"You've reached the quarters of Colonel John Griffin Junior. I am not here, Meg, because I left at 7:50 a.m. to keep our appointment. If you—or anyone else—would like to leave a message, please wait for the beep."

Whoever said silence was golden had never sat beside a ten-year-old girl who'd once adored you and now looked at you like she suspected you plucked the wings off butterflies for fun—when she bothered to look at you at all.

Not a word, the entire thirty-five-minute drive there. There had been plenty of sidelong staring. The kid was going to get eyestrain trying to study his profile without turning toward him.

He knew he didn't deserve her adoration anymore—never had. Though it had done strange things to him that from babyhood on, Meg would break into a smile and launch herself into his arms at his every arrival. That was gone, but he wasn't sure he deserved her distrust, either. Except...

He'd walked into an apparent crisis this morning, with Ben anxiously telling his mother he *had* to go to practice, even as she said thank you anyway to someone on the telephone, and hung it up with a shake of her head.

"That was our last hope, Ben. I can take you, but I'll be working when practice ends, and there's nobody to get you to the library."

"I'll walk."

"That's too far for you to walk alone." Ellyn had explained to Grif, "Ben's ride had to cancel because his friend's little sister is sick—maybe chicken pox."

"But I *have* to go…"

"I'm sorry, Ben, but—"

"What time?" Grif had asked. And in minutes it was worked out that Grif and Meg would be back from their trip in time to pick up Ben at baseball practice. They might even catch the last half hour or so—a prospect that added an extra few watts to Ben's already dazzling smile as he dashed off to get dressed.

Ellyn had given him a smile, less dazzling, but extremely satisfying, and a bag with ham sandwiches for the trip and a surprise.

She'd looked up at him almost sternly, and said in a faintly scolding tone, "You're a good man, John Griffin Junior. The best."

And then she'd kissed him on the cheek.

What might have complicated matters was that the next time he'd looked up, Meg was standing in the doorway staring at him.

Had she seen Ellyn's gesture of affection and misinterpreted it?

He hadn't misinterpreted it, and it still had complicated matters for him. It had complicated reminding his body that Ellyn was a friend when it responded so strongly to her nearness, her scent—the feel of her lips against his skin.

He knew why she'd done it. He'd understood completely. She wanted to make sure they both knew that what had happened the night before hadn't meant anything.

An accidental tangle of one body with the other. Could have happened between two strangers in a crowded hallway. Except it hadn't been a stranger, it had been Ellyn. If her leg had advanced another inch, if she'd swayed another millimeter closer, she would have known that *friendship* was a lie.

Grif spotted Ellyn behind the *Banner's* display table as soon as he walked in the library door, with Meg on one side of him and Ben on the other.

Fran Sinclair entered his field of vision as she leaned over to say something into Ellyn's ear. He thought he heard the phrase ''nice picture,'' but that seemed unlikely to make Ellyn glare at Fran that way, so he figured he misheard.

Ellyn had pinned her curly hair back into the semblance of a bun at her nape. On her it looked anything but staid. Especially since ringlet strands kept escaping. One rested against her cheek. In another second, trying as always to tame the curls, she'd tuck the strand behind her ear.

''Grif!'' Fran moved to meet him, taking his offered hand in both of hers, then pulling him into a hug. ''It's so good to see you. But it's past time you came for a visit.''

''You're right, Mrs. Sinclair, that I should—''

''Mrs. Sinclair?'' protested Fran. ''You'll call me Fran, like everyone else, except these two scalawags.''

''Okay, thank you.'' That would take some getting used to; she'd been Mrs. Sinclair all his childhood. But he'd noticed Ellyn called her Fran. Besides, *Mrs. Sinclair* still applied to Ellyn. He didn't like the taste of that reminder.

Kendra, Daniel and Matthew Delligatti came up just then, saying hello to the newcomers.

''Well, I'll take my grandchildren off for lunch now, if it's all right with you, Ellyn.''

''Thanks, Fran. That would be great.'' She made sure

the kids each thanked Grif politely for the rides, then sent them off.

His reason for being here had ended, but he felt no inclination to leave. He picked up a copy of the supplement that promised an in-depth look at the history of Far Hills, Wyoming.

"Hey, Bub, you read, you pay," Kendra teased.

"I don't want to deplete your stock before your afternoon rush. I'll get mine later." And he'd buy them out if need be to make this a success for Ellyn. It was one way to help Ellyn that she couldn't refuse.

"I hope there is an afternoon rush. It is awfully quiet,"

"I think most people are at lunch," said Ellyn, "I sent Marti for a break, too."

"And she sent me back here with drinks," announced Luke Chandler, walking up with a cardboard tray with cups of sodas and water, which were gratefully accepted.

"If the afternoon's as busy as this morning, we can all use the break," Kendra said. Her grin evaporated as she looked over Grif's shoulder. "Speaking of give-me-a-break."

That was the only warning he had before he was clutched on either side by a pair of unfamiliar hands.

"It's so good to see you!" and "How wonderful to see you!" came from opposite sides of him simultaneously. He looked down into two totally unfamiliar late middle-aged faces.

Ellyn provided a lifeline. "Grif, you remember Helen Solsong and Barb Sandy, don't you?" She nodded first to the woman on his right, then his left.

"It would be better if you were in uniform," said Barb Sandy, with an assessing look that could have made a side of beef squirm. "But at least your haircut is neat."

"Yes, and such good posture. And manners," Helen Solsong agreed with an icy look toward Luke.

"It's so nice to see a young man who's grown up in this

country choose to serve.'' Barb laid her hand on Grif's arm and leaned close, although her voice didn't lower. ''Makes one feel *safe,* you know. That's why we were so disappointed that we already had plans when Marti invited us to your welcome-home tonight.''

''Our calendars are just too full to accommodate last-minute invitations. Even now, we can't be dawdling.'' Helen made the announcement with great importance. ''We have a meeting for the committee reviewing use of the church for all those mothers who leave their children all day.''

''It's a baby-sitting cooperative, in which parents participate extensively.'' The steel in Ellyn's voice surprised Grif. But it didn't seem to surprise anyone else, including the two older women. Unfortunately it didn't cow them either.

''Whatever you call it, it's brought a lot of noise and dirt to the church.''

''Dirt!'' started Kendra, and Grif could see his cousin was about ten seconds from ripping into the women.

''Only way to be sure there's never any dirt or noise is to close the doors and keep everybody out,'' Daniel said cheerfully. Grif noticed Daniel had shifted so he was slightly in front of the others—a barrier between the two women and his wife and child. Grif doubted the other man was even aware of it.

To have a family that was yours to protect... A surge of some emotion washed through Grif. It took a moment to recognize jealousy. God, he was a sad case.

''Course that wouldn't be very generous,'' Daniel added, as if the idea had just occurred to him. ''Not the way most people think a church—and churchgoing people—should behave. I expect that's what you're going to tell that committee, now isn't it, ladies? We certainly wouldn't want to hold you up in doing that.''

Barb Sandy appeared nonplussed, or possibly dazzled by

the winning smile Daniel bent on her. Helen Solsong sniffed her disapproval, and departed with her cohort following.

"Those two nasty biddies!" Kendra muttered. "I'm surprised the church roof doesn't fall in on them when they walk inside."

"Be grateful Helen's working at the commissary at Fort Piney these days. Remember how bad she was when we were kids and she knew even more town gossip to spread?"

"I remember her now," Grif said, "but what was that all about?"

Kendra sighed. "Well, now that those two cats have let the cat out of the bag, you might as well know, Grif. When you go to the main house for that quiet dinner Marti invited you to tonight it's going to be a full-blown party."

"I knew that. I meant—"

"You knew?" interrupted Ellyn. "How? Marti's had everybody standing on their heads to keep it a secret. I've reminded the kids every time they talked to you not to tell."

"Nobody told. Unless you count Matthew."

"Matthew?" Kendra stared at her son. "He told you?"

"Let's say he confirmed my guess. I figured Marti would be up to something before long. But I still don't know what those two were aiming at with their verbal air strikes."

"Stuff about manners and haircut was meant to put me in my place." Luke clearly couldn't have cared less.

"And they were trying to imply Daniel's not a true-blue American, and that he and I had a wild orgy one night last fall," Kendra supplied. "Little do they know he spent the night asleep on the couch."

"Hey, don't say that so loud," Daniel complained. "I have a reputation to uphold."

Kendra grinned at him. "The reality's more important than the reputation, and you do just fine."

The look her husband sent back threatened to ignite the air.

Grif's gaze went to Ellyn without conscious volition. She was watching Kendra and Daniel with a faint smile that also held wistfulness. She glanced at him, as if she'd sensed his watching her, then away, paying careful attention to straightening the stack of special sections in front of her.

"What I want to know," said Kendra, drawing his attention away from Ellyn, "is how did Matthew confirm your guess?"

"He's been saying a word every time he sees me the past few days, and he's either connected the word *party* with me or he's calling me pretty."

"I have something I hear you'd like to see."

The gathering that evening had reached its third stage when Marti appeared at Ellyn's elbow with her announcement.

Marti had been known to lament that modern parties at Far Hills Ranch lacked the longevity of those when guests arrived from their distant homes by wagon at noon, ate and danced all afternoon, evening and night, then had a full breakfast before departing into the morning light. But she did her best.

The first phase had been sorting out the arrivals and their contributions to the spread big enough to cover the big kitchen table, even with extra leaves in. At its center was an impressive roast of Far Hills Ranch beef, carved and ready for eating.

Everyone who'd come through the kitchen door—and they all did, because these were people familiar with Far Hills Ranch—had greeted Grif with a hello and a handshake or a hug.

After catching sight of a faintly hunted look in his eyes when Sylvia Chasen from two ranches over enfolded him in a motherly embrace, Ellyn had moved to his side, whispering a name or phrase to help him get his bearings.

When the flow finally eased up, Grif cupped his warm hand around the back of her upper arm, to bring them hip to hip, so he could say quietly, "Thanks. You should get a lifesaving medal."

She smiled up at him. "You were pretty cool under fire."

The moment stretched long enough for her to realize that the warmth she felt came from more than his hand. It came from where his side met hers, and radiated deep.

He abruptly dropped his hold and backed up a foot.

"We'd better get in line or there won't be any food left."

"You go ahead. I want to check on the kids."

Phase two was the piling of plates and stuffing of stomachs.

For the kids that resulted in rocketing energy levels, so they were banished to the side-yard play area to work off some calories. For most of the adults it meant a mellow slide into phase three, where folks drifted easily from one conversation to another.

Ellyn had been watching the flow of people when Marti came up behind her.

"No reason to jump because I caught you looking, Ellyn."

"I wasn't looking at anything in particular," she lied. Her gaze had traveled often to where Grif and Daniel stood across the room. Two attractive men engaged in a conversation that clearly interested them both was an appealing sight. That's all.

"Well, you should be." Marti's declaration was accompanied by a nudge to a nearby love seat that was temporarily unoccupied. "But never mind that," she added as she slung a large, black tooled-leather photo album around so it rested across both their laps. "Fran said you wanted to see this."

"The Susland album? I saw the old photos when we picked out the ones for the section."

"They all look the same, but this is a more recent book. See, this starts with my father as a teenager. And here he is marrying my mother. Then Nancy and Wendy were born. And me a little later." Marti flipped the oversize pages carefully, but still fast enough to give Ellyn the impression of decades flashing before her eyes in a blur of growth spurts and fashion changes. "Ah, here—Nancy's wedding pictures."

Marti smoothed out the page, so Ellyn could see the photograph of the young bride from thirty-eight years earlier.

"She looks so much like Kendra," Ellyn murmured. "I didn't know…"

"Uh-huh. I took after Mom, but Nancy and Wendy took after the Suslands. Like Kendra."

"Like me what?" Kendra came up, along with Fran.

"Like you looking like a Susland."

"Oh." Kendra sat on the sofa arm. Fran went around the back of the love seat to look over Marti's shoulder. "Aunt Nancy's wedding picture. I remember this picture. My mother had a copy."

"I'd forgotten how little Grif looks like Nancy," Marti said in a thoughtful tone.

Ellyn looked across the room at Grif, and knew the other women were doing the same. He glanced up as if called by the scrutiny, then away before his gaze came back to the group on the love seat.

"He doesn't get any of his looks from the Susland side, does he," added Fran.

Marti slid the book over so the other page of photos was more directly in Ellyn's view, including one of the bride and groom.

"Oh, my—!" Ellyn covered her mouth to stop the exclamation.

"Talk about a spitting image," murmured Fran.

Marti had been thumbing ahead in the album, and now held open another page—Grif's graduation picture from West Point. "Two peas in a pod," she said, as she flipped back to a similar picture of John Griffin Senior.

Kendra whistled.

"What is going on over here?" Even amused, Grif's voice had a tinge of command to it. He expected an answer.

"We're looking at old family photos," said Marti. "Your mom and dad. Ellyn wanted to see them."

Ellyn was aware of his eyes narrowing on her, and she gave a slight shake of her head, but he'd already looked away.

"This wedding picture of your mother is beautiful. You should see—"

"Oh, Grif has a copy, too," said Marti.

"Yeah, but it's your dad who's the shocker, Grif. I hadn't realized you were the exact image of your father. Look at this, Daniel," Kendra added to her husband, who'd followed Grif.

Grif's posture tightened, as if going to attention in slow motion. But no one else seemed aware of the new tension in him. Or that he made no move to look at the photographs.

"Not exact." Ellyn spoke directly to the man in front of her, though he didn't look at her. "Their eyes are different."

"Not that I can see," Kendra argued. "Those graduation pictures look like carbon copies—right down to the uniform."

"Uniforms don't change much."

Ellyn smiled at him. "But the men in them do."

His eyes were aimed at her, but Ellyn had the feeling he wasn't seeing her at all.

"Please, Grif? *Pleeeeeeeaaaaassseeee?*"

Ben's request had caught Grif totally unprepared. He

didn't know what he'd been expecting when he felt the tug on his arm and looked down to find the boy informing him urgently that he had to talk to Grif. In private.

Not that he'd minded the distraction.

He didn't know what he'd been expecting when he'd wandered over to see what the group of women was looking at that had them all studying him, but it hadn't been family pictures.

He hadn't seen those old photographs in years. He had the one of his mother, but seldom took it out. He remembered his mother without a photograph. Besides, the woman in that old picture wasn't the one he remembered—even before the illness had changed her so cruelly, he had never seen her looking at his father the way the young bride gazed up at her groom. And he'd certainly never seen his father smile back at his mother the way the pictured officer did.

Their eyes are different.

Count on Ellyn to try to see the good side. But she was wrong. Terribly wrong.

"Will you, Grif? Will you? *Pleeeeease?*"

Fifteen months ago, pleas from Ben had had to do with a ball stuck in a flower bed where he wasn't supposed to have been playing, or a particular gift on his birthday wish-list that his parents showed no inclination to get him.

But when they slipped outside of the house to sit on the side steps for a while, Grif soon realized that this request was considerably more complicated. Not complicated in its implementation—that wouldn't be hard—but in its ramifications.

And those complications were not ones he could share with Ben. Grif sighed.

Taking Meg to Buffalo had been no picnic this morning, but in retrospect it had turned out fine. But this... Was it worse to endure Meg's mistrust or risk Ben's absolute faith? And what about Ellyn? How would she feel about this?

"Please, Grif?"

Grif looked into a face that blended Ellyn and Dale and came out entirely his own. "If you're sure. And—"

"I'm sure! I'm absolutely, positively, totally sure!"

"And if it's okay with your mother. We have to check with her first."

Abrupt silence yawned hugely between them.

"Ben?"

"Don't tell her, please, Grif?"

More than the appeal itself, the urgency behind it had Grif frowning. "Why not?"

"It's just…it's just I don't want you telling her."

"Then you have to talk to her about it."

"Okay. I will. It'll be okay with her. I know it."

"You can't know that unless you ask her."

Ben clearly took that answer as a parting of the clouds. "Thank you! This is going to be so *cool!*"

That wasn't the word Grif would have chosen, but he was committed now…unless Ellyn overruled him.

He could always hope.

Chapter Six

It wasn't that Grif avoided Ellyn for the rest of the evening. Marti had a lot of people she wanted him to say hello to. At least she wanted him as a prop for some auntly bragging.

But he hadn't minded. He'd caught Ellyn watching him a couple of times, with a faintly puzzled, faintly worried expression in her brown eyes. He suspected that if he got pulled into her orbit, she'd be asking him questions of some sort. And he wasn't in the mood to fend them off right now.

Especially not, he told himself, with this agreement to help out Ben without clearing it with Ellyn first weighing on his conscience. He hoped the boy told his mother soon.

Still, when the bounty on the kitchen table was depleted sufficiently to allow removal of the leaves so it could be shrunk to normal size, then pushed to one side to leave a small dance floor, and the CD player started spinning country-western dance music, he made his way immediately to

Ellyn. She couldn't ask much while they were doing the two-step in such cozy quarters.

"Want to dance?"

"Dance?" she repeated.

He held his arms up in the usual pose. "You know, dance."

An expression he couldn't define crossed her face as her gaze went from the tips of his fingers on one side, traveled across his chest then ran out to the tips of his fingers on the other hand. The sensation that followed the path of that look was all too easily defined. He dropped his arms.

"I, uh…thanks, but no. It's time I get the kids home and in bed. It's been a full day for them."

"You can put them down in one of the rooms upstairs," Fran suggested from over her shoulder. "Marti's got two rooms set up—one for the littler kids who need cribs and such, and one for older kids like Ben and Meg."

Ellyn frowned at her stepmother-in-law. "They wouldn't sleep. We should go home now."

After staying away from her most of the evening, he suddenly didn't want her to leave without some tie, some promise. "How about dinner tomorrow night? I'll take you and the kids—"

"No. No. I don't think that's a good idea. It's a school night, and Fran usually comes over—"

"Fran, too," he said with a quick smile to the older woman.

"Sounds good to me," she said.

But Ellyn was shaking her head. "No, I'm sorry, but… With church and chores and homework to make sure they get done… And we like to make Sunday night family night. Just family." She looked up then, and her expression softened immediately. Her words were gentle, too. "But thank you, Grif. It's very nice of you, but, truly, you don't need to keep feeding us."

He watched as Ellyn gathered her protesting children and

the empty dishes from her contributions, said farewells and thank-yous, gave him a brief smile, then headed out the door.

Not long after, he'd pleaded weariness and headed out himself.

It had been a full day for him, too. After the morning drive with Meg, the afternoon amid the hubbub of the history festival and the evening party, he thought he could use some time alone.

He'd never minded solitude. Maybe because he'd gotten used to it so early, and never broke the habit. Even during the summers he'd spent here as a kid he'd gone off on his own a lot.

But it occurred to him as the car dipped to cross a dried creek bed, that he wasn't looking forward to being alone back in his room.

Ridge House was completely dark except for the safety light that spotlighted the driveway, showing Ellyn's car pulled near the back door.

He took the corner from the ranch road into the driveway and sped up without conscious thought. As he neared Ellyn's car, he saw Meg and Ben standing on the back step, but no sign of Ellyn.

"Where's your mother?" he demanded as he jogged toward them.

"She just went inside—"

"The lights are out," announced Ben.

"I see that. Why'd she go inside, Meg?" If Ellyn had heard a noise and gone inside anyway, he'd throttle her himself—as long as she was okay.

"There's a circus-something that gets broken. It's in the basement."

"Circuit breaker?" Poor Ellyn, she'd hated everything electrical as long as he'd known her. She would have nothing to do with outlets or plugs or wires.

"You kids stay here until I can get the lights back on."

"That's what Mom said, too." Ben sighed. "How come we always have to wait?"

Grif gave him a quick grin. "'Cause you're the kids."

Inside, he groped along the wall for the basement door. It was open. He found the first step with his foot, then reached out to the reasonable spot for the railing to be. It was about six inches lower.

"I told you kids to stay out—"

"It's me, Ellyn."

"Oh." The syllable had an odd note to it.

"Grif," he added, just in case.

"I know. It's awfully dark down here. You better stay upstairs."

"I'm already down." He covered the last few steps. "Damn!"

"What? Did you run into something? You better hold still. This ceiling is awfully low, too."

Basements weren't standard equipment in ranch houses, but the builders of Ridge House back early in the century when root cellars had been particularly handy, had taken advantage of its site on the side of a hill to carve out a partial basement.

"I'm fine. I didn't run into anything. I was just thinking I should have gotten my flashlight out of the glove compartment. It would have made this easier. Do you have any idea where the electrical box is?"

"Yes, but—"

"Keep talking, so I can follow your voice. Then you can direct me to the box."

"You don't need to do that, I—"

"That's good. Just like that."

First he heard a sigh, then, "So, why didn't you get the flashlight?" as he continued making his way across the floor.

Amused and faintly teasing, something about her tone stung him. Maybe because the spurt of fear for her and the kids had made him act instead of think. A stupid mistake. In some circumstances, a dangerous mistake. It was fool's luck that this wasn't one of those circumstances.

"Probably for the same reason you don't have a flashlight available for moments like this."

"Oh?" The light, cool note of this monosyllable gave him a slight warning. "What a coincidence. You mean, you, too, just discovered that someone had used up the batteries in both your main flashlight and the backup by holding them under his chin to make scary faces in the dark during his sister's sleepover party?"

"All right, all right." He was grinning, unable to resist her amusement.

He could smell her now. Not perfume, because she didn't wear any. But the citrus clean of her hair, the soft sweetness of the moisturizer he'd seen her use on her hands and something more…something that came from the *warmth* of her.

His extended hand brushed against the fabric of her sweater. He found the curve of her arm, slid his hand around it. The faintest whisper of an indrawn breath reached his ears.

"Ellyn—"

He didn't know what he might have said, but she forestalled him. "So, you found me."

The cheer of her words didn't sound quite real to his ears. But then he'd been listening to something else—his own accelerated heartbeat.

"Yes, I found you." And he wouldn't let her go again. No matter how often he had to remind himself that he would be—could be—a friend in her life, but no more. And damned lucky to be that. "Now, where's the electrical box, so I can find the breaker and get—"

"Right here."

"—the lights back on for you."

He heard the sound of the breaker being toggled over, then he was bedazzled.

He could try to explain it away by the lights coming on so unexpectedly. But what bedazzled him was to have his sight restored to the vision of Ellyn standing just in front of him. Too late to close his eyes against the fact that her arm was already under his hand, so a gentle tug would draw her into his arms. Her face lifted toward his, a smile curving her lips, so an instant's relaxing of his guard would bring his mouth down on hers.

He didn't know how long they stood like that. Long enough for his body to respond. Long enough for him to sense a ripple of something pass through her. Long enough for unrecognizable sounds from some distant place to resolve into the call of "Mom. Mom!" from Ben and Meg at the top of the stairs.

He stepped back, the motion jerky, then consciously ordered his hand to release her.

Her smile wavered, then shifted, not looking entirely natural. Her other hand drifted up and covered the spot where his hand had been. He didn't think he'd gripped her too hard, and she didn't rub it, simply cupped her hand there, with her arm drawn across her body.

"We'll be right up!"

"Can we go in now?" Meg asked with exaggerated patience. "It's cold out here."

"Yes."

She looked toward the stairs, then to him, still blocking her path out of the corner of the basement.

He retreated another two steps, leaving her plenty of clearance, remaining where he was as she skirted him. Not watching her, but aware when she darted a glance at his face as she passed him.

She was several steps above him before he started up the stairs after her, but that didn't help any. To keep his mind off the view above him, he said, "So, you knew where the electrical box was all along."

"Yes. We have trouble with the power going off a lot."

"So you didn't need me charging in to the rescue at all."

"I did try to tell you," she said shortly, turning on him as he reached the hallway. The kids were nowhere in sight, apparently already in their bedrooms. "But you didn't listen to me. You assumed that I couldn't handle it and—"

"Whoa, Ellyn! I wasn't accusing you. I was the one who was wrong. I thought…well, you used to be afraid of—uh, you didn't used to like anything electrical."

She studied his face a moment, then seemed to release a tension in her shoulders along with a short sigh.

"I still don't particularly *like* it. But as I said, the power goes off here often enough that my choices were dealing with it or sitting in the dark a lot. Besides, when Marti had the house updated after Dale left, they put the circuit breaker box in and Luke explained it all to me. There used to be fuses, and I didn't like those, but the circuit breakers are okay. Besides, it's not so bad when you know how it works."

"No, it's not so bad."

"Can I offer you some coffee?"

"No, thanks, I better get going."

"Okay. Good night then. Grif, I…" The light touch of her hand on his arm stopped him halfway out the screen door. "I'm sorry I snapped at you, Grif. I don't think it was even you I… Anyway, thank you for coming to our rescue."

He smiled slightly, shaking her head. "I tried, but you rescued yourself, Ellyn."

Her eyes widened—hadn't that occurred to her before?

"I suppose I did," she said slowly. Then she smiled at him, that warm smile that had caught him the first time he'd seen her. "I still say thank you. You're a good friend."

"You're welcome. Good night, Ellyn."

Good friend.

The echo of her words accompanied him on the drive to

Fort Piney. Had he been as good a friend to her as he could have been? Had he ever tried to help her defeat the fear, or had he simply taken over?

Ellyn put the freshly rinsed plate in Fran's waiting hands and met her eyes.

"Okay, say it. I can't take this silence anymore."

Fran didn't miss a beat. "Why aren't you happy to see Grif?"

Ellyn dropped her gaze to the next plate in the soapy water in front of her. "I *am* happy to see him."

"You aren't as welcoming as I would've expected from what all I've heard about Grif being part of your lives back East. You practically had to be hog-tied to agree to dinner last week. And all those excuses to not be taken out to dinner tonight!" Fran propped a hip against the counter as she wiped the plate.

"They weren't excuses. It is a school night. And we do like to make this family night."

But she'd have bitten her tongue before saying those words if she'd known they would bring that flash of bleakness to Grif's usually impenetrable eyes. She'd never have guessed that phrase could make him feel like an outsider. Of course, during those years in Washington, if they'd been used at all—unlikely with Dale preferring bigger gatherings than family-only—Grif would have been included.

"Besides, it seemed like an imposition on his generosity," she added. Fran's answer was a disbelieving snort, goading Ellyn into adding, "And I don't want to be treated like a charity case."

"Is that why you wouldn't dance with him? You thought he was asking out of *charity?*"

That struck uncomfortably close to home. Something about the way Grif had held his arms out to her as he'd invited her to dance had flashed into an image of her throwing herself into his arms fifteen years ago.

Or maybe it was her own longing to be inside those arms that had been the same.

No. No! She was wrong. She didn't feel that way about Grif anymore. Hadn't for a long, long time. This was something else. Something else entirely.

Fran shook her head as she set the dried plate atop a pile of its fellows in the cabinet and reached for the next one.

"You don't have any obligation to tell me a thing, but please don't be telling me nonsense. Just tell me to mind my own business."

For a moment, Ellyn longed to do that. But Fran had been so good to her and the kids. Besides, it would be making much too big a deal out of this situation with Grif. And it was *not* a big deal.

"I don't want to see the children hurt and lonely again. He's not going to stay long. So there's no sense getting real close again."

"If you're going to try to protect those two from getting hurt by never letting them get close to people who're going to leave, they're going to have a mighty small circle of friends. Might as well make the most of the time he's here," Fran countered. "Unless…"

Ellyn resisted the tug of that dangling word as long as she could. "Unless what?"

"Unless there's something more here than you're telling me. No—" she held up her hand, stilling Ellyn's protest that got no farther than an indrawn breath. "I don't mean anything like that. I know you better than to think such a thing—him, too. But you seem to be punishing him. I could understand if you were mad at Dale for being so irresponsible—about money and life. I know I am."

"Dale was just himself. There was no point in expecting him to be anything other than the man he was."

"And Grif? You thought Grif was something different from what he now seems to be?"

Ellyn shifted, but Fran's steady gaze didn't. There'd be

no getting around answering the question unless Ellyn said outright that she didn't want to talk about Grif. And that would raise all sorts of speculation.

"I suppose I did. He'd always been there for us, and then he was suddenly gone and, boy, was his timing bad," she said with a shaky laugh. "Grif had always been so steady, so sane, so reassuring, so— Then he disappeared. *Poouff!* Gone. The very last man you'd ever expect that of. I don't know what to expect from him anymore."

Except that he seemed determined to give her help that she didn't want. But she knew better than to raise that argument, since Fran had more than once tried to persuade her to accept money from the older woman's retirement nest egg.

"You deserve some fun, Ellyn. Letting a longtime friend take you and your kids to dinner now and then isn't exactly the high life, but it's a small step in the right direction. Give yourself a break, and stop punishing Grif—and eat dessert!"

"Are we having dessert?" Ben asked from the hallway.

Ellyn couldn't help but laugh as she told her son that if he'd finished his homework, he could have angel food cake and peach preserves for dessert. She carefully made no promises to Fran about any future desserts.

No military genius was required to figure out that if a direct assault didn't work, a flanking attack might be called for.

Having checked Ellyn's work schedule with Larry Orrin, and the rest of her schedule with Fran, Grif had ascertained that Ellyn had no obligations outside her home for Monday afternoon. He was certain she'd say she had plenty of obligations inside it, but that couldn't be helped.

A final phone call, and his plan was set.

When she opened the door after checking through the window who had knocked, she had a tuck between her brows that reminded him of Meg. "I didn't hear your car, Grif."

"No car." He gestured back to the two horses tied to the porch railing. After approving of Luke's choices, he'd ridden one over from the main ranch while leading the other. "We're going riding."

"Riding?"

"Yes. You and me. On horses. Across Far Hills land, like we used to."

"I can't—"

"Yes, you can. I've seen you ride. You're good."

"That was years ago. But that wasn't what I meant, I—"

"You can wear what you have on, but you'll need other shoes, better yet some boots. And bring a jacket."

"Grif, I have things to do this—"

"I know," he said grimly. "You always have things to do. But Luke tells me you haven't been riding even once since you've been back, and you're a damned sight too pale, so we are going riding. And we're doing it now."

She gaped at him for maybe half a minute, then her expression started to harden toward a new determination, and he played his last card.

"Please. You'd be helping me. I want to ride, and I don't want to do it alone."

She exhaled, long and slow, and she relaxed. "Grif... Oh, for heaven's sake."

She pivoted and walked away, leaving the door open. He stayed right where he was. He thought that meant she was going to come, but just in case it didn't, at least she'd eventually have to come back and close the door.

She returned in four minutes, according to the wall clock he could see through the open door, with a jacket under her arm and old, battered ropers on her feet.

She hesitated a moment after he handed her the reins of the chestnut mare Cherry that Luke had suggested for her, but before Grif could consider whether or how to help her up, she'd used the second step as a mounting block and was in the saddle. He swung up onto the back of the brown gelding Fred, and they headed out.

They rode in silence, threading their way from the relative civilization immediately around the house, over the ridge, down the far side and into ranges that spilled one into another.

"Anywhere in particular you want to go?"

As soon as Grif asked it, he knew the question was a tactical error. It left him wide open for her answering that she hadn't wanted to go at all, much less anywhere in particular.

So he counted it as a victory when she simply said, "No."

"Okay with you if we pick up the pace?"

"Yes."

He didn't mind that monosyllable, either, because as they started to canter, he caught the flash of her smile. Even if he had had to bully her a bit, he'd been right to do this.

And he wasn't alone in thinking that.

His call to Larry asking if Ellyn was working today had been met with cheerful disinterest. "Nope. Won't be in till tomorrow. You oughta be able to catch her at home."

His question to Fran had elicited a long, thoughtful silence before she answered. Then she'd added, "I hope you're thinking of something other than asking her to dinner. You aren't making much headway that way."

Headway?

"I'm just trying to make sure she takes some time for herself. Gets some fresh air."

"Good. She needs that."

That answer reassured Grif that Fran hadn't misunderstood his intentions until, just before he heard the click on the other end of the line, she added, "Among other things."

That might have been why an edge crept into his tone

when he tracked down Luke at the calving barn and told him his plan.

"The trail to the flat near Hidden Creek where we used to have campfires is still fetlock deep in spring mud," Luke had told him. "But you could get up to Leaping Star's overlook. That's a nice spot if you have a mind to spread a blanket and have a picnic."

"We're taking a ride. That's all."

The foreman gave him a level look that didn't quite mask a hint of amusement, but said only, "None of my affair."

Ellyn's voice broke into Grif's mental review of these conversations. "Are we heading somewhere in particular?"

They'd not only slowed from the canter, but the steepening trail had narrowed, so they were riding single file.

"Luke suggested Leaping Star's overlook."

"Oh."

He twisted in the saddle to look at her. "He said this is one of the few trails where we shouldn't run into mud or washouts. I don't think he trusts either one of us on horseback anymore. Is the overlook a problem?"

"No. No problem."

Conversation dried up as they both paid close attention to their mounts, picking their route up the winding, rising trail. With the vegetation not fully out yet, taking longer looks at the view was tempting, but not worth the risk of a wreck.

And none of the glimpses would have done justice to the sight that spread below them when they reached the overlook.

"We came up here back in November," Ellyn said when they'd dismounted, secured the horses and sat side by side atop a piece of plastic she spread over a fallen tree trunk.

"We?"

"Marti, Luke, Kendra, Daniel and Matthew, the kids and I. It was the anniversary of Leaping Star's death. Marti started it. I think she wanted to sort of set things right somehow.''

''Set things right? Are you talking about that legend again?''

''Legend, or no legend, your ancestor, Charles Susland, wasn't a very nice man. Marti found out a lot of things while she was doing the research for our special section. And I suspect she isn't telling us everything.''

''What makes you think that?''

''A feeling. Some of the things she's said. Or hasn't said.''

''I'm not sure I understand.''

''You might if you came home more than once every decade.'' Almost before she'd finished the words and he'd felt the sting of them, she was apologizing. ''I'm sorry, Grif. I had no right to say that. It's not my place—''

''It's all right, Ellyn. You're right. I should come back more often. Marti's not getting any younger, and this place is partly my responsibility, too.''

''Don't let her hear you saying that about her not getting any younger. But it is partly your responsibility, and more important it's your *home,* Grif.''

There was that word again. He called on a sure distraction, turning toward the view.

''It's an amazing sight, isn't it?''

''Amazing,'' she agreed.

They sat in peaceful silence for several minutes until Ellyn breathed out a long, soft sigh. Even without looking at her he knew tension had eased from her. He felt something ease in him as well.

He stretched his legs out, welcoming the pull against his muscles. ''I've missed this.''

''Me, too.''

''Then why haven't you been riding before now?'' He hadn't been talking about the riding, but it seemed much safer this way.

"Why haven't you come back before now?"

He looked away. "I've been working hard."

"Me, too."

He covered her hand resting on the tree with his own. She looked at their hands, and slowly drew hers out from beneath his. He thought the move held some reluctance.

"It must have been quite a burden on you when Dale died, besides the grief and the shock. I mean all the things you had to do. It must have made everything all that much harder."

"At first it was actually a godsend. I needed things to do. That way I didn't feel much. And even after... For a long time I was numb. Then... Then I was scared."

"You took on an awful lot all at once. Taking care of a house by yourself, the kids, the car, the finances. Getting on with your life."

She flipped a hand, pushing all that aside. "No. At least... I'm not saying that wasn't all worrisome." Ruefulness tinted her slight smile. "And I won't deny that at times I sat down and bawled in frustration and exhaustion and worry. But that's not what..." He could see her searching for a phrase. "Did you ever feel as if you'd forgotten how to breathe?"

"Forgotten how to breathe?" he asked carefully, not following, but not wanting to stop her, either.

"When I was a little girl, my mother would always tell me if I was nervous or upset or scared, that I just had to learn to breathe deeply and if I did it right, that would calm everything down. So I'd lie in bed some nights and concentrate on breathing in and breathing out."

She demonstrated. And it did nothing to calm down a certain portion of his anatomy. He forced himself to listen to her words.

"And I'd pay such close attention to breathing, trying to get the rhythm right. But I'd have to take an in-breath in the middle of what should have been an out-breath. And the harder I tried, the worse it got until sometimes I thought I'd pass out.''

She glanced at him from the corner of her eye. ''Pretty weird, I know. I bet you never had times like that when you felt as if you'd forgotten how to breathe.''

''I don't remember ever feeling that way,'' he said without inflection. He didn't want to shut down her confidences.

From her ill-at-ease laugh, he had not succeeded. ''No, of course not. I can't imagine you ever feeling like that, ever feeling like you were out of step and couldn't get back—''

''Out of step.''

His voice must have given something away when he repeated that phrase because her head came around and she looked directly at him.

''Yes,'' she said slowly, studying him, ''out of step. Do you know what I mean? No, of course you don't. I remember from the first day I met you, you always knew exactly which step you were going to take next. So sure. So straight.''

''When I was little, not even in school yet, I watched the recruits drill at the base where we lived, marching and turning and marching again, all in step. I started trying to keep in step with my father, everywhere we went, hoping he'd notice. I had to work hard because my legs were so much shorter, but I kept it up for maybe a week. Until the Sunday afternoon when he was trying to watch a football game, and I missed a turn somewhere between the refrigerator and the sofa. His beer spilled. All over my head. I...I remember the smell. And my father shouting at me, shouting at my mother to get me out of the way.

''I went back the next day and watched those recruits again. And this time I noticed that if they got out of step they got yelled at. If they kept in step they were ignored. It didn't take me long to figure out that being ignored was better than being yelled at. And the way to do that was to stay in step.''

She was watching him. He looked out to the view, confident his face showed nothing. He'd had a lot of practice at that.

''I wondered some about the break between you and your father. You never said, even when he died—''

''Break? There was no break.''

''But, you never saw each other. I was even a little surprised when you went to the funeral two years ago, because in all those years in Washington, you never talked about him.''

''Nothing to say.''

''You didn't see him or talk to him or—''

''No. But we didn't have a break the way you're thinking. We just went our separate ways.'' She made a movement beside him. ''You're cold. You want my jacket?''

''No, I'm fine. I...oh, Grif, I'm sorry.''

''Sorry? What for?''

''I never knew it was so bad for you at home. When we were growing up and you were always so good about my problems with my mother, and all the time you—''

''There's nothing to be sorry about,'' he interrupted shortly. ''Nothing like your mother sniping at you constantly, tearing you down. My father paid the bills, gave me money for school and clothes, and otherwise ignored me as best he could. When I got old enough to be on my own, we parted ways.''

''That's terrible. That's—''

''Ellyn, it was nothing like terrible. Don't waste any sympathy on my petty grievances. John Griffin just never should have gotten married, and he wouldn't have if it hadn't been for me.'' He saw both the question in her eyes and the acceptance if he chose not to answer it. ''My mother was pregnant with me. That's the only reason they married.''

She was shaking her head before he'd finished. "I don't believe that. Not after seeing those pictures. Your parents loved each other. Things might have gone wrong later, but—"

"They never should have gotten married. *He* never should have gotten married. And believe me, it was no secret that he only married my mother to make an *honest woman of her,* because I was conceived. And that was the real joke of it, because he shouldn't have had children, either."

"What do you—"

He stood before she could finish. "Let's go. You're getting cold, and I promised you we'd ride, not sit."

Back on Cherry, with only Grif's straight back and Fred's rump to consider as they made their way down from the overlook, Ellyn felt as if her head were spinning trying to assemble the bits and shreds Grif had revealed into something resembling coherence.

There she'd been, cruising along, baring her soul about Dale's death at a good clip, and he'd slammed the brakes on. It would give anyone emotional whiplash.

Of course she hadn't told him the whole truth yet. She'd wanted to. Or at least she'd intended to. To get it all out in the open between them. So at least one person knew the real story.

But even though she wanted Grif to be that one person, getting the words out was harder than she would have expected.

She didn't want him to…to *pity* her.

All her confidences about how she'd felt after Dale died and feeling as if she'd forgotten how to breathe were meant to lead into telling him the rest of it. Maybe part of her had used all the words to postpone the moment.

Now he'd shut that door with a thud. So she could sit

back and enjoy the ride. As much as anybody could enjoy a ride knowing she was a lily-livered coward.

Reaching open ground again, she brought Cherry abreast of his horse. Grif gave her a wary look from the corner of his eye.

"Grif, what we were talking about at the overlook—"

"There's no sense discussing it. It's long past."

She gave an exasperated *tch.*

"Is that why you asked about how I coped after Dale died—because there's no sense talking about it and it's long past?"

His eyes acknowledged that direct hit, but he clearly wasn't about to admit it aloud. "I talk too much."

"Not hardly."

"I don't want to talk about—"

"Then listen."

Without turning fully toward her, he gave her a hard look. She went ahead anyway.

"I thought you should know... I mean you might hear, because a few people know..." She gathered herself and took the jump. "Dale was thinking about leaving—that's why we left D.C., that's why we moved here. To try to make a go of it."

"I know."

"You—?" She swallowed, then started again. "That's good. Then we don't have to pretend—"

"Ellyn—"

"It's okay. It's good you know. We won't be on edge now. We have been a little on edge with each other, don't you think?" Another thought struck her, and she didn't wait for an answer. "How did you know?"

Grif's gaze shifted to between his horse's ears. "He said something one night, but I thought... I thought he'd see the light. And when you all moved out here..."

"Dale wanted to come back to Wyoming," she explained. "I thought it might help."

The words came easier, as she told him a carefully edited version of the night Dale had made his announcement, and the frenetic day that followed. She made no mention of trying to contact him, but his next words showed that the omission didn't fool him.

"I didn't make it any easier on you. Going away like that."

"No, you didn't," she said without heat. "But like I said before, we had—*have*—no claim on you, Grif."

"Of course you could have tried to find me."

"What?" Her raised voice made Cherry's ears flick around like a rotating antenna. "*I* could have— What was I supposed to do? Demand the Army tell me where my friend had gone? Somehow I don't think that would have rattled any cages at the Pentagon."

"Maybe not."

"You're darned right not. You took off and left me no way of knowing where you were, and—"

"Marti always knew where I was. And you knew that. All you had to do was ask Marti for my address and drop me a line."

"Are you saying it's my fault for not contacting you?"

"I'm not laying fault. I'm saying you made a choice, too."

A voice in the back of her head whispered he might have a point—at least part of one. She *had* known Marti was in contact with Grif. She'd considered trying to contact him a couple of times. But she hadn't. Was he right? Had she chosen not to try to get in touch with him? Because his disappearance had hurt? And hurt who? Or were there other reasons? She didn't like the trend of these questions.

"You were the one who disappeared!"

"You could say that."

Irritation at his unyielding inscrutability spurted steam through her—which was far preferable to confusion and self-doubt.

"I could say that, and I'd be right!" With effort, she reined herself in. "Of course, I understand why. The Army held out an important assignment to you, one that you could pull off in a blaze of glory—just like you did."

"No blaze of glory."

"I'll have to take your word for that, but obviously it was good enough to advance your career."

He shook his head.

The steam eased out of her, along with an element of certainty. It left her feeling a little limp, and oddly vulnerable.

"But…but you must have completed that assignment or you wouldn't have been promoted."

"Only achieved half of it, and the Army had nothing to do with it."

"Now you've really lost me, Grif. What do you mean the Army had nothing to do with it. I thought you had orders—"

"No orders, least not until I requested them, and the Army didn't give me that assignment. I gave it to myself."

"Gave it to yourself? What does that mean?"

"The assignment was to forget you…all of you. And to stay out of the way until you and Dale sorted things out. I didn't achieve the first part, but at least I held to the second."

Questions poured through her mind like water over a waterfall. Too fast to get more than a flash of their color, a sense of their mood. One held enough form to be spoken.

"But why leave so abruptly? If Dale told you how he felt, and there's no one he trusted more, so—"

"He shouldn't have."

She blinked up at him, stunned by his fierceness.

"Shouldn't have trusted you? That's crazy, Grif. Of course he trusted you. We both did. Why on earth would you say we shouldn't? That doesn't—"

"So how was the ride?" Luke appeared from the calving

shed so promptly she suspected he'd been watching for them. He'd addressed the question to her, but his gaze went to the horses, like a father who'd lent his prized car to a new driver.

Even before Luke's interruption it had been clear as a cloudless Wyoming sky that Grif wasn't going to explain his comment. And for reasons she didn't care to explore, she was both glad and sorry for that.

It was the closest he'd ever come to letting her know, but he'd left it just ambiguous enough to allow her to ignore the implications. And when she took that opening, he was partly disappointed and totally relieved.

She'd lied about being glad he knew about Dale's thoughts of leaving her. It hurt her pride to have him know, and that hurt him—that she felt guarded with him, but even more that he was in any way a cause of her discomfort.

As for being on edge? Hell, yes, they were on edge. But he didn't think she was anywhere close to hitting on the reason. And even if he'd been stupid enough to tell her what he thought the reason was, she wouldn't want to hear it.

He'd known that for sure when she didn't try to bring the talk back to more personal matters when they were alone in the car as he drove her from the barn to Ridge House.

And that was good, he told himself as he returned to Fort Piney for a shower and change of clothes before having dinner at the home ranch. Excellent, in fact.

He'd come to Far Hills to make sure Ellyn and the kids were okay, and would continue to be okay. Also, to try to restore his place in their lives as a family friend.

Friend. The word mocked him.

It was hard to maintain that illusion when he'd nearly given himself away a dozen times. He had to stop touching her. Stop looking at her. And watch what he said.

Not that any of it seemed to disrupt Ellyn's serenity. All she seemed to worry about was that he might actually do something to lift some of the burden from her shoulders. He supposed he should be grateful she hadn't picked up on his struggle. And he was. Mostly.

Grateful, too, for this time with them. Ellyn, Meg and Ben.

Easing off the accelerator as he reached the edge of town, Grif smiled as he thought of Ben's enthusiasm and Meg's slow, reluctant, but undeniable warming up to him.

A hand extended out the open window of a pickup coming the other way, and a call of "Hey, Grif" floated out. The late afternoon sun glared across the windshield, so he couldn't see the driver, but it didn't matter, as he returned the wave and the hello. Everyone in Far Hills had welcomed him as if he really belonged here.

It was a good place. A good place for Ellyn and the kids to build a life and put down roots.

A good place for him to spend some time.

As long as he didn't let it make him want things that were impossible.

Shouldn't have trusted you? That's crazy, Grif. Of course he trusted you. We both did. Why on earth would you say we shouldn't?

The answer was so loud in his head, he would have thought the words had escaped, except he'd had his mouth clamped firmly shut.

Because I wanted you myself.

Chapter Seven

Marti was in complete agreement with him, so the sole item on his agenda for their talk after Emily went to bed was accomplished in record time. Then, Grif thought wryly, they got down to Marti's business.

"It's been good for Ben and Meg to have you around," she said. "They like Luke and Daniel fine, but they haven't known those two all their lives like they've known you."

"Except for a year when I deserted them as far as they can tell."

"They're already a long way to being over that. As long as you don't intend to disappear again."

"I don't."

Marti showed no sign of needing or wanting the reassurance, as she plowed right on. "It's been especially good for Ellyn."

"I wondered when they first came out here how she'd do—but I knew she'd be under your wing, and Kendra's, and that you'd make sure she and the kids were okay."

"Of course." She sounded slightly insulted at the idea that he might have doubted that. "But that's not the point with Ellyn."

"No, no it's not. The point is she's doing fine. She's got a handle on things."

Marti propped her hands on her hips and stared at him.

"Sometimes, men are so stupid. If bulls had as little instinct about cows as men have about women, there'd never be another calf born in all of Wyoming!"

"What does that mean?"

"It means you are missing the point entirely."

"What point?"

"See! You didn't even know there was a point. The point about Ellyn."

"What about her? She's doing great."

"She is *not* doing great. Not in the ways that a woman worries about deep inside herself."

"I don't know what you're talking about, Marti."

"Of course you don't—you're a man. But I'm going to tell you straight out so you can't miss it. Ellyn's spent a lot of years thinking she's less than a woman because of that fool mother of hers. On top of that, I knew Dale Sinclair all his life."

"What's Dale got to do with it?"

"A lot. Now hush up and listen. No matter how many birthdays Dale had, he never quite grew up. And having a wife like Ellyn, well…any time Ellyn felt she wasn't being loved by him she thought she wasn't being the right kind of woman. Thought it was her fault. So things kept gettin' easier and easier on him, and harder and harder on her. Now he's dead, and she's wondering."

"She's got to know that she—"

Marti jumped on that fragment of a sentence triumphantly. "That's where you're wrong, Grif. She doesn't have to know. Not at all. That's why it's so good for her that you're around. Although…'' She looked at him expectantly.

He leaned back and gave her a level stare. ''I've known you most of my life, and I know you're going to tell me what you want to tell me no matter what I want, so get on with it.''

Her expression shifted, taking on a trace of chagrin, but giving no quarter. ''I've known you *all* your life. And you've always been stubborn.''

''Persistent and tough-minded was on my most recent assessment.''

''That's the Army for you—pussyfooting around the facts. I was being polite using stubborn. Bullheaded's the real truth.''

She turned away, as if that would somehow make him miss the humor tugging at her mouth and creasing the corners of her eyes. But when she faced him again, her expression was serious,

''But you're not a fool, Grif, and you're fair. So I'm going to say what I have to say, and then I'm going to ask you to think it over before you make up your mind.''

The only way to get out of this was to get up and walk out. He wouldn't do that to Marti.

''There's a lot more Ellyn and the kids have lost than a regular income. You can see it with the kids, I don't know why you can't see it with Ellyn.''

When she fell into a silence, he prompted, ''See what?''

''What they need. You seem to know the kids need a man around—a man they can count on, who'll be there for them, make them feel good about themselves. Ellyn needs just the same. No, no, don't go telling me again how she seems to have things taken care of in the house, knows how to do her own taxes and can deal with an old curmudgeon like Ed Bressler. I'm telling *you* now. And what I'm tellin' you is she needs a man.''

''Marti—''

FREE FREE
BOOKS! GIFT!

PLAY
BANGO!

AND CLAIM 2 FREE BOOKS
AND A FREE GIFT!

BANGO
9 19 44 52 71
4 20 32 50 68
11 18 FREE 53 63
7 27 36 60 72
3 28 41 47 64

BANGO
15 19 32 54 73
6 17 41 50 6
13 22 FREE 52
5 24 44 46
8 21 35 47 75

★ No Cost!
★ No Obligation to Buy!
★ No Purchase Necessary!

TURN THE PAGE TO PLAY

PLAY BANGO! AND GET THREE FREE GIFTS!

It looks like **BINGO**, it plays like **BINGO** but it's **FREE!**
HOW TO PLAY:

1. With a coin, scratch the Caller Card to reveal your 5 lucky numbers and see that they match your Bango Card. Then check the claim chart to discover what we have for you — 2 FREE BOOKS and a FREE GIFT — ALL YOURS, ALL FREE!

2. Send back the Bango card and you'll receive two brand-new Silhouette Special Edition® novels. These books have a cover price of $4.50 each in the U.S. and $5.25 each in Canada, but they are yours to keep absolutely free.

3. There's no catch. You're under no obligation to buy anything. We charge nothing — ZERO — for your first shipment. And you don't have to make any minimum number of purchases — not even one!

4. The fact is, thousands of readers enjoy receiving our books by mail from the Silhouette Reader Service™. They enjoy the convenience of home delivery…they like getting the best new novels at discount prices, BEFORE they're available in stores…and they love their *Heart to Heart* subscriber newsletter featuring author news, horoscopes, recipes, book reviews and much more!

5. We hope that after receiving your free books you'll want to remain a subscriber. But the choice is yours — to continue or cancel, any time at all! So why not take us up on our invitation, with no risk of any kind. You'll be glad you did!

YOURS FREE!
This exciting mystery gift is yours free when you play BANGO!

The Silhouette Reader Service™ — Here's how it works:

Accepting your 2 free books and gift places you under no obligation to buy anything. You may keep the books and gift and return the shipping statement marked "cancel." If you do not cancel, about a month later we'll send you 6 additional novels and bill you just $3.80 each in the U.S., or $4.21 each in Canada, plus 25¢ shipping & handling per book and applicable taxes if any.* That's the complete price and — compared to cover prices of $4.50 each in the U.S. and $5.25 each in Canada — it's quite a bargain! You may cancel at any time, but if you choose to continue, every month we'll send you 6 more books, which you may either purchase at the discount price or return to us and cancel your subscription.

*Terms and prices subject to change without notice. Sales tax applicable in N.Y. Canadian residents will be charged applicable provincial taxes and GST.

BUSINESS REPLY MAIL
FIRST-CLASS MAIL   PERMIT NO. 717   BUFFALO, NY

POSTAGE WILL BE PAID BY ADDRESSEE

SILHOUETTE READER SERVICE
3010 WALDEN AVE
PO BOX 1867
BUFFALO NY 14240-9952

NO POSTAGE
NECESSARY
IF MAILED
IN THE
UNITED STATES

"Oh, quit squirming around in your chair like a ten-year-old."

"I'm not squirmi—"

"No, you're not," she said triumphantly. "You're sitting there like a stuffed bear. You're a man, Grif, no matter how much you'd like to pretend you're more soldier than man. And you're just the sort of man Ellyn needs. Being reliable's part of it, but if I thought she just needed reliable, I'd get her a dog. She needs someone to look at her the way a man looks at a woman when he thinks she's hot. And don't bother being appalled I'd talk about such things. I'm your aunt, but I'm a woman, too, you know." She flipped her hand, as if dismissing that topic, but she was far from through. "I'm not talking about you needing to marry Ellyn. I'm not even talking about sex. Although…"

"Marti."

"Well, you and Ellyn are two consenting adults and I don't see why you couldn't… But that's neither here nor there."

The hell it was. It was very much *here* on his mind when he let his vigilance drop for even a moment, and sometimes he thought it was very much *there* between him and Ellyn, an underlying hum to everything they said to each other or did together. Unless that was his mind playing tricks on him, which was entirely possible.

But he was *not* going to talk about this with his aunt. He stood. "Marti, I've got to go."

She didn't budge. "Go ahead. But remember, Colonel, the planet's round. So you can only retreat so long before you come back to where you started."

The day was mild enough and the noontime sun was strong enough that Ellyn and Kendra decided to eat their sandwiches at a picnic table in the small park across from Far Hills Market and a short walk from the *Banner* office.

"So, I hear Grif dug in manure in your garden for you—now that's a friend!"

Ellyn sighed. "He's driving me nuts with this helping. He wants to take us out to dinner all the time. He's volunteering to pick up the kids at school. And he wants to buy me a dryer for heaven's sake."

"That's great! You sure could use one. What?" Kendra studied her. "Not great?"

"Definitely *not* great."

"What's the big deal? It's not like accepting a dryer from an old friend makes you a kept woman or something."

There was no logical reason for heat—surely accompanied by color—to rise up her throat and into her cheeks. But logic never defeated a blush.

"Of course," Kendra added with an assumption of airiness that Ellyn didn't buy, "accepting help can take a lot of courage."

"What does that cryptic remark mean?"

"Are you sure you want to know?"

Ellyn hesitated a moment, then sighed. "No, I'm not sure. But I know I've hit you with some observations that you probably didn't want to hear, so it's only fair."

Kendra nodded, acknowledging the justness of her words. "Using myself as a prime example, I think it's safe to say that the people who are the most touchy about getting help are that way because they know they need it. And that makes them feel like they're failing."

Ellyn winced.

"Sorry, Ellyn. *I* don't think you are failing, but I wonder how you're feeling—"

"Like I'm struggling. Maybe not failing exactly, but certainly not succeeding."

"And I don't know why. You're holding down a job, running a house, keeping up with your finances, being a terrific friend whenever I've asked to lean on you, fulfilling all your duties for the baby-sitting co-op and school, not to mention raising a couple amazing kids.''

"I just want to make sure Meg and Ben don't feel an unbridgeable gap in their lives because of Dale's death. I want…'' Her throat clogged with tears and the words stopped coming.

"There's no way they can not feel a hole in their lives with their father dead. But we've talked about this. And about how well they're doing—and they are! So are you sure this is all about the kids, this feeling that you're not succeeding? What about you, Ellyn?''

Hesitating usually persuaded her to tell less rather than more, but this time even after hesitating, Ellen opted for opening a new level to her friend.

"Things…things weren't very good between me and Dale during those last few months.'' She made a sound that didn't come close to a chuckle, although that's what she'd intended. "Even before the last few months, only I didn't know it then.''

"Was that why you moved back? Trying to make things better?''

Ellyn looked up, surprised. "Yes. How did you—?''

"Wasn't hard to figure out.'' Kendra gave a wry smile. "And you've got to know if I figured it out—the Queen of Not a Clue when it came to romance—that most folks around saw it, too.''

"But no one's said anything.''

"It's not the sort of thing you bring up over casual hellos at the Market.''

"No, but…''

"But how about those of us who know you a lot better than casual hellos? Like Marti and Fran and me?''

Ellyn nodded.

"I suppose I didn't pry because I had my own secrets I wasn't telling. As for Marti and Fran, I have no idea. Surprised the heck out of me that they kept quiet!''

Ellyn gave a real chuckle this time, and Kendra joined in. Then Kendra's expression shifted to slightly speculative. "Unless…"

"Unless, what?"

"Well, I think we all were surprised when you ended up with Dale. Everybody thought you and Grif would make a match of it. So maybe that had something to do with it."

"You're thinking that because we were buddies as kids. I don't see how that could have anything to do with it. Not basing some expectation on when we were barely even teenagers."

"How about basing it on after Grif graduated?"

Ellyn hadn't known Kendra had been aware of her feelings that summer. But it was silly to feel awkward now about Kendra knowing about the failure of her romantic overture.

"That was foolishness on my part. But what do you expect at eighteen?"

Kendra was shaking her head. "Not you. Grif."

"Grif what?"

"Grif was the one everybody said was head-over-heels."

"Head-over-heels? With who?"

Kendra laughed, then took another look at her face and said firmly, "Grif showed every sign of being crazy about you."

Now Ellyn shook her head. "Every sign except that when I threw myself at him he politely but oh-so-clearly said thanks but no thanks."

"He what? You're kidding? No, I can see you're not. And it's even consistent, given the Susland family knack for romance. But let me get this clear, you're saying you made a pass at him, and he didn't respond?"

Something in Kendra's words snagged at the fabric of Ellyn's subconscious, but she left it there for now.

"Oh, he responded. He made it absolutely clear that there wasn't anything like that in his feelings for me."

Kendra whistled. "Boy, my cousin Grif is more mixed up than I'd ever thought. Even for a Susland. Grif looked at you during that visit in a way that not even I could mistake. What in the world was his problem?"

Kendra's words echoed in Ellyn's head long into the night.

The obvious answer was that Kendra had gotten it wrong all those years ago. As she readily admitted, Kendra had not been the least interested in or attuned to matters of the heart at that point in her life.

Grif had looked at her like a man who was interested romantically in a woman?

No, Kendra must have had gotten it wrong.

But what if she hadn't?

That answer had to do with timing.

With pillows stacked behind her back and her knees drawn up tight to her chest, Ellyn faced that answer.

Maybe Grif had looked at her that way… *until* her overture. Maybe in those moments when she'd kissed him, and pressed her body against his, the feelings he'd had for her evaporated.

He might have thought he wanted her until faced with the reality. The reality of Ellyn Neal, the least sexy girl in four counties.

She had been sobbing out her pain at Grif's rejection on her bed when her mother returned home unexpectedly early from her date with Paul Brindford.

Rose had been subtly pressuring Paul to marry her for several weeks. Now, from the few, vehement words Ellyn had heard them exchange at the doorway, Rose's tactics had shifted to withholding sex.

Rose had sounded tearful in her farewell, but when she pushed open Ellyn's door moments later to demand, *What's this all about? I can hear you all the way down the hall!* she was dry- and clear-eyed.

Ellyn could not say the same.

Nothing, Mom.

Rose had heaved an exasperated sigh. *Must be about a boy. Ellyn, I despair of you, I truly do. When will you learn?*

That had started a new spurt of tears, because she was painfully aware she'd been inexperienced to the point of clumsiness.

A woman has to learn how to please a man. She has to show him she can please him. And a woman doesn't learn how to do all that without making sure she has some discrete experience. If you'd been paying half as much attention to boys as you have to horses, and learning what you need to know, this wouldn't have happened.

Vindication of her mother's creed had come two weeks later when Paul Brindford asked her to marry him.

Ellyn had married Dale as a virgin. The wedding night hadn't reached her dreams nor her fears. But the next several months had made her feel slightly more secure and certainly bolder, as they explored each other and their new lives.

Then she'd gotten pregnant. They'd had a vague plan to have children several years down the road. The reality came much sooner and harder than either had anticipated. But for Ellyn, the reality also blossomed into a full-blown love affair with her baby-to-be.

Halfway through the pregnancy, all sexual contact ended. Dale had claimed he didn't want to hurt the baby. She had been convinced he found her repugnant. She worked hard at regaining her slenderness after the baby, and they seemed to have regained their zest in bed, when she became pregnant with Ben.

After that they never regained that zest.

For a long time she blamed it on the physical changes in her body. Then on the drains on her energy of having two small children to care for. Eventually the busyness of their lives seemed the logical explanation.

Only after Dale came to her that night in Washington and said he'd decided to give her a second chance before he asked for a divorce did she recognize that it was something else—her inability to please and hold onto her man.

Just like her mother had warned.

When Ellyn awoke, a different phrase of Kendra's circled through her mind. One spoken with wry irony.

The Susland family knack for romance.

That sort of oblique reference was about as close to acknowledging the Susland curse as skeptic Kendra ever got. Marti, on the other hand, was convinced that Daniel's actions in finding and winning Kendra had set to rest the first element of the curse. Ellyn supposed she fell somewhere in between them.

But what had floated to her consciousness during the night was the suspicion that it wasn't the Susland side of his family that Grif would blame for any inherited flaws. He'd made that clear even in his truncated comments about his father.

Those thoughts kept rattling around her head all morning during the usual rush to get the kids off to school, then herself off to work, during a routine morning of work, a quick brown bag lunch with Kendra at the *Banner,* then a review of the week's ad layouts before heading home.

She spotted Grif's rental car before she pulled the Suburban into the driveway to Ridge House. But she didn't see him until she was out of her vehicle.

He was on the crest of the ridge, not far from the empty clothesline. He was outlined against the dramatic gray, black and white clouds of a fast-moving system. A stark, solitary figure.

Lonely.

I know one thing, Fran had said of Nancy Griffin, *she*

*loved her son more than anything else in the world. She'd
hate to see him lonely.*

Ellyn was climbing the hill before she even knew she'd
made a decision.

"Grif!"

He turned toward her, wariness showing in the set of his
shoulders. "It's ranch property, and I'm going to fix it so
don't give me any grief. Talk to Marti if you don't like it."

That stopped her. "Don't like what?"

His brows dropped. "Me rebuilding the path from the
house."

"Oh." She took stock then, putting together the sheets
of paper on a clipboard where he'd obviously been taking
notes and the retracting steel tape measure he held. "Well,
I will talk to Marti, because it's on property that's my responsibility. But that's not what I want to talk to you
about."

His brows relaxed. "What did you want to talk to me
about?"

"The other day, when we were riding, you said— No,
don't do that."

"I'm not doing anything."

"Yes, you are. You're closing down, like Ben and Mcg
do when they don't want to hear what I have to say."

"It's not worth discussing, that's all."

"How do you know?" She pushed her windblown hair
out of her face with both hands, as she pointed out with
some triumph, "You don't know what I'm going to say."

"Nothing I said is worth discussing. That's how."

"Grif—" He'd started to turn away, and she caught him,
her hand on his forearm, below where he'd rolled back the
cuff of an age-softened khaki shirt. Impulsively she laid her
other palm against the line of his jaw. "Please, listen."

He froze. She took that as acquiescence.

"When I said you're the most honorable man I know,
and you said I didn't know things... I've been wondering

if that had to do with your father. No, don't say anything yet, let me finish.'' She dropped her hands from him, wishing she'd thought out the words a little better. This had all been so clear in her head a moment ago. What was the matter with her? "I know it's not really my business, but I care about you, Grif. And I know you. You're a good man. Don't confuse yourself with failings you saw in your father. I'm a pretty good judge of character and you—"

"You?" he scoffed. "You're Pollyanna—a *blind* Pollyanna.''

That left her flat-footed for a second, then she jammed her hands on her hips and demanded, ''What do you mean by that? Give me one example where I—"

"Dale." The single word was hard, unrelenting. So were the ones that followed. "Dale Sinclair. The man you married. You knew him all your life. But you didn't see what he was? I don't call that much of a judge of character."

"I saw."

"Then why by all that's holy did you marry him?"

"Because he wanted me. And he showed me he wanted me. And I needed that."

He stared at her, his gray eyes hard and desolate. "Yeah? Well, now you know wanting's not enough. Not nearly enough." He turned his back to her.

She tipped her head back, drawing in a long, deep breath. "Yes. Now I know."

After a moment, she heard him sigh. He shifted so his side was to her, but still didn't look her way. "Oh, hell, I'm sorry, Ellyn. I shouldn't have… I can't blame you. I knew what Dale was. I kept hoping that with you, he'd become something more, something better."

"Me, too," she said quietly.

He nodded. "But I shouldn't have let you take the chance."

Her mood crackled, like a charge of lightning had passed through her. "Let me take the chance? *Let* me?"

"You know what I mean."

"No, I don't. I have no idea what you mean. You're letting the Grif-the-Protector role go to your head twenty years retroactively."

"Grif-the-Protector?"

"From when we were kids." She waved one hand impatiently. "Looking out for all of us. Arranging things the way you thought was best for us. Well, let me tell you, Grif-the-Protector or no Grif-the-Protector, my marriage wasn't something you arranged. You had nothing to do with my marrying Dale. That was—"

"Nothing?"

The soft question stopped her dead in her tracks, but it didn't hurt as much as when he'd first brought up her foolish mistake. The implicit taboo they'd observed against mentioning it had been broken. The surprise element had evaporated.

"I know—we both know—I had a crush on you for years, Grif. A schoolgirl crush that I let get out of hand. If I'd been more mature, I would have read the signals better, and I never would have put you through that embarrassing scene. But I didn't turn around and marry Dale in a rush the instant you made it clear you didn't return my feelings."

His face had gone still as stone, and just as hard.

"Oh, I'll admit I was more vulnerable for a while. That's not easy on any girl's ego." She forced a smile that drew no response from him, and hers faded.

"Dale took advantage of you."

She shook her head emphatically. "No, he didn't. He came along at a time when his attention gave me a real boost—" Like a cool stream of water to a fish left flopping high and dry on a hot riverbank. "But that was three years before we married. I loved Dale when I married him."

She caught a shadow of something in his face. "You

don't think I was still carrying a torch for you then, do you? Is that why—?''

''No.'' The word stood stark for a moment before he added, ''I know you weren't. I knew for sure...the week before the wedding.''

Another awkward memory in their path to friendship.

She tried to smile about it now. ''I never understood where that came from, Grif. It was so out of character.''

He was silent long enough that she thought he might not answer.

''I don't know. Maybe I wanted to know for sure that you really loved him before I stood up for him at your wedding.''

''I did,'' she said simply. ''And I loved him for a long time afterward. I'm not quite sure when I stopped loving him, but it was after he stopped loving me. If I hadn't let him slip away, I think I'd still love him.''

''Let him slip away? You didn't let him slip away. It's not your fault.''

She curved her lips, knowing they didn't achieve a real smile. ''There are things,'' she said, echoing his words, ''you don't know.''

Stalemate.

Jotting an occasional note, Grif automatically absorbed the items Lieutenant Shaw was enumerating with one portion of his mind, while the rest considered yesterday's encounter with Ellyn.

It didn't matter what Ellyn thought he didn't know.

He knew Dale and he knew her. And he knew which of them was responsible for making the last few months of their marriage uncertain and miserable for her.

Not to mention the past year.

If he'd known Dale was going to end up hurting her...

You don't think I was still carrying a torch for you then, do you? Is that why—?

Was that why four days before the wedding that made her his oldest friend's wife, he had kissed Ellyn Neal? Not a kiss-the-bride kiss. Not an old-friends kiss. Not even a basically innocent kiss like she had bestowed on him three years earlier.

He'd been helping her move her things into Dale's apartment that Tuesday night, while Dale was at a ball game in one of his series of bachelor flings. They'd been working along steadily when she looked up with a slightly misty-eyed smile, and said, "This is like when we were kids, riding side by side for miles without saying a word. I've missed that, Grif."

His mind had been far from the innocence of those days. It had been on the permanence of the step she was taking. On the finality of the door closing behind her...between them.

And somehow her words broke something in him. He'd shoved aside the box in front of her with his foot, trapped her against the wall next to the closet door with the weight of his body, and kissed her like he hadn't kissed her three years earlier. With all the heat and passion and desire he hadn't let himself show her then.

She didn't fight. She didn't freeze. She accepted, but she didn't participate.

And when that realization reached into the small part of his rational brain that was still functioning, it took only a heartbeat for all that heat to freeze to solid shame.

It seemed to him that it was over before it had even begun. And yet when he pulled back from her, her lips were reddened and puffy.

He made himself meet her eyes, because he owed her that.

She made a small sound, and reached a hand toward him. He backed away. Never saying a word.

I never understood where that came from, Grif. It was so out of character.

And that showed what a lousy judge of character she was, because it was precisely *in* character—his father's character.

Dog in the manger. That's what they called it. A man who wouldn't take something himself, but didn't want anyone else to take it, either.

Was that why he'd kissed Ellyn four days before she married Dale Sinclair?

Whatever his reason, there'd been no excuse.

Whatever he'd hoped to gain, he'd only lost.

Whatever he'd thought to learn, the lesson had been that he'd made his choice three years earlier and there was no going back.

And the fact that he'd kissed her that way, in that place, at that time, showed he'd made the right choice to start. Ellyn deserved better than him.

So, he'd stood beside Dale Sinclair as he made Ellyn his wife. He'd kissed the bride on the cheek. And he'd become her friend. Knowing there could be no more.

Until Dale called him to a smoky bar one night, and the demon of letting himself dream got loose.

"…the release date for the base-closings has been delayed."

That non sequitur from sequitur-prone Lieutenant Shaw offered escape from his thoughts.

"Delayed?"

"Yes, sir. No new date for release yet. I thought if your trip to Wyoming was involved with Fort Piney being on the list, you would want to know that. Unless…" Chagrin took over the younger man's voice. "I suppose you already knew."

Grif could trace Shaw's thinking process exactly. He had a superior officer, who rarely took leave, suddenly decide to take leave. And to Far Hills, Wyoming, of all places. Then the sharp lieutenant notices that a base in the same community is among those the Army plans to announce will be closed. To Shaw's knowledge, Colonel John Griffin Junior did not exist beyond the Army, so of course his leave had to involve the Army. And the only thing to do with the Army in Far Hills was Fort Piney. Which was about to close.

Grif didn't apprise Shaw of his error as they completed the call. No sense making his junior officer feel stupid…especially since you never knew when Shaw's mistaken impression might produce some information along the way.

So, Fort Piney was on the closings list.

He wondered if the lieutenant colonel in charge knew that. It didn't much matter. He wouldn't be able to reveal the information to civilians, even if he did know. Just as Grif could not reveal it. The Army decided when the news should be released and any individual member of the Army who knew the information was honor-bound to adhere to that.

So he couldn't tell the people of Far Hills that the Army base, which was such an integral part of their economy, was about to be yanked out from underneath them. And he couldn't warn Ellyn that one of the major advertisers in the newspaper where she did advertising layout was about to disappear.

He grimaced and paced the five feet to the window. The immediate view was a parking lot, pockmarked by Wyoming winters and gritted by Wyoming dust. But beyond that showed a ridge of hills to the north, with a hint of the Big Horns at the left horizon.

His immediate prospects were about as unattractive as the parking lot, and without any inspiring uplifts in his future.

He had to get out of here. What good had he done? A game or two of catch with Ben, a couple of reassuring follow-throughs with Meg, a few meals provided for Ellyn. What else he could do for them, Ellyn resisted. What he couldn't do for them taunted him during the long, still nights. His self-discipline was eroding like a wind-scoured bluff. Crumbling a little more with each breeze.

They wouldn't understand if they found out he'd known about Fort Piney and hadn't told them.

Not only Ellyn, but all the others. All of Far Hills, the ranch and the community.

His leaving would be best for everyone concerned.

But the honor that bound him not to reveal what he knew about Fort Piney also meant he had to keep his word. And that meant he had at least two more obligations. One was to fix that path up to the ridge. The other was to an eight-year-old named Ben.

Chapter Eight

Ellyn had timed it perfectly.

The fact that it was a result of luck rather than planning didn't matter. She'd actually meant to arrive fifteen minutes earlier than she did at the elementary school for her stint of bringing treats and helping supervise a Fun Friday session. That's what second-grade teacher Joyce Hammerschmidt called the once-a-month time when the kids ate goodies and sang songs. The kids loved it. That level of excitement in a class full of second-graders meant parent volunteers were essential.

She let out a huff of relief as she opened the classroom's door and discovered it empty. The other parents had obviously already arrived, because there were plates of brownies and cookies laid out on a long table at the back of the room.

She was rearranging the cupcakes she'd brought when the teacher walked in.

"Oh, Ellyn, I'm so glad to see you arrived in good time."

Joyce Hammerschmidt was a forceful woman nearing sixty. Ellyn was secretly a bit intimidated by her. Somehow when the teacher said *Ellyn* it made her feel as if she should sit up straighter and not be talking. But Ben had flourished in her class.

Before Ellyn could form a coherent response, the teacher continued, "And I was even more glad to see Ben has come out of his funk over this."

Ellyn stopped with a cupcake in midair. "Funk?"

"Nothing major." The teacher gave an odd little laugh as if she'd said something clever. "Although at this age there's nothing minor in their lives, is there? Especially after losing a parent. I have kept my eye on Ben, but he's been doing quite well."

With the exception of that one bed-wetting episode, Ben had seemed to be doing well, especially since—she might as well admit it—Grif had shown up.

"Although, I feared this incident with Billy Dayton might throw him into a tailspin."

"Incident?"

Billy Dayton was the boy Ben talked about the most, the one whose house he most frequently asked to eat dinner at, the name listed first to come to the ranch. Except, Ellyn thought with a loud click of belated recognition, Ben hadn't mentioned him in a while. She searched her memory. The last time she could remember for sure had been a couple of days before Grif's arrival. And Ben had been unusually quiet right before that. But Grif had changed that.

"Of course," Joyce Hammerschmidt continued, "most people think these relationships are more important to girls, but not those of us who work with children. Especially at a certain age, and especially if the boy is vulnerable. Boy or girl, that can make a betrayal devastating."

"Betrayal?"

Oh God, she was a terrible mother. Her son had been betrayed and she didn't even know it. Except she had. At least she'd seen the signs. The quietness, then the relapse on bed-wetting, the lack of Billy Dayton's name. But she hadn't put it all together.

Because she'd been too taken up with Grif. With the surprise of his return, the mystery of his disappearance, the memories of their past.

"Ah, I thought perhaps you hadn't heard about it." Joyce laid a hand reassuringly on Ellyn's arm. "That's not unusual. At this age, some boys still take every problem to Mom, but some are starting to think they need to work things out for themselves. Ben and Billy didn't tell me, either. If it hadn't been for overhearing a few of the girls talking at recess, and then what Daniel Delligatti said after Billy brought him in this morning, I wouldn't have known."

"Daniel? What does he have to do with this? Please, Joyce, tell me what happened. I'm totally in the dark."

It must break some rule of motherhood to admit that, but she needed to know so she could help Ben.

"It started with the assignment to bring in something that had been created outside of Wyoming, and give a short presentation to the class explaining how it had come to be in Far Hills. Ah, I see you hadn't heard about the assignment. It's a bit of show-and-tell, which the children love at this age, but requires some research on their part, as well as presentation skills. I picked up the idea at a seminar—"

"Yes, but what does this have to do with Ben? And Billy Dayton? And Daniel Delligatti."

"Well, from what I can gather, the children were talking about what they would bring in, trying to figure out things that hadn't been created in Wyoming, and Ben became very excited and said he had a great idea. And it *was* a good idea," the teacher said with a smile.

"What was his idea and what did Billy do?"

"Ben wanted to bring in a person instead of an object. He decided he'd bring in Daniel Delligatti, who most definitely wasn't created in Wyoming," she added with a smile that seemed to appreciate the newcomer's exotic good looks.

"And the only person he told his idea to was Billy," the teacher continued, pitching her voice louder as the thunder of small footsteps rumbled in the hall outside. "Then Billy turned around and asked Daniel to be *his* project before Ben could. The poor man. He told me he already felt badly that Ben asked, too late. This morning, when he found out Billy had stolen Ben's idea, he felt *truly* terrible. But, of course, it was too late."

"But you said Ben had—"

The door at the front of the classroom swung open with a thud and a ragged stream of second-graders flowed in. Ellyn searched the stream for her particular just-turned eight-year-old, with no luck, though she did see Billy Dayton come in, by himself. Three mothers followed, taking grown-up size seats along the side of the room that they'd already staked out with purses and jackets.

At last, Ben came in, but he stopped just inside the door, with that mixture of excitement and anxiety on his face that always scraped a little at her heart. Once, Ben's excitement had never left any room for anxiety. He spotted his teacher first.

"Mrs. Hammerschmidt, is it okay for me to check if—" Seeing his mother, he broke off to wave.

"Yes, Ben, I believe someone is waiting for you at the principal's office next door. Please, accompany your guest in."

Ben's smile exploded in the instant before he dashed out.

"Class, settle down, please. We want to be polite to the guest Ben is bringing us this afternoon."

Ellyn looked at Joyce Hammerschmidt. "Guest?"

"Yes. And that's what I think we need to look at in this

whole incident. It did drop Ben into a funk for a period, but that didn't last. He's shown initiative after adversity, and that is *so* important at this age.''

Ellyn was glad to hear that assessment, even if she still had no idea *how* her son had done that.

''But who…?''

The door opened again, and Ellyn could hear Ben's excited whisper, saying, ''Put your hat on, please. Pleeseaaase.''

A figure stepped in, familiar and unknown, at the same time.

Grif.

No, not Grif. Not the Grif she knew. But Colonel John Griffin Junior.

In full uniform. That neutral green the Army wore. With his hat on, as requested, and toting a regulation duffel bag—at least she presumed it was regulation. What she knew about the Army was basically limited to the fact that Grif had chosen to make it his life…and his love. This was a part of him she'd never even fully seen before, much less understood.

He set the duffel down, then was taking off the hat when his eyes met Ellyn's. She couldn't interpret any message in his cool gaze—in fact, she was certain he made it unreadable on purpose. Her own expression, she hoped, displayed her gratitude that he'd come through this way for Ben. Her other emotions she'd as soon keep to herself. At least until she sorted them out.

He tucked the hat under his arm and stood as if a general had popped up in front of him instead of five rows of kid-occupied desks and a handful of adult women.

''Ben, won't you introduce your guest?''

''Yes, ma'am. This is Colonel John Griffin Junior of the United States Army. He used to come to Far Hills all the time as a kid, but he wasn't born here,'' Ben hurriedly assured the teacher. He looked at note cards he held tightly.

"He was born at Fort Hood—that's in Texas. He's visiting now, while he's on leave—that's what they call vacation in the Army—and he's been my friend my *entire* life."

A flicker crossed Grif's face that caught Ellyn's heart by surprise. At that moment she wanted more than anything to hug man and boy. But all she could do was stand at the back of the room and beam, as Ben consulted his note cards in telling the class about some of Grif's assignments.

She was soon caught up as much as the children in what Grif began drawing out of the duffel bag. Using Ben as an undersize mannequin, he outfitted the boy for "duty" in camouflage fatigues—shirt only, since the tail reached the top of the boots he had Ben step into. He showed a canteen and various tools, as well as rations, an emergency shelter, a compass, and gave a brief discourse on the importance of socks to a marching soldier.

"Thank you, Colonel," the teacher said from her spot at the back of the room beside Ellyn, as Ben and Grif started returning the items to the duffel. "And thank you, Ben. That was a wonderful presentation. Colonel, we would be honored if you would stay as our final two students give their presentations, then join us in the special treat our mothers have brought us."

Grif looked directly at her, and Ellyn managed a smile, despite the odd sensation that seemed to take hold of her facial muscles. And her knees.

"Thank you, ma'am. I'd be happy to."

"Wonderful," Joyce Hammerschmidt said in her classroom voice. Then she dropped it to a whisper only Ellyn could hear: "There *is* something about a man in uniform."

Uncertain what her voice might sound like, Ellyn nodded.

As Joyce made her way to the front of the room, a small part of Ellyn's mind recognized that the teacher's comment had relieved Ellyn of ever feeling intimidated again by the older woman. The rest of her mind was occupied with thinking:

At least there was something about *this* man in uniform.

And no doubt something even more about him *out* of uniform…or better yet, out of any clothes at all.

Oh, my God, I didn't just have that thought, did I?

Her mind circled around from shock to something that might have edged toward glee, then caromed away from that with renewed shock. What was *wrong* with her? To think that way about Grif. And to be honest, not just to think it but to envision it in full, glorious Technicolor.

Grif.

She glanced at the quarter-profile that was all she could see of him seated at the front of the classroom, hoping that would remind her who she was having these unseemly thoughts about, would restore her to sanity.

It didn't work, and she spent the remaining presentations carefully not looking anywhere near where Grif sat.

Still, she did notice, as the teacher finally released the kids from their seats to thunder toward the baked goods at the back of the room, that the three other mothers went the opposite direction, heading toward one U.S. Army colonel.

That held him long enough for the first wave of cupcake, cookie and brownie marauders to plunder the table, retreat with their booty and reform around the star attraction. Soon Grif was surrounded by a ring of chocolate-smeared fascination about waist-high.

Ellyn's attention shifted as one member of that ring broke away and headed for her.

"Wasn't that great? Wasn't that great?" Ben demanded. "I had the best one of *anybody*—even better than Billy, who thought he was so smart getting Daniel before I had a chance to ask him."

"It was great. And it was very, *very* nice of Grif to do this for you. But why didn't you tell me about this assignment, Ben? I would have helped you."

"I know, but you've been having that worried look a lot lately and I've gotta start taking care of things on my own."

"Oh, Ben" was all she got out around the clog in her throat.

"Besides," he added, dropping from sounding approximately two decades older than his chronological age back to eight, "you'd have said I could bring you in, since you were born somewhere else, and that'd be so *lame*, having my *mother*."

A chuckle eased her throat. "I can see that it wouldn't have been too exciting. But you have to promise me that in the future you'll tell me about projects likes this—no matter how worried I might look. I'll be even *more* worried if I think you're not telling me things. Do you understand?"

"I suppose."

"Do you promise to tell me from now on?"

He met her eyes. "I'll try, Mom."

"You see that you do, young man."

He grinned at her, and she grinned back.

"Gotta go, Mom, or there won't be any of your cupcakes left, and they're the *best*."

"Flattery will get you everywhere," she muttered to herself as he took off for another pass at the table.

From the corner of her eye, she caught the movement of muted green. Turning, she saw the broad-shouldered, straight-backed figure of Colonel John Griffin Junior leaving the room.

She cast a practiced glance over the room, assured herself that whatever mayhem might break out in the next five minutes, Joyce and the other mothers could handle without her, and hurried after him. She didn't catch up until he'd almost reached his car.

"You didn't get a cupcake, Grif."

He stopped and turned, his face unreadable. "No, I didn't."

"That's okay, I've got more at home. I'll save you one."

"I'd like that."

She considered the formality in his manner and her own discomfort. Might as well hit them both head on.

"You didn't tell me about this."

"No, I didn't. Ben said he'd get your okay, and he asked me not to talk to you about it."

She sighed. "He didn't say anything. He thought I..." Somehow, telling Grif that her son was worried about *her* being worried did not seem a good idea when she'd spent so much time and effort telling him she was doing fine. "He was afraid I'd make him bring me in as his presentation. And that, of course, would have been *lame*." That drew a quirk of amusement from Grif's otherwise stern mouth. "As for Ben *asking* you not to talk to me, that sounds awfully mild for what I suspect happened. A blood oath, maybe? Swearing on your sacred honor? Agreeing to forfeit your firstborn?"

She'd been prepared to go on, but that last image stopped her.

"Well," Grif conceded, "pledged me not to tell you. I'm sorry, maybe I should have anyway. Do you mind that I came like...?"

"Mind? That you came like a knight in shining armor for my son? Now, I could understand why *you* might mind—being coerced into this by my relentless son, as I know perfectly well you were. I know how persistent that child can be."

"That can be a good trait."

"Not if it drives the people around him crazy or makes them do things they'd rather not."

"I was glad to do this for Ben, but he should have told you. I could tell you were surprised and..." A slight shift of his hand seemed to indicate the uniform.

"Maybe I was a bit taken aback. When I saw you standing there, it struck me how seldom you wore your uniform around us back in Washington. Almost as if you weren't comfortable in uniform. But seeing you now... You certainly look at home in it.''

"I am."

The words had an odd finality to them.

"You deliberately didn't wear your uniform around us?" She'd rarely asked him about the Army or his role in it during all those years, and now she couldn't seem to let the subject drop. Like pushing at a sore tooth with her tongue.

"It seemed better to wear civvies. Around the kids. Uniform never seemed to fit with a family life."

"There have got to be thousands and thousands of military families who don't agree." She smiled, but he didn't. "As for making my kids uneasy—especially my son—you can see after today how wrong you were about that."

He grinned slightly. "He did seem pleased."

"Pleased. There you go with hyperbole again, Colonel. You've got to stop overstating situations. He was flying higher than any kite. Although, you could have done one thing to make him happier."

"Yeah?"

"If you'd just had a spare canon or bazooka lying around that you could have brought along."

They were both laughing then.

Oh, it was so good to see Grif laugh. If his grin transformed his face, his laugh transformed his soul, lifting the sadness, the weight that seemed to cling to him. She loved to see him laugh.

Ellyn tipped her head back and laughed, too, and Grif felt an unfamiliar lightness combine with the all-too-familiar tightness in his chest. God, Ellyn's laugh was something he'd give his life to protect. Light, but real. Inviting, including. Wrapping around his heart the way her arms reached now to wrap around his waist.

She hugged him as she had a thousand times. He

schooled his arms to return the gesture with the reassurance of friendship as he had a thousand times. He could do nothing about the sensation of heat wherever her body pressed against his. Could do nothing about the instinct rushing blood to his groin. She released him and eased back. His arms obeyed his command to loosen their hold on her.

Then she stopped moving away.

For one beat of his heart, everything remained as it always had been.

With the second beat of his heart, the door to changing everything opened. Ellyn stretched up, one hand steadying herself against his upper arm, and her lips touched his cheek. But just barely his cheek, because somehow he'd turned. Or she had. Or they both had. Her lips, which had meant to brush across his cheek, grazed the corner of his mouth.

Her mouth no longer touched his skin, but she hadn't pulled away. She was still right there, so close, her breath, coming in short, light puffs, brushed across the faint dampness her lips had left. So close, he smelled the tangy spice of her shampoo, blended with the rumpled, clean sweat of the kids she'd been hugging and shoulder-patting as she'd dispensed cupcakes, juice and love.

For one beat of his heart, everything remained as it always had been.

With the second beat of his heart, he turned his head that final degree, and touched his lips to Ellyn's.

She didn't retreat.

Their lips parted a moment, then came back together. *Together.* Not a mistake. Not a misdirected innocent kiss. Not him kissing her. The two of them kissing each other. Her lips warm and soft, moving against his. Giving and taking.

The reality of that bolted hot and triumphant through him.

She might have felt it, because her hands tightened their

hold on him, her fingers digging in, gaining support. Holding on.

He shifted toward her and she balanced by moving in, too.

He touched his tongue to her lips, and they parted, just barely but immediately. Taking a welcome from that slight opening, he slid his tongue inside, feasting on her. She hesitated, just long enough to make him consider dropping to his knees and begging. Then her tongue answered his, and a pulse of distilled heat shot through him.

He wrapped her tighter, aware of the sweet press of her breasts against his chest, of the fit of her hips against him, of her hands on his back and into his hair. They adjusted to each other, angling to make the kiss deeper, harder, then softening it as they both grabbed air before the kiss consumed them again.

A kiss that seemed to search, almost frantic. And then they found it. A deep, driving rhythm that echoed the throb of heat in his body. It was blatant, undisguised, raw. A mating of mouths.

Desire shouting to find someplace, anyplace, to push aside the layers of clothes, to join. A soft, straining sound escaped Ellyn, telling him she felt it, too.

He lifted his head, discarding his car as too exposed, gauging the distance to her more enclosed Suburban.

But before he could start, she made another sound. Born as a gasp, but dying as a sob.

And her hands no longer held him, but held him off.

"Ellyn—"

"Please... Please..."

She didn't look at him, her eyes locked on his nameplate over his heart. Head back, eyes closed, he swore. Harsh words in barely a whisper. It didn't help.

He straightened his back and, against every instinct rioting in his body, he loosened his hold on her. She backed away three unsteady steps, then stopped.

"I have to go. I have to…"

"Ellyn—"

Her voice had ground to a halt before he spoke, but as soon as he said her name, she was off again.

"Back to the room. I should— I mean, I left my post— that's a court-martial offense, isn't it?" As if afraid he might answer, she rushed on, backing up another step, starting to turn. "Leaving those other mothers with all those kids. Have to guard against sugar highs, you know, or—"

"Right now. Ellyn." His voice had enough of the bark of command that she stopped in midflight. Her eyes came to his face for a flash, then away, before he could read their message. "Whatever you've got to say, just say it."

She paused long enough then to stammer out, "There's nothing to say. I mean, I didn't… I shouldn't have… I'm sorry."

Still not looking at him, she turned and walked away. Purposeful now, no longer a flight, but not looking back. He didn't try to stop her again.

"Yeah," he said to the school door after it had closed behind her. "I'm sorry, too."

Ellyn stood in the girls' bathroom, feeling like Gulliver in the land of Lilliputians. The mirror was too low for her to see her face without crouching down.

She was glad she couldn't see her face. Especially as her hand went to her lips, touching their newly tender surface.

Her fingers trembled and she balled them into a fist.

What was the matter with her? What had possessed her? Those old feelings for Grif had disappeared long ago, faded like delicate spring flowers giving way to the sturdy blooms of summer. As her girlhood fantasies were replaced by the reality of their friendship.

That kiss was no daffodil or crocus, clamored a voice in her head. *It was roses entwined with jasmine and orchids. Rich and heady and delicate.*

Could he possibly have meant to kiss her that way?

What? You think roses and orchids get into a crocus bed by chance?

She shook her head, trying to clear it, of the voice and of the aftereffects of kissing Grif. She had to think.

He didn't exactly push you away.

Grif wouldn't. He'd never want to hurt her that way, with that kind of rejection. Even when she'd thrown her eighteen-year-old self at him, he'd been so gentle, taking all the blame.

Even a non-femme fatale like you can tell the difference between a man who's not rejecting and a man who's turned on. He was turned on.

That didn't need much explaining. He was a man. Men didn't need emotion for that particular reaction.

Not Grif.

No! He was a man like any other man. No saint, as Dale had told her. Perhaps he was lonely, being here. Away from…someone.

She'd never thought to ask. He'd so rarely mentioned other women to her. But that didn't mean there wasn't someone. Someone beautiful, dazzling, exciting. Someone who offered much more than cookies and lemonade, someone who didn't need a new dryer or a path rebuilt, someone whose kids didn't drag a man into chauffeur duty and show-and-tell—if she even had kids. Someone who knew how to hold onto a man.

No, Grif couldn't have meant the kiss that way. It had been her own longings—longings she had thought long ago dead and buried—that had betrayed her.

Twice before had they kissed, and each time had taught her an important lesson. That first time had taught her that Grif didn't share her feelings.

The second time, that stunning kiss the week before her wedding, had taught her that her feelings were more complicated than she'd thought. But that kiss had also taught her a critical lesson about Grif. With her blood and nerve-endings fizzing like champagne, she'd seen the immediate regret and self-recrimination in his eyes. He'd hated himself at the moment. Ellyn would never again be a party to anything that made Grif feel that way about himself.

That moment had been the end to her younger feelings for him, making it possible for them to build their true friendship.

And now she'd betrayed that…*why?*

The answer wasn't comfortable, but it wasn't too hard to find. She'd selfishly wanted a man's body to respond to her as Grif's had responded. She'd needed that reassurance. And maybe some part of her deep down had picked Grif because she knew he wouldn't reject her.

Not like Dale had in the end.

Whatever the reason, it was contemptible that she'd used Grif that way, had abused their friendship that way.

She had to make it right. Somehow.

"Ellyn?"

The pause on the other end of the line told Grif more clearly than words that she recognized his voice. And was uncomfortable.

He strung together mental curses that did nothing to improve his mood. And his mood was none too good to start with, since he'd gotten little sleep last night. He'd tossed and turned until he drifted into a restless doze that brought fragmentary dreams of a man in uniform kissing a woman he knew he had to leave.

"Hello, Grif."

She sounded tentative, making him more grimly determined.

"Will you be available in the afternoon the day after tomorrow to go look at materials for rebuilding that path up the ridge? I'll pick you up and—"

"Grif, I haven't changed my mind—"

"I know. Nothing's changed." He thought he heard a slight indrawn breath from the other end of the line at his emphasis on the last two words. "But that path's Far Hills land, and—"

"Grif, let me say something, please?"

He didn't want to hear it. Damn, he didn't want to hear it. "Sure."

"Grif, what happened yesterday… I'm sorry. I shouldn't have… Marti and Fran have been after me for spending so much time alone, and I guess they're right. But that's no excuse," she added hurriedly, "for abusing your friendship that way. I'm so sorry. All the years we've been friends and then to put you in that awkward situation. I truly am sorry that—"

"Forget it." It *had* been an awkward situation…awkward for walking for several minutes after she'd disappeared. Awkward for his peace of mind.

"I hope we both can forget it and keep on being friends. I promise it won't happen again. I'm so sorry it happen—"

"We'll be friends any way you want if you stop this damned apologizing."

His harsh words brought silence for a moment.

"Okay, Grif." She sounded strained now. Perhaps even a little peeved. "I'm done apologizing."

"Good. Now, about the path. I talked to Marti, and we're agreed it needs to be fixed, and I'm going to do it. She and I also agreed you should have some say in how it'll look when it's rebuilt, since you're living there."

"Then I'll pay for it."

"Talk to Marti. I have nothing to do with the money."

The sound he heard this time was definitely a snort. "I won't be able to budge her, either, if she's made up her mind."

"You might be right. Either way, that path's going to get rebuilt. The question is if you want any say in what it looks like. If the day's not good—"

"Day after tomorrow's fine." Her voice sounded surer now. Brisk. "About one."

"Okay. I'll see you then."

"Goodbye."

"Goodbye, Ellyn."

Forget it? She wanted him to forget how it felt to hold her, to have her body snug against his, her lips on his, her tongue in his mouth? He could take abuse like that every day for the rest of his life and consider himself well used.

But from the moment she'd backed out of his arms, he'd known she didn't feel the same. She didn't feel as if letting go of each other might rip something open inside.

Yet even as he cursed it, he knew that was for the best.

It might bruise his ego that the burn of desire that threatened to jump all the fire walls he'd erected was not as powerful for her, but it truly was for the best.

This way he could continue helping Ellyn and the kids without letting loose emotions he was so ill-equipped to handle.

Holding one corner of the kitchen window curtain aside with the back of two fingers, Ellyn watched as Grif emerged from his rental car. It reminded her of the day he'd arrived in Far Hills.

Only this time, she knew he was coming, so she wasn't exposed on the hillside open to ambush from an unexpected visitor or unresolved emotions. This time, she could watch him without being watched herself. This time he wouldn't be a surprise soldier, so straight and handsome, who'd come to the rescue of her son. This time she was ready for him.

Not like that first day, when her mind had so strangely obsessed on his casual touch on her drying clothes, and certainly not like three days ago at the school.

Now she knew the dangers lurking inside her. From those moments in the bathroom and her initial recognition of why she'd kissed him, she'd spent a lot of time setting herself straight. Those wayward longings wouldn't ambush her again.

He moved more slowly than he had that first day, almost stiffly. His face looked as if he might have gotten too much sun. He must have been doing something strenuous outdoors yesterday. She hadn't seen him all day…not that she'd been on the lookout. But every other day of his visit she'd at least heard from him.

The knock on the door seemed a long time coming. It still made her jerk slightly. When enough seconds had ticked by to pretend she'd come from another part of the house, she drew in a calming breath, and opened the door.

But when she stepped back to let him enter, she blurted out the first thing that came to mind. "I wasn't sure you'd come."

"I said I would."

"Of course, and you always keep your promises. But really, Grif," she added hurriedly, straining for a lighter tone. "I don't need you to—"

"I know you don't. I know you'd do fine on your own. Without me at all. But I said I'm doing this, and I am."

"You haven't changed at all from the time you were Ben and Meg's age. You're stubborn as all get-out."

"I haven't changed," he said, the slow words oddly chilling. "I never will. But you have. You've changed, Ellyn."

"Yes, Dale pointed that out numerous times, too."

She snapped her mouth shut on the final word, caught off guard by her own tone. Stunned by her own feelings. Bitterness? Where had that come from? She hadn't been bitter with Dale. Sad, frustrated, scared, heartbroken, disappointed, hurt and even impatient. But never bitter. So why on earth would bitterness have surfaced toward Grif, of all people?

If he noticed the vinegar in her voice, he didn't react to it, but continued looking at her steadily.

"You're stronger."

She blinked at him in surprise, or maybe in shock at the warmth of underlying approval in his words.

"I didn't have a choice. I had to be—for Meg and Ben."

"No, I don't suppose you did have a choice."

He turned away with the same stiffness she'd noticed when he'd gotten out of the car. If he was that sore—

"Grif, are you okay?"

He half turned back toward her, slowly. "Sure. Fine."

"Grif—" She put a hand on his arm below his rolled back cuff, hoping to get a better look at his face. What she felt drove all other thoughts from her mind. "My God, Grif, you're burning up."

Chapter Nine

She moved around to face him and put her palm to his forehead as she would with one of the children. "You have a fever. Why on earth didn't you call and postpone this?"

He looked at her, and she realized how glassy his eyes were.

"It's warm out."

She tsked once—at his stubbornness and her obtuseness, then she got busy, leading him to sit on the couch before she retrieved the thermometer from the medicine cabinet.

"I'm okay. We've got to get going—"

"We're not going anywhere. Sit down." In familiar territory now, she slipped the plastic cover over the end of the digital thermometer. "Hold this under your tongue," she ordered in the same tone that quelled the kids. When he opened his mouth to protest, she slid the thermometer in—a ploy that seldom worked with the kids anymore. He was obviously new to this.

"Ellyn—"

At least she thought that's what he said. He reached toward the thermometer, and she grabbed that arm, putting her fingers over the pulse point at his wrist.

"Be quiet so I can count."

He subsided long enough for her to take his pulse—twice. The first time she was sure she had to be wrong that it could be that high. She checked a second time.

"Okay, that should be it."

He gave her a look as she removed the thermometer that was probably meant to be intimidating, but reached merely doleful.

"Now can we get going? There's—"

She barely heard, all her attention on the thermometer's figures. "Oh, my. I'm calling the doctor."

"I don't need a doctor. I'm—"

"The hell you don't, John Griffin Junior."

"Don't call me—"

"I'm calling the doctor." She overrode his words and any other objections he might try to make. "You stay right there."

She dialed the number of Doc Boyd, and got his head nurse, Laurel Vega, on the fifth ring.

"Laurel? This is Ellyn Sinclair. I've got a...ah, friend here visiting. He's got a temperature of a hundred and four."

"An adult with a hundred and four? Better let you talk to Doc. But it might be a while—it's a zoo here. You're lucky anybody answered the phone at all. You want to hang on or wait until Doc has a chance to call back?"

"I'll hang on. Thanks."

She stretched the extralong telephone cord to reach the aspirin she kept in the cabinet by the sink, then filled a glass with water and trailed the cord into the living room to Grif.

"Here."

He took the water, but balked when she held out two small white pills. "I don't need those. I'm just thirsty."

"Grif, you take these and don't give me any grief about it, do you understand?"

He took the pills from her hand, but ventured another protest. "Ellyn, I don't—"

"You do. Take the pills and drink all that water."

He grimaced as he popped the pills into his mouth, but swallowed them with water immediately. Then he kept drinking like a man who'd been in a desert.

With his head tilted back, she watched the rhythmic motion. The sinews and muscles of his strong neck at contrast with the vulnerability of his exposed throat.

"Ellyn? What's this I hear about you having a patient? Not one of the kids, I hope."

It took her a moment to adjust her mental focus from Grif to the voice on the phone. "Oh, uh, Doc. No, not the kids. Grif, uh, Colonel Griffin is a friend of the family. Marti's nephew."

"Mmm-hmm."

What did he mean by that? Had he heard something? Or—

"Symptoms?"

His terse question settled her immediately. She related the figures of temperature and pulse, along with her observations and what she'd given Grif. He asked a series of questions that seemed to eliminate his worst concerns.

"Has he been around Ben the past couple of days? Ben or other second-graders. Say, the past two days?"

"The past two days? No. He gave a presentation to Ben's class three days ago, but Ben hasn't seen him since, and there wasn't a lot of close contact even then."

"Could be longer than two days if he's otherwise healthy. How about you? Have you been around this Grif? Close contact?"

"No. I told you. We're frie—"

It wasn't just a memory of their kiss that stopped her words, it was the full-blown sensation. Grif's lips pressing against hers, his body around hers. Heat as high as his fever now, and sensations more potent than the most powerful drug.

Doc Boyd's pragmatic voice snapped her out of her trance.

"Well, that's probably how he got it," he said, apparently reading her aborted denial with unerring accuracy. "Sounds like the strep infection that's got half the second grade in my clinic. You'll probably get a note from school with Ben this afternoon."

"But Ben's fine—*I* feel fine."

"Sure," he said cheerfully. "You're carriers. You've built up immunity to lots of these germs from having your kids bring them home all the time. But sounds like this colonel of yours—"

"He's not mine."

"—hasn't been around kids. Right?"

"Not for a while," she confirmed.

"So he doesn't have much immunity. Come to think of it, with a fever like that, he doesn't have *any* immunity to this bug no matter how healthy he is normally."

"I'll bring him right in and—"

"Whoa, there. That's not a good idea. This clinic is teeming with kid germs. Not only the second grade, but the kindergartners. Some virus is going through them like a hot knife through butter. This is the last place you want your colonel. Way I see it is you can take him up to the hospital in Billings—"

"The hospital!"

Grif roused himself enough to say sternly, "No hospital."

"—or you can take him to the base. But they're not any better than here, since those kids have the same stuff. Or—"

"I'll go. BOQ. My room." Grif leaned forward as if to rise.

"Stay still." She pushed back on his shoulder, and he fell back against the couch's cushions like a rag doll. "Doc, he's so weak... Are you sure I shouldn't bring him in—"

"Not unless you want to load another disease on this one while his immune system's kerflooey. He's better off there, as long as you can keep an eye on him. He shouldn't be alone, and he sure as hell shouldn't be driving with that kind of a fever. You'd better keep him at your house."

"My house! But how can I—"

"Best place for him. Make sure he gets plenty of rest. Drinks lots of fluids—especially water. Keep an eye on that temperature and if it goes up, you call me back. I'll write a prescription for antibiotics. Allergies to any medicines?"

His impatient interruption hadn't answered her objection, but even if he'd let her finish, Doc wouldn't have had a solution to the concerns swirling through her mind.

She relayed the question to Grif, and his answer to Doc. "No, but—"

"The prescription will be waiting for someone to pick up at the Market. But don't leave him alone—get someone else to pick it up. Watch that temperature! If it doesn't start dropping, call and do what you'd do for the kids."

With that he was gone. Leaving her to contemplate the idea of giving Grif a cool bath the way she did for the kids if their temperature shot up.

"Oh, Lordy." The whisper did little to block out the image, but it did remind her of her immediate problem.

Having Grif here. No, there had to be another solution.

Of course! The home ranch. After three rings, Marti answered, sounding weary.

The reason for Marti's weariness was soon apparent— Emily had the virus, which was making the rounds of the baby-sitting co-op as well as the kindergarten. Matthew had also been exposed and Kendra wouldn't know for a couple of days if he was contagious, too.

But at least the call solved one problem.

"Fran's bringing out medicine and other supplies about two, so call and ask her to pick up Grif's prescription," Marti suggested.

With a fatalistic sigh, Ellyn did that.

"Might as well pick up clothes for the kids while I'm there, and I'll have 'em stay with me here in town for a few days," Fran said. "You wouldn't want to risk exposing them all over again to this bug."

It sounded so negligent to even consider having the kids stay home when they had a place to stay with Fran that Ellyn couldn't think of a good argument that didn't involve admitting she was wary of being alone with a man—this man—even this sick.

After hanging up the phone in the kitchen, she returned to the living room to find Grif with his head back and his eyes closed. But not ready to admit defeat.

"Give me a minute, and I'll get out of here, Ellyn."

"You're in no condition to drive."

"I'm fine. I'll go to my quarters. Stay in bed."

"Doc said you shouldn't be alone. Somebody's got to watch your temperature, take care of you."

"I'm not going to stay here—"

"Oh, yes, you are." Funny, how the more he argued, the more determined she was that he wasn't going to get out of her sight. "I thought maybe Marti could…but Emily is sick, too. Doc Boyd said staying here was best, and that's what you're going to do."

Only, where was he going to stay?

She pushed her hair back with both hands. Meg's bed was barely big enough for her. Grif would be miserable. Ben's room…she closed her eyes as she considered the state that reigned within those four walls. The guest room had no furniture. That left the couch, which wasn't long enough for him, besides being decidedly lumpy. Or her bed.

"C'mon, Grif." Before she could consider the ramifications, she took him by the hand and tugged. He stood without needing much help from her, but he weaved a bit with his first steps. She wedged her shoulder under his arm, and draped it around her, then looped her arm across his back, grabbing a fistful of waistband at the far side so she'd have a good hold if he started to go down.

"Ellyn, this isn't—"

"Hush. And keep walking."

He said nothing more as they negotiated the living room, hallway and into her bedroom.

She eased him down to the side of the bed. He sat there, his eyes opened, but not focused. His skin flushed. If she asked him if he needed help undressing, he'd deny it if he had to use his last breath.

She scooched down and pulled off his shoes and socks, then straightened. Telling herself this was no different from dealing with Ben, she started unbuttoning his shirt.

Her fingers brushed the bare, heated skin of his chest below the shirt, reminding her of the necessity for this, and keeping her mind on the straight and narrow. At least until she tugged the shirttail out of the waistband of his chinos and felt a new warmth in the material there. Firmly putting aside the thought of where that particular warmth came from, she pulled the shirt off him in an awkward attempt to touch him as little as possible.

Not letting herself think, she reached for the waistband tab of his chinos, and unbuttoned it.

Grif jolted like a sleepwalker awakened from a trance. "Don't. I'll...do it."

She relinquished the task—gladly, of course. With no feeling other than pure relief.

He levered himself up from the bed, and she busied herself with pulling down the covers and plumping the pillow on that side.

When she turned around from placing his shirt on a hanger, she found him with his back to her, his thumbs hooked in the waistband of his pants, slowly drawing the material down. Only the deepening view of the bare flesh of his lower back and then the top of his butt revealed he'd hooked more than his pants.

"Stop!" He did. And remained still. "Grif, you can't…I, uh, I think you'll be more, uh, comfortable if you leave your…your shorts on."

He dropped his head forward, as if checking out her assessment. She heard him mumble a few words, a curse by their tone. Then his hands shifted, and the tops of white boxer shorts appeared as he kept pushing the pants down.

She started breathing again, realizing only then that she'd stopped.

He tried to pull the pants free, and sat hard on the bed, instead. She finished the task, then gave his shoulder a gentle push to get him to lie flat.

"Ellyn?"

"Yes, Grif?"

"I don't feel good."

"I know you don't, Grif." She pulled the sheet and light blanket up over him until they rested under his chin, but left the comforter off. "Get some sleep and you'll feel better soon."

He put his hands over the top edge of the sheet as if he might push it away, then subsided.

His voice wasn't much more than a raw whisper as he added, "All the times I dreamed about being in your bed…this wasn't what I had in mind."

He hadn't wanted anything covering him, but his nose had caught the faint trace of Ellyn's warm spiciness on the sheet, and he'd let it stay.

And then he'd told her the truth. For the first time in a long, long time, he'd told her the full truth.

He turned his face into the pillow that smelled like Ellyn's hair, and let the dreams come.

"How's the patient?"

Ellyn took the pharmacy bag from Fran.

"Asleep. I almost hate to wake him up to give him the pills."

"Sometimes sleep's even better for folks than medicine."

"I don't know," Ellyn said, hearing the doubt in her own voice. "I think he might have been delirious."

Fran gave her a sharp look. "Delirious? What did he say."

"Oh, nothing, really. Nothing. He was just so weak."

"I see."

Ellyn sincerely hoped not. Grif's words had stunned Ellyn, but not nearly as much as the sensation that followed them, like a starburst in her chest.

She'd forced herself out of the room, keeping occupied by packing the necessities for Meg and Ben to stay at Fran's. Twice she'd ventured to the doorway of her room to check on Grif.

"I'd better get going if I'm going to pick up the kids from school," Fran announced.

"Have them call me when they get to your house, will you? So I can explain. Not that they ever mind staying with you." She raised one brow. "I'd almost suspect you did things like let them eat dessert without having their vegetables and staying up late."

"Me? I'm as strict as can be."

"If you say so." Ellyn laughed as she gave the other woman a hug. "Thanks for everything."

Grif was still sleeping when she took the pills and a fresh glass of water into the room. She sat on the battered side chair, oddly hesitant to wake him.

Without reason, she told herself. His words before he fell asleep had been the product of his illness. Good heavens, with a temperature of a hundred and four, he could be babbling nonstop.

Although… Could she have been wrong to dismiss that kiss by the school? Could he have meant to kiss her that way? *Wanted* to kiss her that way?

No, no. She'd been right before. And she'd been right to tell Fran he was delirious. Which meant he truly needed this medicine. And yet she waited, looking at his face, strong and so familiar. And yet different in some way. She studied him, searching for the difference. And then she had it.

With his eyes closed, he looked less like himself and more like his stern father. The father he regarded with too much coldness to truly be indifference. As little as Grif usually let show in his eyes they still gave such a sense of *him.*

She laid her palm across his forehead, smoothing back the ends of the thick hair she'd so rarely seen this long.

She started to pull her hand away, but Grif gripped her wrist and held it there.

His eyes opened slowly. Still glazed, but aimed directly at her face. She turned away, using the shaking out of the pill from the plastic bottle as her excuse.

"I have your medicine here. Can you sit up?"

He gave her a look that should have been withering, but didn't pack half its usual wallop. He levered himself up on one elbow and took the pill, then reached for the glass of water. Once again he drank it all.

She put the glass back on the bedside table, pretending she didn't hear his sigh as he sank back.

"Stay."

No plea, but not enough power to be a command. She made her answer carefully neutral. "Okay."

She sat beside the bed, one hand resting on its edge. After a minute, he pulled his nearest arm from under the covers and laid it down on top of them. His hand was less than an inch from hers as he closed his eyes again.

The first half hour he was restless, seeming to sleep in short snatches that would end with his eyes jerking open. He'd see her still sitting there, and soon his eyes would close again, only to repeat the cycle.

Finally the medicine took effect, and he slept peacefully. Ellyn remained for another hour.

Twenty-four hours later, Grif's temperature had dropped to a hundred and one. He was starting to sleep more naturally. But he continued to sleep more than he was awake, as his body battled both the effects of the fever and the disease itself.

Ellyn had been reluctant to stray too far. She called in to work, explaining the situation and warned Larry she might have to take a few days off. In between checking on Grif, giving him his medicine and helping him twice to the bathroom—then having the door closed firmly in her face—she made soup. Overnight she slept on the couch.

The next afternoon, in a spurt of domesticity, she made two batches of lasagna and some spaghetti sauce for the freezer. Fran arrived as she was cleaning up and putting together a supper tray for Grif.

"I dropped the kids off at the home ranch. They're going to ride with Luke while he checks the heifers that haven't calved yet. Emily's bouncing back. How's your patient today?"

Ellyn filled her in, including his habit of trying to get to the bathroom on his own, stubbornly refusing to admit his legs felt like rubber.

"Smells great in here," Fran said. "That should help give Grif a good appetite."

"I had trouble getting soup in him, much less anything else. This is for the family—for me and the kids."

"Uh-huh."

"It *is*. I make things ahead so we'll have them." What was she doing, explaining? Fran knew all this. "What brought you here today, Fran?"

"I brought some of Grif's things." She placed a familiar-looking duffel bag on the floor.

"You went to Fort Piney? And they let you into his quarters?"

"That soldier thought he might want to go citing regulations all over the place, but we got that straightened out. Grif needs clean clothes, and other things. But I couldn't find that boy's pajamas anywhere."

Ellyn swallowed at the thought of what *that boy* was wearing—and not wearing right now.

"Ellyn? Are you okay?"

"Yes. I'm fine. A little preoccupied."

"Make sure you're getting enough rest. Takes a lot out of you taking care of somebody who's sick. Running back and forth, toting and fetching, giving 'em medicine, and with a fever like this, the sponge baths. You know how much easier the kids rest after one."

Sponge baths?

She caught a definite glint in Fran's eyes, and directed the conversation in another direction.

After Fran left, Ellyn took the duffel bag to her room.

Grif was awake, and looked decidedly rumpled, and possibly cranky. Beard stubble was in full bloom on his jaw and cheeks. His hair had lost its tame constraint and fell down over one eye. He looked both younger and rougher. Not at all like himself and yet in some strange way more like himself than he had since he was a boy.

He ate both the soup and chicken sandwich with hungry concentration, leaving any talking until after he'd finished.

"I don't remember ever seeing you like this before."

He gave her a sour look that had the perverse effect of making her grin, since it was a duplicate of ones Ben gave her when his male pride had been offended.

"I don't mean sick. Although that applies, too. You were never sick all those years in Washington. I mean—" She waved a hand toward him. "Unshaved and your hair this long."

"I ran out of time to get my hair cut before I left Washington. I'll go to Mike's in town." A sly look came into his face. "Tomorrow."

"Next week. You're nowhere near strong enough to be driving into town. Besides, I kind of like this look."

"It's not military."

"No, it's not." *Was that why she liked it?*

"I could at least take a shower and shave."

"No shower. You're too weak. But I tell you what, I will give you a sponge bath. You'll feel a lot better."

He gave her a look that included an element that in anyone else she would have said was fear. But this was Grif. And this was her. And as Fran had pointed out, a sponge bath was a standard way to make the patient more comfortable. And since nothing had changed—or would change—between her and Grif, giving him one made absolute sense.

She kept telling herself that even after she'd gathered the pan of lukewarm water, two washcloths and a towel. Even after she'd started applying them to his broad shoulders, the lightly tanned planes of his chest, and his muscled arms. Finally she blanked out her mind and operated on automatic pilot. Until Grif's large hand clamped over hers as she wielded the towel in the final motions of drying him.

"You'd better let me finish that or we're going to start something very different."

Sudden realization flooded her with heat. Under her hand, the towel had followed the track of an errant trickle that had slipped under the waistband of his boxers, and headed south.

She jerked her hand back, leaving the towel. He picked it up, but she refused to watch what he did with it. Instead she found a plethora of tidying that needed to be done on the bedside table. After a moment he handed over the towel, and she folded it in quarters, decided she didn't like it and refolded it long-ways.

"Ellyn."

He was trying to lever himself up to a more straight-backed position, and that gave her another excuse to avoid meeting his eyes, as she fussed with rearranging the pillows behind him.

Only when she felt the tightening, tempting breath across her breasts did she realize that the combination of their movements had put her chest immediately in front of his face, and that he was breathing hard and fast. It took her entire stock of self-control simply to stay still. Her nipples were taut and tender against the inside of her bra, as if they strained to meet the mouth expelling the air that teased across them, even through the layers of cloth.

At last, she started slowly to pull back. Tension rode across the hard lines of his face, the lines around his mouth dug deep. Instinct, not thought, dropped her gaze to where a bulge showed between his legs, blatant and unmistakable under the smooth expanse of sheet. When she would have continued her withdrawal, away from him, away from the side of the bed, maybe out of the room, the house and the county, he captured her wrist in his hand, and held her there. His grip was surprisingly strong for someone who'd been so sick. Or maybe her resistance wasn't that strong.

"Are you going to ignore this, Ellyn?"

"I thought I would," she admitted.

A faint smile touched his lips without removing the tension, and he didn't release her wrist. "Maybe that would be best. Pretend I never said anything, either, and everything will go back to the way it was before."

Abruptly she sat on the chair beside the bed, goaded by something inside her. Something that she hadn't known she had until the past year—the strength to face facts.

"The question is, before what? Do you want to go back to the way things were before Dale...before Dale died? I don't think that's practical, do you? We'd all have to move back to Washington, and even then of course—"

"Ellyn—"

"Okay, so not that far back. All right then, go back to the way things were before you came to Far Hills? Well, I can do that, but I'd miss you. I know the kids would hate it. Marti and Kendra would definitely not be pleased. So, what does that leave? Putting things back the way they were before...before I kissed you?"

He frowned. "You said that before—that *you* kissed *me*. That's not how I remember it."

"Well, we kissed each other, but I know you didn't... I mean, you're a very generous man, Grif."

"Generous?"

She ignored his apparent disbelief. "And I love—I *like* that in you. It's part of what makes you you, but..."

"But?"

"I don't... Generosity might not be the best thing, Grif. Honesty would be better. So much better. Because pity isn't something I—"

"Pity? *Pity!*" Implacable, his grip on her wrist brought her hand to his bare chest, then drew it down his body, over the sheet covering his abdomen, below his waist, and lower. "Does this feel like pity?"

By instinct or need her hand curled around his hot length.

His other hand caught the back of her neck and brought her, unresisting to him. "Dammit, Ellyn." His mouth took hers, open and demanding from the start, his tongue plunging into her mouth with a hunger that made her moan. It was as if the kiss in front of the school had never ended, but was continuing now, building on itself and their desire.

She was draped across him. Then with a twist of his hips and a shift of his shoulders, she was beside him, lying on the open side of the bed. He followed her, one knee sliding between her legs, one hand sweeping up her rib cage. With the tips of his fingers brushing against the lower curve of her breast, he hesitated long enough to make her gasp. And then his hand covered her, and she gasped again.

And all the while their mouths held each other, each touch fueling the driving hunger.

She stroked her palms across his back, pressed them into his hard flesh. Tangled her fingers into his hair, then used their tips to follow the firm lines of his jaw and cheek.

He'd opened her shirt, pushed down her bra, with a need that knew no finesse. But his capable, strong hand feathered her nipple so softly that she arched and moaned. His knee came higher, and his hips rocked against her, taking up the rhythm of their tongues.

He tore his mouth from hers, and put his lips around her nipple, wetting the pebbled ring, then closing his mouth around her and drawing on her strongly.

She cried out, nearer the edge than she could have believed. As if he sensed that, he sought her other breast with his hand, but the bra intruded. Impatiently he rolled her a few degrees toward him, and yanked loose the hooks at the back. A sound escaped him as he brought his mouth back to her nipple and stroked his hand over the other straining tip.

She dragged her hand down between their bodies, following the same path he'd taken her on earlier. And finding him even hotter and harder and bigger. She pressed her palm against him, and shifted, trying to ease the ache inside her.

He groaned, deep in his throat, the sound vibrating against

her. His hand covered hers, holding it still, as he slid down the bed, his head resting on her rib cage.

"Ellyn…" His panting breath across her nipple made her shudder, incapable of answering. "If we don't… If we don't stop now, you'll be washing sheets again."

The words penetrated slowly, but finally reached the grain of sense not drowned by her senses. She levered away from him enough to see his face. It was etched hard and taut. The lines stretched thin by the power of his self-control. Self-control that was about to snap. As if to confirm that thought, the flesh under her palm pulsed hot and hard.

"Sorry, Ellyn. I'm sorry."

He was sorry. And she was shuddering with need.

He was sick. And she was crawling all over him.

She jolted away from him, off the bed, pulling her outer clothes together without taking time to deal with her bra.

"You're sick. And I— Oh…"

She dragged in two deep breaths, staring at the dent in the pillow by his shoulder that had held her an instant ago. A flexing in that shoulder alerted her, and before he could reach for her, she'd bolted.

She had to come back eventually. She wasn't going to leave him lying here in bed forever, not after treating him as if he were as weak as a kitten.

Which, in the area of self-control, he was.

At first he'd felt so bad he hadn't cared. But after the first couple of pills he could feel his strength returning— too slow for him, but steady. And he wasn't dead for God's sake. He was a little drained from their…exertions, but he sure could have managed to continue until he was drained in a much more satisfactory manner.

No wonder she ran away, Grif. With a lecher in her bed.

It was more than an hour before she came back, with another pill, more water and a dish of cottage cheese and peaches. God, he hadn't had cottage cheese and peaches since he was a kid. He used to love it…and she'd remembered.

He felt such an urge to wrap her in his arms and pull her down to the bed beside him, so her body nestled close against his, that his voice came out raw.

"I'm sorry I shocked you."

Her chin went up, and she put the tray down with a *thunk*.

"Shocked me? What do you think I am, Grif? Some naive little girl? You think I never had sexual feelings? You think I never had temptations? Everyone thinks I'm such a Goody-Two-Shoes, but I have urges, too. I feel things, no matter what Dale might have told you about—" The stricken look she sent him was like a kick to the gut. "Oh, God—"

"Dale and I never discussed that, Ellyn. Never."

She gulped twice. "It's not that I can't talk about those sorts of things—I can. I do! But…"

"But you wouldn't have wanted Dale talking to me."

"No. I wouldn't have."

She sat in her chair, handing him over the pill, then the water. When he'd finished, she gave him the dish.

He'd almost finished all of that when she spoke in a soft monotone, absent the life and passion of earlier.

"Dale was leaving me. The night he left here, and had the accident. He said he'd given the marriage another chance, tried moving back here and it just wasn't going to work."

He heard her words, understood the importance of them, but something about her tone made the hairs along the back of his neck rise. Carefully he set the dish on the bedside table. He'd heard her talk this way before, but when?

"He'd met someone. Someone who gave him what he wanted, what he needed. What I couldn't. He was going to San Diego to join her. Then the accident… If I'd been able to hold onto my husband, he'd be alive now."

And then he knew. He remembered the tone from when she'd repeated the viciously stupid things her mother had told her about herself—how she wasn't sexy, how she needed to make up for her lack of physical attributes, how hopeless she was as the sort of siren Rose considered herself.

"What sort of damned crap is that?"

His anger widened her eyes, and when Ellyn spoke her voice was back to normal, even a trace tart.

"It's the truth. It wasn't a fairy tale marriage cut short by tragedy like everyone else views it. I don't want to shatter their illusions, but I couldn't..." She looked down at her hands. "I didn't want to pretend anymore with you, Grif."

He watched her, seeing the new strengths and the old vulnerabilities. Wishing she could see herself through his eyes. He almost smiled to himself then. She'd have an ego the size of Montana if she could.

"You don't have to pretend with me, Ellyn. Not ever. Not about anything."

Her chin quivered so slightly that someone not feasting on the sight of her would have missed it.

"Thank you, Grif. I knew you'd understand."

Early the next morning Grif returned to the bed from the bathroom, almost stumbling over the duffel bag.

Curious, he pulled it up beside him and checked out Fran's sensible choice of underwear, a pair of sweats and his toiletries. He pulled out a paper bag marked Far Hills Market Pharmacy and looked at in surprise. The surprise deepened when he opened it and discovered two multipacks of condoms.

...you and Ellyn are two consenting adults and I don't see why you couldn't...

Clearly Fran agreed with Marti. And was even less subtle.

He put the bag back, careful to fold over its top so its contents weren't obvious to the casual observer.

It struck him then—perhaps because his thoughts had steered in that direction—that he hadn't heard Ellyn stirring. He ventured down the hallway. He'd managed this trip once before without her knowing—sure she would object if she caught him.

She was curled on her side on the couch, sleeping.

He pulled the multicolored quilt up so it covered her flannel-clad shoulder, then brushed two curling strands of hair back from her cheek. She stirred, making a mumbling sound, then settled again.

If he was smart, he'd turn around and go back before she woke up and gave him a tongue-lashing.

He sat in the overstuffed chair that gave him a good view of her, even in the thin, gray light.

I knew you'd understand.

He'd thought he did until she'd said that. But there'd been a significance to those words that made him feel he'd missed something along the way.

He had to think this through. He'd been trained too well in the necessity of anticipating what dangers might lie over the next hill, or around the next bend or under the next bush to go plunging ahead.

The first step was to gather the available facts. That wasn't always easy with people, but sometimes there were hints.

Like yesterday when she'd looked at him that way, and made that ridiculous comment about being kissed out of *pity* and he'd decided he had to show her how wrong she'd been.

Decided? mocked his conscience.

He hadn't decided. He'd responded. There'd been no thinking. Only afterward, putting together her words and remembering her expression did Marti's words about Ellyn feeling unsure of herself filter back through his haze of lust. Only then did anything close to *thinking* get accomplished.

And then she'd come in and talked about Dale leaving her. In the same tone she'd used the times she'd confided to him how her mother had belittled her.

I was never that kind of woman. A mouse to start, a bit of a tomboy later, then a haphazard housekeeper and, as a wife—

She didn't know... Good Lord, she didn't know...

She truly didn't know what it cost him to stop from making love to her yesterday. She didn't know what kissing her in the school parking lot had done to his body. She didn't know what her offer of herself and her love all those years ago had done to his heart.

"I think I do understand now, Ellyn."

She stirred again at his whispered words, so he kept his pledge unspoken.

And now I'll make you understand—and believe.

Hell, all he had to do was tell the truth.

As long as he didn't let himself forget that he wasn't the kind of man to give her what she deserved—a home, with a great husband and the right kind of father for her kids.

Ellyn took advantage of Grif's sleeping late to plant seeds for early season crops in a protected corner of the garden he'd dug for her. When she came back in, she was surprised to see how much time had passed.

After washing up, she headed for her bedroom. The bed was empty, and there were the remnants of a sandwich she hadn't made on the bedside table.

Before she could do more than observe those facts, the bathroom door opened to a clean, damp, shaved male dressed only in clean boxer shorts.

"What do you think you're doing?"

"I thought I was getting showered and shaved so I felt

human again." He grinned, but she also saw how he leaned his shoulder against the support of the doorjamb.

She went to him, putting her shoulder under his arm and wrapping her arm around his waist as she had that first day.

"And," he added in a tone blended of amusement, peevishness and something else, "I *thought* I was getting back to bed on my own."

Peevishness was generally a sign that a patient was starting to recover. And being impatient with his weakness was a very clear sign that Grif was getting back to himself.

"I never would have known if you hadn't told me."

She could feel the steady pulse of his heartbeat against her. That was another good sign, one any nurse would appreciate.

"I didn't use up your stuff," he said, as if she'd complained about his using the soap and toothpaste she could smell on him. "Fran brought me everything I'd need. Everything I could want."

His tone changed on those last words, and she noticed his pulse picked up. Maybe he'd overdone it with this foray out of bed.

"I'm glad, but this was very foolish of you, Grif."

"I'm too much of a burden on you."

"No, you're not. You're hardly leaning on me at all, and anyway, here we are. You want to lie down or sit?"

"Sit. And that's not what I meant, and you know it."

She shifted around and bent to help lower him in case his legs were weak.

And before she knew what was happening, she was on her back on the bed, one of his legs across hers and his torso looming over her as he held himself up on one elbow-locked arm.

"Grif! What are you doing?"

"Getting some things straight between us. Not generosity, not pity, not you kissing me. Me kissing you." He brushed his lips across hers, innocent and light. Then he lined her bottom lip with the tip of his tongue, darted it against the seam of her lips, and innocence fled. "Me wanting you." He shifted against her, and she felt the proof of that against her thigh.

"But…but men can…"

"Yeah, men can. But I'm not. Look at me, Ellyn."

"But…"

That word held a couple of decades worth of being so sure what his feelings were, and weren't. "But you said… Not to care about you, you said—"

"That wasn't a lie. You shouldn't care about me." He gave those words a fierceness she didn't understand. "I didn't lie then. Unless it was letting you think I didn't want you—because I needed you to think that so you'd be strong enough to walk away. If you're smart, you'll walk away right now."

"That summer… That night. You—" she studied his face above her "—you wanted me?"

"I wanted you so bad my hands shook with it. And God knows my body ached with it. You must have known."

Maybe she had. At some level. But she'd been so utterly inexperienced and unsure that she'd discounted instinct. "But then, why?"

"I knew it couldn't work out. Not the way you deserve."

"Because you'd be leaving? Because you were starting your career?"

"That was some of it. You were so young. And so innocent."

"I was a bumbling idiot."

"You weren't and you aren't. You're…you're *Ellyn.*" A lifetime was in the way he said her name. "I wanted to make love with you then. I want to make love with you now."

Maybe if he'd pushed she'd have resisted. But this…she had no heart left to resist because it was all in her throat.

His lips touched her throat, as if he sensed that. "Make love with me, Ellyn."

She touched his cheek, then his lips. He caught two fingertips with his mouth, flicking his tongue across them, then sucking. She replaced her fingers with her lips, and it began. It continued.

Amid the wonder and strangeness of a first time was the bedrock of decades, of rides and confidences and sharing and silent understanding. They fumbled with the newness, her shyness when he drew her top over her head, his so capable hands struggling with the button on her jeans. But they also burned with it. His jolt when she ran a fingernail lightly across his nipple. Her moan when he slid his hand inside her open jeans and gently cupped her.

There was time for gentleness. Her kiss to the small of his back where a bullet had gouged from some encounter his duty wouldn't let him talk of. His voice and hands when she tried to cover the silvery threads that tied her to childbearing.

She spread her hand across her breasts. "Having babies…"

"You are never more beautiful than when you're pregnant." He kissed her belly, now passably flat, then used his tongue to trace a line from the inside curve of her breast, holding aside her hand, reaching the tip, and circling there with tongue and lips. "How could you be anything less than beautiful now?"

Hot tears pricked at her eyes, but something hotter pushed her hips up against him, demanding, asking.

He ran his hand down her naked body to brush across the curls between her legs, and her moan would have embarrassed her if she had not seen such fierce pleasure at it in his face. He slid a finger inside her and the lines on his face etched deeper as she met its rhythm. Without releasing her, he rolled to reach a hand into the open duffel beside the bed, and came out with a package of condoms.

She didn't realize she'd raised her brows until he leaned over her and pressed a kiss to the underside of each arch. "I didn't have these. Fran must have put them in. She must have thought I might have use for them."

"Fran! Oh, no. Then she thinks—"

"Ellyn." The dark strain in his voice stopped all thoughts but of him. "This is the time, but it better not be because of Fran or anybody else except the two of us."

"Time?"

"For you to say you want to stop."

She stiffened involuntarily. "Do *you* want to stop?"

He kissed her, slowly sliding his tongue against hers, as his finger pressed a fabulous friction inside her. "Like I want to cut my arm off."

She tried to smile when he ended the kiss. "Then it's a good thing Fran packed for you. Do you…may I help you?"

He growled and shifted away just enough to rip open the packet. "Not this time."

Her entire body pulsed at that implicit promise of a *next time*. And then there was nothing but him as he moved over her, between her legs. Beyond the tension and desire, she saw the edge of desperation in his face, felt it in the tension under her hands. She would have calmed it away, soothed him, if she hadn't felt it, too.

Driven to take what had been so long denied, afraid to have it end after so much waiting.

She pressed her fingers into the hard muscles of his rump, and opened herself to him. He slid inside her with a slowness that showed its cost in the shudder of his muscles and the longing ache of hers.

When he nearly withdrew and would have started a second slow, tormenting stroke, she curled her fingers to press her nails into him and raised her knees.

He held over her an instant, his eyes on hers.

"Grif."

She saw the taut self-control snap, felt the plunge of his body into hers. And then there was nothing except the two of them. Separate bodies moving against each other in order to be together, straining and guiding and tantalizing each other to reach that one moment, one place, one sensation, one...

The starburst caught her hard and somehow unprepared, radiating from the center of her in a series of continuing starbursts until each atom glowed with the charge and shimmered with the colors.

Head back, Grif went rigid and still above her, a bead of sweat sliding down his throat, dropping from his collarbone to her heart. Then the starburst shattered the tension in his muscles, as she felt him pulse inside her, and she gathered him into her arms.

He woke to find her gone from his bed—*her* bed, he reminded himself.

Their bed. The phrase stole into his mind and wouldn't be dislodged by logic or discipline.

It had certainly been *their* bed last night, he told himself as he sat up. They must have used every square inch of it—as well as two more condoms. Touching, caressing, loving, stroking, climaxing.

He'd pay for this down the road, and pay hard with the memories that would both sustain and torment him. But for right now, he was—for once—going to think of *right now*.

Right now and *their bed*.

He was almost allowing himself to enjoy the implications when she appeared at the doorway. Fully dressed with another of those big shirts topping gray leggings, her hair curling more tightly as it would if she'd had a shower in the past hour. And not inclined to meet his eyes.

Her gaze slid over the portion of his body exposed above the sheet he'd retrieved after the last time they'd pushed the covers to the floor. The direction of her look shifted lower, and he felt a stirring in his groin that made him want to moan. Again.

Pink tinted her cheeks, not entirely masking the sleepless shadows under her eyes, as she looked away. But he'd already seen what he wanted to see, a flame adding gold to her brown eyes.

"We need to talk, Grif."

Enjoyment fled. "Okay. Come back to bed, and we'll talk."

"I...I think I'll sit here."

She pulled the battered chair up and took her place, as if she was still the nurse and he the patient.

"Go ahead and talk, then."

Chapter Ten

Ellyn didn't approach it head-on. Head-on collisions could do a whole lot of damage.

"I talked to Meg and Ben on the phone." He knew they were at Fran's, so she didn't have to explain that. "I told them they could come home tomorrow afternoon."

"And you don't want them to know that you and I have been sleeping together."

So much for avoiding head-ons.

She parted her lips to dismiss that "sleeping together," which sounded so much more enduring than the single night—no matter how amazing—they'd had. The look on his face stopped her—that was just the argument he wanted to have.

"I don't want them hurt," she said instead, knowing that was unfair, because it was an argument Grif would never dispute. "I don't want them confused. They've been through enough."

"I understand. I know you want the best for Meg and

Ben. You want a man who can be a great father to them. And some men aren't suited to family life.''

Especially men who were still little boys themselves, like Dale.

It took her a moment to recognize that their thoughts had obviously followed different paths.

She'd been thinking of the disappointments the kids had sustained at their father's hands, well before his death. But that didn't fit Grif's words.

''You mean you? Because you've never wanted to be a father and—'' she overcame the urge to skitter away from the next word like a nervy horse away from paper fluttering in its path ''—husband.''

Grif's silence was like a wall. It kept her out completely and efficiently, yet she had the sense of a great deal of activity taking place behind it.

''Grif...''

''It's the way things are, Ellyn. The way they've always been.''

And that's how it'll always be.

That's what he'd said to her that night when she was eighteen. He'd been starting his Army career then, and telling her that there could never be any future between them. Because the Army came first with him, leaving no room for her.

And now he was telling her again that there was no future for them. Because the Army still came first, certainly leaving no room for a demanding family.

He moved fast. He swung both legs over the side of the bed, leaving a corner of the sheet to trail haphazardly over his lap. He took both her hands and tugged, hard enough to pull her out of the chair, then used one foot to tip it over and out of the way.

''But we still have some unfinished business from last night.''

"Unfinished." She couldn't think of a thing they'd left unfinished last night.

His hands were already at her waist. In one, smooth, long, enticing stroke of his hands over her hips, then down her legs, he stripped her leggings and panties off.

In another second his mouth touched the juncture of her thighs, and she grabbed for his shoulders to hold herself up when her knees buckled.

She held on to him, because he was all that sustained her. And because she wanted him.

Time and sense first parted, then dissolved, before the power of timeless sensation.

When she cried out, piercing and sharp, then melted so completely that her hold on him had no strength, his arms tightened powerfully around her as he raised a face triumphant with her pleasure.

He carried her boneless body down to the bed beside him, removing the last of her clothes, which had after all provided no barrier to her desire as she'd intended. She drew him, so hot and hard, to her and into her, until they found triumph together.

She woke up slowly, in the luxury of feeling him behind her, around her, and in the reluctance to do what she knew she had to do.

She couldn't believe they'd spent the entire day yesterday in bed. Well, she could believe Grif had, considering how sick he'd been. Not that he'd shown any signs of it. Except for an insatiable appetite…and all he ate seemed to feed another insatiable appetite.

She had never experienced a time like this. Had never felt that her look could ignite a fire in a man. Yet, each time she had disbelieved it in these past thirty-six hours, Grif had disproved her disbelief.

But none of that changed the result.

If this went on much longer, she'd start dreaming of just

the sort of future he'd made clear couldn't exist for them. His leave would end, he'd return to his life in the Army, and she'd be left to pick up the pieces. At least if she ended this now, the pieces might not be quite so small. And maybe they could preserve the future he *could* provide.

She shifted quietly, turning in his arms, making sure no sudden moves would wake him. She wanted just once more to see him asleep. To see the long straight lashes casting lush shadow along the top of his cheekbone. To watch the rhythmic rise and fall of his chest. To enjoy the faint easing of his discipline.

Anticipating all that, she didn't wait until she had turned all the way to her other side, but looked over her shoulder and encountered a pair of watchful gray eyes.

"Oh. You're awake."

"I'm awake."

How could a voice so even sound grim?

It doesn't matter how. It doesn't matter if he sounds grim. I have to do this. Now.

Now while she had the strength.

No longer bothering with stealth, she turned onto her side to face him, drawing a fistful of covers to her neck and draping the excess into the valley carved out between their bodies.

"I have something to say, Grif."

"Okay."

She had his complete attention. She had all the words and reasons and logic. She just didn't have a voice.

She cleared her throat once, then again. If he'd said something it might have been easier, but he held his silence.

"I, uh, I've been thinking, Grif. I don't—"

She stopped herself, took a slow, deep breath. His eyes flickered as they followed the movement of her breasts under the covers she still held tight. A warmth bloomed in her, in the vicinity of his gaze, and lower, both at once.

And that finally unstuck her tongue. She had to get this said. Now. Fast. Before...

"Grif, we've made a mistake. It's my fault, not yours. We have a connection, a tie that goes so far back, nearly our whole lives. And at one point, I wanted that connection to be something other than it was." *I wanted you to love me.* "But it isn't. I mean, it has been because of this—" without releasing the fabric, she spread her fingers to indicate the two of them in bed "—but it shouldn't be. Not really. Because what we really are, what we've always been, what we always should be, is friends."

She saw something brewing in his eyes, like clouds boiling up across the horizon. But clouds could be almost anything—a punctuation on fair weather, the bringers of gentle, sustaining rain or the creators of punishing, cruel hail. She hurried on.

"I think we both know how this happened. I've been lonely. For a long time. And you've been the one I turned to for so long—as a friend, I mean. And you're such a good friend, that you've always come through for me. Even now, even when I never should have...I'm sorry, Grif. That's all I can say. I'm truly, truly sorry. And I hope our friendship can survive this in some form."

His silence was ominous. His tone was worse. "So you're saying you led me on?"

"Led you on? I don't—"

"You said you're *sorry,* didn't you? You said you made a *mistake,* didn't you? You said it was your *fault, didn't you?*"

"Yes, but—"

"Ellyn, you keep telling me my motives. Generosity. Pity." He practically spit out that one. "Friendship. No. This is exactly what it feels like. It's desire. Wanting. Lust."

"Yes, but—"

"The kids will be here this afternoon, but there's *now.*

Do you want me, Ellyn? Right now. Inside you. Making love with you.''

"Grif.''

"Answer me. Do you want me? Right now.''

"Yes.''

His lips on hers stopped any hope of a *but*. Stopped anything but *now*.

Grif dropped his duffel bag on the floor of his quarters and grimaced.

He'd gotten spoiled, and he better get over it fast. This was his life. This was where he lived. This was who he was.

He also better get used to not kissing Ellyn very often or learn to be sneakier about it.

He had a strong suspicion Kendra had spotted him kissing Ellyn this morning on the landing to the basement stairs as everybody got ready to head in their different directions. At least she'd seen enough to draw conclusions.

Conclusions that were right for now, but not for the long run. He had to remember that, and take care.

Twice he'd kept Ellyn from calling a halt to this interlude. Twice he'd delayed the inevitable. That wasn't very smart.

He was showing Ellyn how he felt because she needed that, to counteract the corrosive influence of her mother and the foolish pain Dale had left behind. When he succeeded at that, it wouldn't matter how he felt. He'd have to step back from her, leave her free to find what she deserved.

She'd given him the words he'd been searching for. Why hadn't he taken them?

Taken them? Hell, he'd fought like a demon to escape them.

Because of how she'd said it. She'd still needed him. Eventually she wouldn't. Eventually…

But he'd taken every drop he was spared until "eventually" came.

Ellyn was working Saturday to make up one of the days she'd lost caring for him, so Grif volunteered to take the kids riding.

He was inordinately pleased to find he remembered the subtle trails through the wide land. They took a picnic and he let them choose the trails to follow.

He was even more pleased that both Meg and Ben seemed comfortable and relaxed in his company. Ellyn had confided some of her concerns about them missing a man's companionship, and it pleased him to meet that need, at least for a while.

In the afternoon, they followed the trail to Leaping Star's overlook. He let them tell him the story he already knew so well.

"He left his kids. Just like..." Ben didn't finish the sentence, staring down at the ground.

"Dad died," Meg said harshly, seeming to warn him. "It's not the same."

But then, belying her tough stance, she eased closer to her younger brother and put her arm around his shoulders. The two stood like that for a moment, both looking down. Two small figures, with the mountain dropping away at their feet and the land spread out to an endless horizon.

"My father, too."

Grif's own voice surprised him, sounding raw with a pain he'd sworn he'd discarded long ago.

Ben and Meg turned to him in unison. "Yours?" Ben voiced the question in both sets of eyes.

"Yeah."

"But...did your dad...die?"

A better question was if the man had ever been anything but dead to him. But Grif was telling this now to help these two kids feel less alone, not to vent his own grievances.

''Not until a few years ago. But when I was about your age, my Mom got real sick.'' He weighed his next choice—cushion the reality or tell them the unvarnished truth? ''She died when I was eleven.''

Meg's eyes widened, and Grif felt as if he could hear her thought: *A year older than me.* What had Ellyn said about the two of them and there being a connection, a tie? Now a new connection, borne of his honesty and her sympathy.

''And then your father left you, too?'' Ben's stricken voice pulled Grif back to the matter at hand.

''Not the way you're thinking, I lived with him, but he was away a lot.''

''Who took care of you then?''

''He hired different people, at first. After a couple of years, I'd stay by myself for short stretches. We lived on Army bases, so there were neighbors around.''

''Didn't you get lonely?'' Meg asked

''Yeah, I did get lonely.''

''But then he'd come back,'' insisted Ben. ''He always came back.''

''He came back. But it wasn't much different when he was there. He wasn't like other dads. He didn't talk to me much. He'd give me some money, and I'd buy food and stuff like that.''

''You cooked your own food?'' Ben was amazed or appalled, or both.

Grif nodded, fighting down the first urge to smile he'd felt during this conversation. ''Not very successfully to start with.''

''Do men always leave?'' Meg demanded.

Something in the stance of the two youngsters examining his face as they waited for his answer made Grif believe that Ellyn was wrong in thinking she'd been the only one to know Dale was leaving his family the night he died. He knew from firsthand experience how easily kids could overhear conversations—especially arguments—the adults meant them not to hear.

He looked out across the land where he'd done some of his most important growing up, a lot of it next to the boy Dale Sinclair had been. And he considered the man he'd come to know during the years of being the Sinclairs' family friend.

Then he met Meg's eyes.

"Not all men, Meg. But some do—too many."

"Will you?" The small voice asking the huge question came from Ben.

"I won't always be here like this in Far Hills. You know that. Like I told you when I first came, I'm here on leave. When that's over I have to go back to my job. But—" he held the word until Meg's eyes, which had slid away with his first sentence, came back to his face "—I will always be part of your lives. I won't ever let a year go by without seeing you like I did before this visit. And if you ever have a problem, any kind of problem, I promise you I'll do my best to help you solve it."

He saw that they were torn between their pride at being spoken to as an equal and the pain of the unvarnished truth. More slowly he recognized their belief in his pledge. The knowledge of their trust swelled in his heart until he thought it might burst—and he wouldn't have minded at all.

Brigadier General Pulaski didn't care for small talk, so Grif simply outlined his proposal. After he finished. Grif told himself silence was better than cursing.

"I suppose I should have expected something this insane after you took that lunatic leave, but I didn't. I'm disappointed in you, Colonel Griffin."

"I'm sorry you're disappointed, sir."

"But not sorry enough to change your mind?"

"No, sir, not that sorry."

"Your career won't recover, Grif."

"I know."

And didn't care. This interlude with Ellyn, loving her the way he'd tried to not even allow himself to dream about, and sharing this time with Meg and Ben, was worth more than a career. Oh, he'd stick in the Army. It gave him something to belong to even if he didn't have somewhere or someone. The fact that he'd never resume the climb up the promotion ladder didn't matter.

"You'd be at Piney for one thing—to close it. There's no way to make more enemies than to be in command of a base-closing. And you know it."

"Yes, sir."

This interlude would end. But Ellyn and the kids would still have needs. Needs he knew Ellyn wouldn't let him fulfill. One way to safeguard them was to make sure Ellyn didn't lose her job. That meant making sure the *Banner* didn't lose so much revenue when the Army base closed that Larry Orrin couldn't afford to keep her on. If Grif was in command of closing the base, he could implement ideas he had to ease the transition and help the community's economy as a whole and Ellyn in particular.

"You can't let anyone know Fort Piney's on the list for closing until it's cleared through the politicians."

For the first time, Grif hesitated. But before the general could exploit the pause, Grif said, "I understand, sir."

The general heaved a sigh. "All right, dammit. You're a fool, but I've known you too long not to know you're a stubborn fool. I'll put it through." There was a pause, then the general's tone shifted. "Are you going to tell me what this is about?"

Grif hesitated before telling some of it.

"I spent a lot of time around here as a kid. It's where my mother grew up. I have a part share in a family ranch not far from Fort Piney. I feel a…responsibility to these people."

"I can't do anything about Piney being on the list—wouldn't even if I could—"

"I know that, sir."

"Quit interrupting, Griffin. I might be able to do a thing or two to help the transition go better for the civilians. Business development and such."

This was no idle offer. Pulaski's high voice had caused some under his first command in Vietnam to nickname him Squeaky. They'd lived to regret it. They'd lived because Pulaski had gotten them out of a fix. They'd regretted it because he'd held a grudge, even against men returned to civilian life more than thirty years ago, including one now a U.S. senator and another running a Fortune 500 company. And he exacted compensation for that dismissive teasing by calling on these powerful debtors now and then for favors.

"That would be extremely helpful, sir."

"You put some ideas together—but not for release until this is official—and I'll see if there are people you can talk to."

"Thank you, sir."

To Grif's mind the conversation had ended, but Pulaski didn't cut the connection. After a noticeable pause, he said, "So that's where your mother grew up? She was a good woman. Nancy Griffin was real good to my wife and son."

Grif knew that Pulaski's first wife and their son had been seriously injured in a house fire on base. He'd been about six at the time, and remembered the fire trucks and the ambulances. Both Mrs. Pulaski and Will died of their injuries after agonizing weeks.

"You've got a lot of your mother in you."

An answer was clearly expected; Grif gave his carefully. "I've always been told I resemble my father."

"You look like him. But hasn't anybody ever told you looks aren't everything?"

Chapter Eleven

"Ah, baseball in Wyoming," said the mother of one of Ben's teammates from three rows behind them on the bleachers at Veterans Park. Her voice was muffled by a scarf wrapped around her face against the raw wind.

"At least we didn't have to shovel the field," remarked another. "And thank heavens it's the last inning."

From beside Ellyn, sharing two woolen blankets under them and a comforter over them, Grif chuckled.

"Grif, you don't have to stay," Ellyn said. "Ben would understand if you're not here after the game."

He faced her. "Would he?"

No, but as it was, *she* didn't understand, and at least Grif leaving would remove the constant reminder of that, like a burr under her saddle. Which made her a horribly selfish mother.

"You know he's thrilled you're here. I just don't want you to get sick again."

Heat glittered his gray eyes to silver. "That wasn't all bad."

There—that was exactly what she didn't understand.

For these past ten days, he would make comments like that and then just as abruptly he'd withdraw behind his wall so completely that she wondered if he might die from lack of oxygen. He worked on the path only when she was gone or the kids were around, too.

Oh, she knew he would be leaving. That had been clear from the start. After all, the *Iron Warrior's* true love was the Army. And it would be beckoning anytime now.

But dammit, she wasn't going to passively wait for him to announce his departure date.

"So, Grif, when is your leave up?" Not subtle, but it did the job.

For a moment she thought he didn't hear her, or was going to pretend he didn't. Then he slowly turned his head. When he still didn't answer, she pushed a little harder. "When do you leave?"

"I don't."

She gaped at him. "You...you don't?"

"I'm staying when my leave's up."

"But, how?"

"I'm taking over command at Fort Piney."

"Piney?"

"Not so loud. They made it official this week, but I'd rather let the Army make the announcement," he said with a touch of wry humor.

"I don't understand. It's such a small post." His brow started to rise, and she amended that. "It's not small to us. Piney's the center for a lot of activity around here. After ranching, it's a big part of our economy. So a new commander's a big deal to us, but it *is* a small post. I wouldn't think there'll be potential for a man with your ambitions at a place like Piney."

Grif seemed suddenly intent on the field, even though

the only action was a player clad in multilayers moving toward the plate.

"Depends on what your ambitions are."

The man made no sense. He didn't believe in a future for them, but he was going to tie himself to a go-nowhere job? Before she could digest that, he was adding words that she had no trouble understanding.

"Small post or not, it's going to keep me busy. Very busy. Once I report, it won't be the sort of regular hours I had most of the time you knew me in Washington. There'll be a lot of demands on my time."

"Okay, Grif. You've always made it clear that the Army comes first with you. That you want—"

"*Want?* What I want has nothing to do with it."

Stunned at the vehemence of words spoken so low she barely heard them, it took her an extra beat to recognize them for what they were—a crack in his wall. "What *does* it have to do with, then?"

"Reality. The way things are. I've seen…"

She prompted, "You've seen what, Grif?"

He shook his head. "None of this makes any diff—"

"You've seen what, Grif? I think I deserve at least that much, don't you?"

She saw that landed a blow. One he didn't try to shake off.

"I've seen what happens when a man like me tries to mix with a woman like you."

She froze, Dale's voice overlapping Grif's.

A woman like you just doesn't understand that a man needs more in his life than this. He needs excitement, variety!

"A woman like me," she echoed.

"Yeah, a woman like you." Something had stripped Grif's voice of its usual patience. "A woman who should have the kind of life we all dream about—not worrying about having enough for your kids, not trying to make a rattletrap last another five years, not making do in a house that isn't your home—''

''You don't consider Ridge House a home?''

''You could make a home out of a shoebox. But you deserve better. You deserve a place that's yours for good. A place where you and the kids can put down roots and never worry about leaving.'' His voice dropped again. ''You deserve the best.''

Ellyn scrambled to try to sort this all out. Remembering. Putting together phrases, impressions. Coming back to the same conclusion. He considered *a woman like her* a compliment, not a jibe.

I've seen what happens when a man like me tries to mix with a woman like you. That's what he'd said, so if he considered *a woman like her* to be a compliment, what could the rest of it mean?

''Grif.'' She took hold of his arm with both her gloved hands, only then realizing that he'd stood, as had everyone else in the bleachers. The game was over. Blankets were being folded, stiff limbs shaken out. She stayed where she was, holding his arm until he looked at her. ''What did you mean, a man like you?''

Faint surprise crossed his eyes for a flash before their gray turned an impenetrable leaden shade. His voice crisp and distant, he answered as if her question didn't interest him. ''Ellyn, you know what kind of man I am.''

She thought she did, but did *he?*

''I thought it went well,'' Kendra volunteered as they left the school after a program on newspapers for Meg's class.

Ellyn looked at her from the corner of her eye. ''I think you were nervous. I can't believe it—a former network TV reporter, and you were nervous about talking to a class of fourth-graders!''

''Hey, I didn't want to embarrass Meg.''

"No, that's a mother's job," Ellyn said, getting into the passenger seat of Kendra's car for the return to the *Banner*.

"You must not have done so bad, I saw her give you a hug—in public no less."

"I know. It's so nice to have a break from the world-weary twenty-seven-year-old who'd been living in my house. If this recent bout was a preview of her as a teen-ager, I think a convent might be the only answer."

"For her or you?"

"Me!" They both laughed, then Ellyn turned serious. "At the start I thought Ben missed Dale more. But his sadness seems to be easing—Grif's helped. But Meg…Meg still has a lot of anger about losing her father. I suppose I should be glad she's letting some of it out instead of holding it all in. I know how bad that can be for a kid."

"Is that what you did?"

Ellyn looked at her friend, surprised. So much of this past year-plus of living close had been sharing the daily travails of kids, work and house. That had started to change when Daniel arrived, and Kendra began opening herself up more, including to her friends. But sometimes this new aspect to their friendship still caught Ellyn unprepared.

"Yes, it is. That's why I hope letting it out helps Meg."

"And now? How about holding in what's going on with you and Grif?"

"Grif? What makes you think something's going on?"

"Maybe," she suggested, "because your voice just visited both ends of an octave. Maybe because you and Grif spend so much energy trying to convince yourselves and the world that nothing's changed between the two of you that I'm amazed you don't both fall over in a heap like people at the end of a marathon. Maybe because I saw you two kissing, Ellyn."

"That must have been some time ago. Grif hasn't kissed me in weeks," she said with remarkable calm.

"So that's why he's so cranky."

To her own amazement, Ellyn laughed a little.

"What's wrong with him?" Kendra asked.

"Why does it have to be with him?"

"Because I know my cousin. And because he clearly has been nuts about you, ever since we were kids. Maybe the amazing thing is that he let down his guard to act on it at all, after he'd spent so long pretending it didn't exist. Unless... Of course!" Kendra's face, always beautiful, became almost beatific with the beaming smile spread across it.

"Of course what?"

"He had his defense against what he feels for you all nicely fortified during those years in Washington. But then you two were apart for more than a year, and the old friendship facade got a little porous. It couldn't hold up against the assault of seeing you so suddenly and so often. Now he's back there trying to shore the thing up, trembling in his boots," Kendra concluded happily. "So, what do you think?"

"You mean other than the fact that you make me sound like a cross between a virus and an invading army? I think this was the result of a complicated set of circumstances, not because Grif really wanted—"

"You know, one thing I've learned from getting together with Daniel is that sometimes the simplest explanation is the right one." Kendra planted her zinger as they walked into the building where Ellyn would have no chance to respond. "Sometimes we do things not for all the complex reasons we tell ourselves we did it, but because in the end, it's what we wanted."

Ellyn got two surprises at work the next day. She could have done without both.

The first was literally running into Grif as he and Kendra headed toward the main door to go out to lunch.

She hadn't known that's where they were headed. She

hadn't even known he was in the building when she walked out of her office door and collided with the hard, male body. It was frightening how quickly her body recognized it as *Grif's* hard, male body. Their tangle was a near duplicate of when they'd been doing dishes at her house. Except now, they both knew what it felt like when such an alignment of hips and chest, such an interlocking of arms and legs, was anything but an accident. And the knowing was like a crackle of electrical charge through her nerve-endings.

The second was when Larry came bustling up, with her and Grif no longer touching and looking anywhere but at each other, while Kendra barely stifled laughter.

"Hey, Grif! Great news about you being named CO at Fort Piney! What a story! I'll go through channels, but I'm going to want a nice long interview." Larry looked around, apparently reading some of the sudden tension. "It's not a secret, is it?"

Grif gave her a hard look, and Ellyn returned it. *Don't look at me. I didn't tell a soul.* Even now she wasn't saying anything, leaving Grif room to deny it if he chose.

"Not anymore," he said sourly.

"Grif's been away so long," Kendra interposed, "he's forgotten how anyone's business is everyone's business in Far Hills."

"Especially when you work for the newspaper," Larry added.

"Or when the Army has an inveterate gossip like Helen Solsong working in its commissary." Kendra frowned significantly at Grif.

"I've got to say," Larry was going on, "I won't be sorry to see Lieutenant Colonel Reardon going, especially being replaced by somebody like you. Somebody who did a lot of his growing up around here—a native!"

"Having family and ties around here won't change any

orders I get,'' Grif said bluntly. ''Orders are orders in the Army.''

Ellyn turned toward him. He shifted so Larry Orrin blocked her line of sight, as Larry concluded, ''I don't mind the orders—I just want to know about 'em.''

Ellyn answered the knock at the back door at ten o'clock Friday night already knowing it was Grif.

She'd had no reason to expect him to come. She'd only had hope.

The kids were at separate overnights, and he reported to duty Monday as CO at Fort Piney. If they were going to sort out what had been happening—and not happening these past weeks—this seemed a good time to try.

When she opened the door, the first thing he said was, ''I shouldn't have come.''

The urge to soothe and the urge to rant hit her simultaneously. She compromised. She didn't slam the door on him. ''Then why did you?''

''Because I owe you an apology.''

''Fine. Apologize.''

For the first time, he seemed to take in her mood. And then he gave a half smile. ''Don't rush me, I'm new at this.''

She fought down her responding smile. ''Maybe we should sit down.''

She led him into the living room, where he sat beside her on the couch.

''I shouldn't have doubted that you'd keep your word about not telling anyone about my assignment to Fort Piney, Ellyn. I know you better than that.''

She looked up as he finished. His direct gray eyes were on her. He *did* know her. All of her. In ways no one else did or could. The strengths and the weaknesses. The successes and failures. And he accepted all that in her. A strangely fierce satisfaction swept across her like a fine mist of heat. It took another instant to realize it was the recognition that *she* accepted all that in herself.

She supposed the new Ellyn was largely a product of that acceptance. But it had taken the mirror of Grif's eyes to see it.

"Yes," she said with deliberation. "You know me better than anyone else."

"So you have a right to wonder why I was such an ass." He grimaced. "Oh, hell. I think I just wanted to take it out on you after running into you, holding you like that and feeling…"

"I suppose we're both still feeling our way with this…this." She spread her hands to encompass both of them. "These are new feelings for us—"

"The hell they are."

Her head snapped up, and she stared at him. The bones of his face showed hard under sudden tension.

"Are you saying—?"

"That I wanted you all the time you were married to my best friend? Yeah, that's what I'm saying." Derision embittered his chuckle. "How's that for honorable?

"That's why I left, Ellyn. That's why I stayed away for a year. When Dale told me he thought your marriage was over, that he was going to leave you, I couldn't believe it. He had everything—*everything*—and he was going to throw it away? It caught me off guard. I didn't have a chance to stop the thoughts." He met her eyes, and she put a hand to her throat, as if that would ease a sensation like her lungs had been singed from breathing superheated air. "I let myself think about you being free. After that I couldn't stick around. I couldn't stand to watch you and Dale together. Worse, I couldn't be sure I wouldn't try to make sure you ended up apart."

More questions pounded in her head, but one was answered. And the certainty of that moved through her like a warm, sweet balm.

Only with that release did she realize part of her had held back from Grif. Only with the end of fear did she realize how afraid she'd been. Afraid of seeing that she'd been disloyal in her heart to Dale long before he was unfaithful in action.

But now she *knew*.

She placed her palms to either side of Grif's face so he met her eyes. "Grif, I swear to you that you never showed that once in the time Dale and I were married. Nothing you ever did or said or felt hurt my marriage. And I can swear to myself the same thing."

His eyes bored into hers, searching. "Ellyn, are you…?"

"Yes, I am sure."

He dropped his head forward, resting his forehead against hers.

"I've tried so damned hard not to want you."

She looked at him in wonder, remembering Kendra's theory about his facade of friendship. Except it hadn't been wholly a facade, because the friendship was true and enduring. It had been like a handsome brick gatehouse that she would have enjoyed living in for the rest of her life, until the gates creaked open and revealed the magnificent estate beyond as her potential home.

"You know, Grif, there's one thing about you that bothers me—sometimes you try too damn hard."

He glanced up, and with a flash as fast as gunpowder, the uncertainty in his eyes ignited to heat.

She stood, and extended a hand to him. He took it, and she led him down the hall.

"My mother—"

"Your mother doesn't know a damned thing about you."

Still holding his hand, she stopped and faced him in the doorway to her bedroom, smiling. Not only at his Grif-the-Protector defense of her, but because his interruption had allowed the full, wide impact of what she'd been about to say to spread its wings in her mind. In fact, a smile hardly seemed enough. She wanted to laugh, maybe sing.

"Ellyn?"

"You're right. I was going to say that my mother doesn't say what she thinks, but I do. My mother has been scared all her life. She doesn't think she can stand on her own, so she needs a man to hold her up. And she doesn't think she'll keep a man unless she uses her *womanly wiles*."

At that phrase, she looked at him through her lashes, hooked her fingers over his belt buckle and tugged him toward the bed. His grin flickered, and the silver fire in his eyes blazed.

"So she lies and manipulates. She tried to teach me to do the same, but even as a child I knew somewhere inside that being that way hadn't made my mother happy. So I didn't use my womanly wiles. And because of that, she always thought I was a fool and a failure. Especially when Dale wanted to leave me."

"You—" he stroked her cheek, then dropped his hand to her shoulder, let it brush the side of her breast, before settling at her waist "—are no fool and no failure. Dale was an idiot and—"

Her fingers on his lips hushed him. "I know." She smiled as she saw that trailing those fingers down his throat, over his shirt placket, his belt buckle and tooth by tooth on his zipper produced an entirely satisfactory result. She pushed at his shoulders so he sat on the bed. She straddled his legs, leaning her knees against the side of the bed, holding his face between her palms. "I didn't know that, but you helped me see it. And you helped me see that I'm not scared. I don't lie, and I don't manipulate."

She dipped her hips to rest against his straining lap, brushing her breasts across his chest in the process. He groaned, and gripped her bottom, and rose up to meet her as she repeated the motion.

"But I do have some womanly wiles, don't I?"

"If you had any more—" He put his mouth over the tip of her breast, and she felt every nuance of his tongue through the cloth. They rocked against each other, finding their rhythm. "I'd be dead. Happy, but dead."

He dropped back to the bed, and she went with him.

"Are you ready for more happy now?"

He raised his hips against her, and she had her answer. "Just pretend I'm too sick to do much—not as sick as I was but just so you do most of the work."

But it was nothing like work, and she certainly didn't do most of it. Not with his hands and mouth on her. Not with him inside her.

"What is it, Grif?"

She'd been awake for a while, watching him through nearly closed eyes as he moved silently around the room, getting dressed, looking at photographs on her dresser, pulling some sort of armor around himself.

He looked at her, then away, picking up his shoes and socks and sitting on the bed by her knees before he answered.

"I have something to tell you. I shouldn't. But I'm going to. And then I'm going to tell you that you have to do what I'm not doing—you can tell no one. I know it's not fair, but..."

She sat up, using the covers as her shield against a sudden chill. Not so much from his words but his crisp, distant manner.

"Okay. I won't tell anyone whatever it is you're going to tell me."

He finished tying one shoe and put his ankle across the other knee to draw on his second sock.

"Fort Piney is closing."

"What? Why? But you've just gotten there! Can't they give you a chance to make it worth keeping? Or—"

"There's no question of making it worth keeping. It's

on a list that will be announced any day now. I'm there to close it. I knew that was the job when I took it.''

"But if you knew, why would you take a job like…'' Her heart thundered with the hope before her head found words for it. "You did it to stay here with us."

"No." His harsh tone drove the hard word home. "I took the job because there's a chance that with me in command, the transition won't wipe out the economy of Far Hills and everyone here."

He finished putting on and tying his second shoe. His foot met the floor with a thump that brought her back to life.

"But that still means you care, about Far Hills, about—''

"Don't."

"Don't what?"

"Don't hope." He took her hand, the one not holding the covers to her, and laid it across his other palm, then stroked it, as his voice changed completely, yet lost none of the iron beneath it. "I have always, will always care about you, Ellyn. Every day of my life. It's you…''

"It's me? What does that mean, *it's me?*"

"It's not right for you to care about me."

She tried to hold back the pain that threatened to flood her, to operate by the lesson he'd taught her. To not interpret every word as criticism. "Why?"

"Because of who I am."

"Who you are is the reason I *do* care, the reason I care so much! You're Grif. You're—''

"John Griffin *Junior*. United States Army officer. Devoted to his career. Just like the old man. A chip off the old block."

Still holding the covers to her, she came up on her knees, to bring her face closer to his.

"You're not your father, Grif." She'd known him so long and thought she'd known him so well, yet she'd never seen any of this. "I never met your father, but from everything I've heard, from the little you've told me about him, you're nothing like him. Not in the way you are with people. Not in personality. Nothing.''

''Don't fool yourself, Ellyn, I'm just like him.'' His smile was grimmer than a frown. ''What were the chances I could be anything else? When it comes to nature and nurture, I've pretty much covered the bases. I look just like him. I was brought up just like him. And I've lived just like him.''

''But...but you *chose* the Army.''

''What else was I suited for? Except for the summers here, I'd spent my whole life on bases. The Army was what I knew. It didn't ask things of me I don't have to give.''

Oh, God. All this time she'd blamed the Army for making him feel that he wasn't meant to have a family or a home. But he'd gone into the Army *because* he felt that way.

She sat back on her heels, dismayed, but with a strange sort of excitement running through her, too. If she could make him see—

''Ellyn...'' He smoothed her wild hair back from her cheek with a slow, gentle stroke of his palm. ''You are... You are the best part of my life, the best part of me. I won't let you and the kids suffer for that.''

''Suffer? How could we possibly suffer from having you in—?''

''I saw my mother miserable for years because of my father, and God knows the man wasn't much of a father to me. You and Meg and Ben deserve a hell of a lot more than that. A hell of a lot more than a man who couldn't even make himself go into the hospital room where his wife was dying. But night after night sent his young son in there alone to fill visiting hours.

''That's when I learned the real truth of what she'd said.''

He fell into a silence, his eyes unfocused. "What she said?" Ellyn prompted gently.

"It was before she got sick. Maybe a year or two. I heard them arguing. I got out of bed and went down the hall. I don't know which base we were at, I only remember the dry smell of that dark, narrow hall, and the lights on in the living room. My mother crying, and my father looking totally blank, like his mind was a thousand miles away. Then Mom got real calm, each word so clear. *Some men never should get married, never should have children. They don't have the heart for it. You're one of those men, John Griffin. Like father, like son.*"

Through the man before her, Ellyn felt the pain of that boy. How could a mother say that, even not knowing her son was listening? How could she even think that?

"Grif..."

She reached to him, but he was already standing and heading toward the door.

"I have to go."

He didn't look back.

Her timing sucked.

A fine time to realize she was in love with John Griffin Junior, when he'd just declared himself unworthy of being in her life or her kids' lives, and walked out, determined to *protect* them.

She'd loved him most of her life. She'd fallen in love with him...when? When they'd kissed by the school? When she'd seen him walk in the classroom, coming to her son's rescue? When she'd kissed him on the cheek in the kitchen for being so wise and patient with Meg?

Or a little at each of those moments and a thousand others in these weeks since he'd come home.

Home...

She'd been sure for so long that he considered the Army his home, but now... She wasn't sure of anything.

He was here, but he held himself apart from her.

He was staying, but only to close down their fort.

He confided in her, but he thought that knowing he was going to close Fort Piney would make her turn away from him.

The last thought finally lifted a corner of her gloom. Grif wouldn't bother with trying to make her turn away from him if he wasn't running out of strength to turn away from her.

He'd stayed away more than a year, why had these past ten days been so damned hard? And why did coming back to Ridge House now make his heart hammer like a carpenter on fast-forward?

The closings list had come out this morning, but that should have made Ridge House his one refuge, since Ellyn was the only person the announcement hadn't caught unaware. He'd spent the morning making and answering tough phone calls.

That had delayed him and Luke on their way to Sheridan, so they'd returned to the ranch nearly two hours later than they'd planned. Which was the reason Ellyn's beat-up Suburban was in the driveway instead of still parked by the *Banner* as he'd wanted it to be when he and Luke wrestled this new dryer into the house.

They'd bumped the thing up the back steps on the dolly Luke brought, and were crossing the threshold when Ellyn came running from the far side of the house.

"What on earth—Luke? What are you—?"

Her words stopped abruptly. Grif didn't know if it was because she'd spotted the dryer that answered her questions or because her eyes had met his and she'd felt a similar jolt of joy, lust, regret and longing.

"Back up, Ellyn," Luke ordered.

She obeyed automatically, and he rolled the new dryer into position to block the doorway between the kitchen and the back hall, the way they'd planned when they realized Ellyn was home. Grif helped tip the dryer so Luke could free the dolly, then Luke passed it over the top of their temporary roadblock.

Grif got the dolly into place under the old dryer Luke had already disconnected and started easing it out of place.

"Wait a minute! What are you doing, Grif?" From her voice, Ellyn was trying to peer around the new dryer to where he was working. "You can't do this. Luke, listen to me—"

"He's the boss," Luke interrupted. "Part owner of Far Hills Ranch, so that makes him part-payer of my wages."

Grif didn't hear the rest, because he was wheeling the useless old dryer out. He brought the dolly back and handed it over the new dryer to Luke.

As Luke passed Grif's spot pressed against the back door to give man and machine room to pass, he said in a low tone, "Keep her occupied."

This, too, was part of the plan they'd put together out in the truck. Luke had read the manufacturer's instructions, then they'd removed the packing material so installing would be as quick as possible, but he'd still need some time. Preferably without Ellyn standing over his shoulder ordering him to take it out and protesting his every move.

Grif stepped in between Luke and Ellyn, and she stopped immediately, hands on hips.

"Grif, I can't take this from you—I won't."

"Then I'm paying you for feeding me and nursing me and changing my sheets and—"

"You most certainly are not."

"Why?"

"Why? Because I did that out of...out of friendship."

"Fine, then I'm doing this out of *friendship*." He met her eyes at the last word, and got another jolt from that emotional cocktail.

"Grif, it's not the same."

"You're right. I come out too easy. I figure I would've been in the hospital two, three days, and that's about the cost of three dryers. In fact—Luke? How're you at installing dishwashers?"

Luke's voice was partly muffled by his position behind the dryer, but audible. "I could manage."

"Don't you dare, Grif! That's completely out of the question. I won't—"

Grif wasn't sure if his luck was good or bad when the back door opened to Ben and Meg.

"Grif! You're back!" Ben said with such open joy that Grif felt his throat close. The boy wrapped both arms around his waist and hugged tight. "I knew you'd be back. I knew it was all a lie about you being the one to close up the fort and take the Army away. I've missed you, Grif. You haven't heard about our game last week, and the last kids finally did their presentations and I got an *A* from Mrs. Hammerschmidt for you coming to class, and Bobby got a *B* because he made Daniel do all the work, but me and him are friends again and—boy, there's a lot to tell you."

Unable to stop himself, Grif drew the boy closer with his hands on his shoulders. He'd written them a couple notes each in the ten days, but he hadn't let himself see them. He had to start pulling back from their lives. He had to...

"Hi, Grif."

He looked around to see Meg in the doorway. Wariness and hope warred on her small face. "Hi, Meg."

He stretched out a hand to her before he knew he intended to. But she didn't move.

"Can you stay for dinner, Grif?" Ben asked.

"Don't be stupid, Ben," Meg said before either adult could answer. "Can't you see he's going away again? Just like everybody in town said."

He met Ellyn's eyes. In the telltale sheen there, he saw

pain. In a flash as bright and stunning as lightning, he knew the pain was for him as well as her children.

"Meg—"

He reached for her, but she ducked away and ran past her mother through the kitchen and out of sight.

Ben had backed away from him and now looked up. "Are you, Grif? Are you going away again?"

"I'm going back to Fort Piney," he said evenly. "And eventually, I'm going to close it down. Those are my orders."

"But you could—"

"Ben, don't you have homework?" Ellyn asked, firm but even.

"But, Grif, you—"

"Benjamin."

The boy gave him one more look that Grif feared might bring him to his knees, then headed slowly in the same direction as Meg.

The silence was broken now only by the sounds of Luke working behind him. He didn't look at Ellyn, afraid of what he'd see in her eyes, afraid of what that would do to him.

"Grif—"

"I know. I shouldn't have come. And I shouldn't come back."

"I would never tell you that. You're welcome here anytime. Anytime you can stay for a while."

Then Ellyn left, too.

Grif didn't let himself think as he helped Luke with the final installation steps. Within minutes they were trying it out. And Ellyn finally had a dryer that worked.

They loaded up the old dryer and headed to the home ranch, where Grif had left his car—and had promised Marti he'd stop by. He'd called her as soon as the news about Piney closing was official, but he figured he owed her more than that.

"You coming in?" he asked Luke.

"Nah. I've got some work waiting."

"Well, thanks, Luke." He extended his hand. "I appreciate your help."

The younger man studied him a moment before meeting his grip. "Glad to do it for Ellyn and the two kids. Maybe you'll appreciate some advice, too—don't be a horse's ass."

Grif wouldn't have had anything to say to him even if Luke hadn't turned and walked away then.

Braced for more of the same from his aunt, it was a relief when she merely grilled him about the closing of Fort Piney and his role in it. Only after an hour or so could he start steering the interrogation toward his ideas for Piney's future. When he told her about the community meeting he planned, she gave his forearm a firm attaboy pat.

The pinch between Marti's brows had eased and she was actually starting to look intrigued when the back door opened. Without coming in, Luke Chandler addressed Grif with his usual directness.

"Ellyn needs you. Meg's locked herself in her room. Won't come out."

Chapter Twelve

Ellyn knew it was Grif, not Luke returning, even before she could see him, recognizing something in the rhythm of his movement despite his taking the stairs two at a time.

He gave her a brief, hard hug. "Are you okay?"

She answered in the same low voice he'd used. "I'm fine. Meg's just so upset—"

"Do you want me to break the door in, are you worried she'll hurt herself?"

"No, no. I can't believe she'd… But if it comes to that I can take the door off. But I think it would be better if she came out on her own steam."

The muscles around his mouth shifted as if under other circumstances he might have smiled. "Like the circuit breaker. Nothing for me to do because you have it all taken care of."

"Not hardly. She won't talk to me at all."

He glanced toward the closed door down the hallway. "Ben?"

"He was tired. He's taking a nap." She saw no need to tell him that Ben had cried himself into a deep sleep. "Maybe if you tried to talk to her…?"

His expression stiffened an instant, then slowly relaxed to an unreadable neutral. He didn't meet her eyes as he stepped across the landing to the locked door. He stood there a moment with his head down. When he raised it, he also raised his hand and knocked briskly.

"Meg?" His voice was steady and normal.

"Why are *you* here?"

"Because I'm worried about you. Your Mom—"

"Why? You're not my father."

He winced. His voice gave none of that away. "No, I'm not. But I'm still worried about you. Remember what we talked about up at Leaping Star's overlook?"

"It doesn't matter what I remember, because it was all a lie."

"It wasn't a lie. I love you, Meg."

"Why should I believe you? All the things you said that day—you said you'd always be around for us. But you *lied!*"

"I didn't lie to you, Meg. I told you I would have to leave. I told you I was here just for a while. That I'd have to go back when my leave was over."

"But that was before you started working at Fort Piney. You could be here, you just don't want to be. So you *lied*. You could be here if you loved us like you said you did, but you *don't!*"

"Meg—"

"Go away. I don't want to talk to you. I don't want to talk to anybody."

"Okay, then you can listen."

"No! No, I'm not going to listen to you. Why did you even bother to come back when you're just going to go away again? Everyone goes away. Everyone…" That trailed off into a sob.

"Sometimes people don't have choices about going away, Meg. Remember what we talked about on the overlook, how your dad—"

"My dad had a choice! And now you're just like him. I heard him arguing with Mom about a divorce the night he left." Ellyn covered her mouth with her hand to keep from crying out in recognition of the extra burden Meg had carried all these months. "He said he was going to find something better. Something better than—" another sob broke the next word, but Meg defiantly repeated it in a near shout "—*us.* So go ahead and do the same. We don't need you. I don't need you. I don't need anybody. I'm strong!"

He backed away from the door slowly.

"Grif—"

"This is why, Ellyn. This is... I never wanted to hurt her—any of you. You warned me, and I knew better, but I was too—" She stepped toward him, reaching, but he held out a hand to ward her off. "No. Take care of your daughter."

Ellyn brushed her hand across the top of the headstone where her husband was buried.

In the numbing shock when Dale's death followed so close on the heels of his leaving, Ellyn had gladly agreed to Marti's suggestion that he be buried here on Far Hills Ranch in the plot that held four generations of Suslands as well as ranch hands. Marti had said it would be easier for her and the kids to visit his grave this way.

She hadn't been here since the day of the funeral—not even when the headstone was erected—and she didn't think either of her children had, either.

Maybe they would after last night's long, tear-filled but cleansing talk among the three of them.

Meg had finally opened her door, the timing of it making Ellyn suspect she'd watched Grif drive away, then unlocked the door and fell into her mother's arms in a gale of tears, exclaiming that she'd driven Grif away just as she'd driven her father away—and to his death. Ben emerged from his room, sleepy and rumpled and looking entirely too young and vulnerable to cope with these revelations.

And then she found out Ben had known about Dale leaving all the time, too.

The three of them sat on the landing at the top of the stairs, crying and talking and crying some more, as the secrets came out one by one and turned to dust.

Then they'd talked about Grif. She'd tried to explain what she could of what he faced, hoping they'd understand a little.

Instead they'd given her insights, recounting revelations he'd made to them about his years growing up with a father absent in all ways but the physical.

Closer to midnight than dinnertime, they ate soup in their pajamas around the table, and then they had ice cream with whipped cream on top, and she tucked each of her children in bed as she used to when they were babies.

They all slept in so late that she drove them to school after lunch. And then she came here.

"It's okay, Dale. I know you cared. Not the way I wanted you to, but you cared the way you could. And I want you to know we're all okay now. I'm sorry... I'm sorry we hurt each other. I'm sorry we disappointed each other. I'm sorry you're not going to have another chance the way I do now."

She touched her fingertips to her lips, then brushed them against the letters of his name carved in the stone.

"I will always love you because we created Meg and Ben together. Thank you for them."

No tears dropped, though her eyes were full. She felt lighter somehow. *And right.*

Farther along, she kissed her fingertips and pressed them to the center of another name. "We miss you, Amy."

She moved away and found the other headstone she'd

been seeking, the one in the large grouping of interconnected Suslands, reaching back four generations. She placed a spray of blazing star and long-leaf phlox on the grave, then stepped back, one hand cupping the other.

"I don't suppose you remember me. I would have been just a baby the last time you were at the ranch. I'm Ellyn. Ellyn Neal Sinclair. I love your son. He needs your help. And I need your help, so I can help him."

Marti was waiting for her when she got back to Ridge House. Ellyn poured herself a cup from the fresh pot of coffee Marti had made while she waited, just as Ellyn would have done at the home ranch or at Kendra's.

"Looks like you can use the caffeine," Marti commented as Ellyn sat beside her at the table.

"I can. The kids and I were up late—talking." She'd answered the question behind Marti's statement, now she answered the question in her eyes. "It was good. We'll be okay now."

"And Grif?"

Her eyes teared up so suddenly she had no hope of stopping two from spilling over. "I don't know."

"I thought when the boy came home... *You turn away from my people, so your blood will have no home.*" Marti covered Ellyn's hand in the warmth of mutual comfort, and heaved a sorrowful sigh. "The past isn't always what we think it is."

Ellyn waited for more, but when Marti spoke again, it was in her usual brisk tone.

"I have something for you, Ellyn." Marti took an envelope from her sweater pocket. She stared down at it, making no move to hand it over. "Going through all the old family papers for the special section, at the home ranch and in the archives in Sheridan, got me thinking about more recent history."

She breathed in sharply. "This is my sister Nancy's last

letter to me, before she died. I flew out there. I was with her when she died, but she couldn't say much. When I came home to Far Hills after the funeral, this letter was waiting for me.''

Now she did hold it out, but Ellyn shook her head word-lessly.

"Go ahead," Marti urged. "You read it. Then I'll leave it to you to decide what—if anything—you want to do with it.''

"I can't. This is private...personal."

She'd asked for help, but this...

"It's family," Marti said, placing the envelope in Ellyn's limp hands, then curling her fingers around it. ''You read it.''

Ellyn didn't know how long after Marti left she sat there, with the aging envelope awkwardly held by fingers that felt nerveless. A shudder passed through her, then she walked down the hallway to her bedroom.

She hesitated in front of the bed, then turned away. The old sliding rocker in the corner was strangely absent of folded clothes waiting to be put away. Taking that as an omen, she sat there and extracted the sheets covered by handwriting in blue ballpoint.

Dearest, littlest sister Marti,

Remember how I used to call you that when you were little and you hated it because you wanted to be so grown up? And now you are grown up. So grown up. And now Amy is the littlest and you're the older sister.

It's almost morning, and still sleep won't come. Or I won't let it come. Everything is a balancing act now. How much pain I can bear, how much time I will lose by killing the pain. And there is so much still to do. So much I can't do. Can only ask others to do for me.

Marti, with all you carry and all you've given up to raise Amy and to run dear Far Hills, I ask more of you now. Please look after my Johnny as much as you can. Make sure he has Far Hills in his heart wherever he goes. I worry about him. He's so serious, so good, so grown up. He carries too much weight on his shoulders. I've tried not to add to that weight, but I know I have. I hope he finds a love in this life that will help ease that, help him find joy.

John was here. First, sending Johnny in during visiting hours, then later, when he slipped past the nurses again as he does most nights. I've let him think I was sleeping the other nights. He cries. Tonight I touched him, and he held my hand. And we both cried. Oh, Marti, I regret so much, but mostly I regret that I could not have been a better wife, a better love to John. He has so much to give, and he doesn't believe it. And I didn't know enough then to teach him how to believe, I didn't know enough to overcome what his father did to him. If you could see the scars, Marti, you'd start to understand. And to my shame, in my frustration and anger and hurt I've even thrown that monster up to him, as if he were somehow responsible for what that vile man did.

I made it so much harder for him to give, when I should have been making it easier. I didn't know any of that until this disease became part of my life. It finally made me grow up. Maybe now, if I had the time… But there is no time, and I must accept that. I wish he could. I am grateful we can touch again.

I don't ask you to look out for John, because I know he won't let anyone do that. That's the worst of this dying—fearing what it will do to John, and Johnny. But I've complained of John so much—too often, I fear from my own selfishness and insecurity—that I wanted you to remember this, too, when I'm gone. To know I love him.

I love you, Marti—always my dearest, littlest sister.

I drift so much these hours, not awake, not yet gone, and in that time always I'm home with everyone at Far Hills.
Love, Nancy

Ellyn rocked as the tears came, wrapping her arms around herself and feeling the pain. The pain of Nancy Susland Griffin. But even more, feeling the pain of those who suffered when she died. For Marti, who'd lost a dear sister. For Grif, who'd lost a beloved mother. For John Griffin Senior, who'd lost his love and his chance at living.

The tears and the rocking motion slowed to a stop.

She carefully ordered the sheets and folded the letter along the old creases, then returned it to its envelope.

...I'll leave it to you to decide what—if anything—you want to do with it...

She'd asked Nancy Griffin to help her help Grif. And the letter had arrived. A letter that told of opportunities lost. Of a woman who wished she'd been stronger, a woman who wished she hadn't squandered her chance to love a difficult but good man.

Maybe Grif *was* like his father. He certainly needed to learn how to believe that he had much to give.

If she showed the letter to Grif would he see that the burden of blame between his parents was not so one-sided, that the *should-haves and shouldn't-haves* were not so clearly divided, that the story wasn't entirely as he'd believed it, and the outcome had never been preordained?

Would he see that *their* story wasn't preordained?

Would he see that even if he was exactly like his father, that things could be different for them? Because they would have time. Because she was a different woman from Nancy. She'd already grown up, matured not by disease, but by troubles and time.

A figure burst through the door of Colonel John Griffin Junior's office, with the sergeant who was supposed to prevent such interruptions trailing behind making sounds like a fish.

"What the hell is this?"

For a fraction of a second, Grif's own words brought the memory of General Pulaski using very similar words when he'd entered another office not so long ago. But this figure had no papers, and looked nothing like the barrel-chested, bald officer.

It was Ellyn, hair wisping around her face, cheeks flushed and eyes bright with challenge and something else.

He didn't try to squirm out from under her look, but returned it as he dismissed the sergeant in a tone that reminded him of his failure yet suspended retribution.

"I know you're a busy man, Colonel Griffin—" She slapped her palms on the desk and leaned forward. The scoop neck of her top gaped, revealing the ivory silk curves of the tops of her breasts as well as a fragment of lace. She couldn't know the view her position gave him, could she? "Especially with that community meeting about the closing of Piney tomorrow night, which you didn't bother to tell me about when you and Luke were hijacking my old dryer, and exercising your strategy."

He'd fully intended to tell her, until things went so wrong so fast.

"Ellyn—"

"But that's not why I'm here today."

Why was she here? Here, where he never would have envisioned her. He'd kept the special segment of his life where Ellyn, Meg and Ben, and a few others resided so rigorously separated from the military existence that took up most of his life, that he could barely accept this reality. She was here, at an Army base, in the commanding officer's office—his office—with him in uniform and doing his military duty.

"I have something to say to you. Something I need to say."

Her voice made a remarkable transformation during those two sentences, going from chastising to tender.

"I understand your being scared, Grif. I'm scared, too. But you know what they say about heroes? They're the ones who go ahead and do something even when they're scared. So I'm about to be a hero."

She drew in a breath, and he wanted nothing more than to put his mouth over hers and capture that breath when it came out, take it deep inside him, as if to capture some part of her in him.

"I love you, Grif. I love John Griffin Junior. I have loved you most of my life, but the way I love you now... It's not the way I loved you as a girl. It's not the way I loved you as a friend, though both of those are part of what I feel now."

"Ellyn, I've told you—"

"I know what you've told me, and I know it's crap."

She couldn't have thrown him more off balance if she'd landed a punch to his solar plexus.

"You say you're not suited to dealing with a family. You say you are like your father. I say look at the facts. I say look at how you've acted with Meg and Ben—all their lives you've been honest with them, kept your promises and cared. That's what a father—a *good* father does. And me?" Her voice dropped. "You've been my friend, you've been my lover. I could never ask for more than that you continue to be both of those all my life."

He was glad this happened surrounded by the accoutrements of his Army life, where he was used to keeping his responses dispassionate, no matter how passionate the cause. "And if you're wrong and I'm right? Then what? Meg and Ben get kicked in the teeth again? You said it yourself, Ellyn, they can't take that right now. Neither can you, sweetheart."

Sweetheart was a tactical error. He saw it in her eyes. Worse, he felt it in his gut.

But she gave no quarter.

She started shaking her head even before she spoke. "You're a coward. You're afraid to give it a chance."

He slowly rose. At least it made her straighten so he was no longer distracted by that gap. "I won't gamble with the welfare of those two kids—or you. If that makes me a coward, I'm a coward."

"Okay, Grif." She looked at him directly, with great calm and a faint glint in her eyes as if she knew he needed the desk between them. "But I'm not going anywhere. And you're not going anywhere. At least for a while. In the meantime, I think you should read this."

And now she did put something on his desk, placing it gently instead of slapping it down. A single envelope yellowed with age.

"Read it, and consider that maybe you've been wrong. That maybe what you're so afraid of isn't that the kids and I might get hurt, but that we'll start feeling about you the way you've felt about your father. And that's why you don't think you're suited to being a husband and father, because you're afraid of being judged the way you've judged John Griffin Senior.

"You told me up on Leaping Star's overlook not to worry about your petty grievances about your dad. Something about that kept nagging at me. Finally I got it. Grievances come from a form of grief. You're grieving, too, Grif, just like Meg and Ben. Only you've been doing it for a long, long time.

"So read this letter, and then consider that maybe you have to let yourself forgive and even love your father before you can think about taking on his roles as a father and a husband."

Her voice cracked at the final word. He clenched his fists

to keep from reaching for her. He dropped his head to keep her from seeing how much he wanted to reach for her.

The envelope stared up at him, the faded writing legible enough to read the address, the handwriting taunting him with its familiarity.

"How did you get this, Ellyn?"

He looked up, but where she'd been standing was empty. A hammer of loss pounded his heart with two painful blows before he saw her at the door, watching him.

"That doesn't really matter. You know, you've made a couple tactical errors in this battle, Colonel."

"Yeah, what're they?" His voice was raw, but he kept it steady.

"You taught me about strategy." He could almost hear an echo of *dirty, underhanded maneuvering* in the faintest edge of amusement that touched her voice even as she said words he knew she meant in absolute seriousness. "And you helped me believe in myself. And I believe with all my heart that you'll come to believe in yourself, too. You'll be a hero, Grif."

Grif sat alone, out of sight in the darkened staff office, watching the people of Far Hills file into the library to hear what he had to say. Looking to him for guidance.

That was a joke. Him giving anybody guidance when all it took was a letter from out of the past to make him wonder if he'd known anything his entire life.

He hadn't let himself read that letter until he'd finished the day's work. As it was he hadn't been his most productive with Ellyn's words and image haunting his every second. The letter made it worse.

Sometime after midnight, he'd driven to Far Hills Ranch. One light showed in the back of Kendra and Daniel's house, but Ridge House was dark. Everyone there safe and sound in their beds. Ellyn...in *their* bed, alone.

He'd forced himself to drive on, parked without paying

much heed, then started walking. Sometime after the moon set, he stopped. He sat on a low rise overlooking a creek. It wasn't until dawn grayed the night skies that he realized he'd found the spot where they used to have summer campfires.

He couldn't remember a complete, coherent thought from the long night, just flashes of memories and images. He'd certainly reached no conclusions, made no decisions before a quick cold shower and a cup of scalding, strong coffee started him on a workday that hadn't stopped for a second until now.

Ellyn came in to the library, with the kids behind her. She looked around—for him, he was certain of it. Then she sighed, deep enough to raise and drop her breasts. His hands tingled as if they'd rested on her soft, smooth skin and absorbed that movement.

An echo filtered into his mind, and he recognized it as his own words to Dale about what a fool he'd be to give up this woman and these kids. And now it was all offered to him. The family he loved, the life he'd dreamed about, and never thought could be his. All he had to do was accept it.

But would that be what was best for them?

"This doesn't have to be the end," Grif told the people of Far Hills in concluding his official announcement of the decision to close Fort Piney. "It can be the beginning."

Ellyn wished he would make eye contact with her so she could make him see that his statement could apply to him as well as to Fort Piney. But he had studiously avoided looking at where she sat, with Meg and Ben beside her.

"Of what? Some big promotion for you?" jeered a voice from somewhere behind her in the audience.

Ellyn shifted in her folding chair. That was so unfair. Almost any assignment Grif could have taken would have been better for his career. And he could have sat in his office and issued reports, met with a delegation, insulated himself from the people and their sense of betrayal. He could have done that—except he couldn't, because it wouldn't have been Grif.

Couldn't the people of this community see that? Couldn't they see how tired he was? How heart weary?

"A beginning of new ways of using Fort Piney," Grif was saying evenly. A discontented mutter rose, and Grif raised his voice. "The Army's leaving, but it's not taking the buildings or the airstrip or any of the other facilities. The question is what Far Hills wants to do with them. Let them crumble and decay? Or try to make something of them?"

"Like what?"

Ellyn felt a surge of hope so strong at those words that she didn't know if it was her own or if she'd sensed Grif's.

"I'm glad you asked that, Roberta." Grif's faint smile at the local postmistress and his laid-back drawl drew a reaction. Nothing as overt as a smile or a chuckle, but a faint easing of tension. As if a few minds might have opened a crack.

"I've been talking to Daniel Delligatti about the search and rescue operation. It needs room to grow. It—"

"You told *him* and kept the rest of us in the dark?" demanded Helen Solsong from the front row.

"No." Grif's tone left no doubt. "My conversations with Daniel Delligatti were in general terms about search and rescue. He told me the operation needs a bigger facility— for planes and for housing volunteers during training. Fort Piney has both of those. We talked this morning for the first time about how one could help the other. Daniel, will you tell them what we talked about?"

Daniel Delligatti stood from a spot about three rows back on the left side. Ellyn also saw Kendra, Marti and Fran nearby.

Daniel nodded to Grif, then looked around at the faces

in the audience. "The colonel filled me in on how an Army base like Fort Piney can get turned over to civilian authorities. I've got the application right here that he gave me for a grant that would help us finance refitting a couple of buildings for search and rescue's needs." He held up a sheaf of papers and gave them a rueful frown. "Looks like I'll be doing a lot of paperwork the next few weeks."

That drew a ripple of laughter as Daniel sat down.

As the sound ebbed, Grif called on their state senator to talk about a proposal for a state highway patrol barracks and auxiliary training facility at Fort Piney. A buzz rose as the audience speculated on how that could help the local economy.

"That's fine, if the Army will cooperate and turn it over to us," said Ed Bressler from the back. "But why should it?"

"The Army will cooperate," said Grif. "The Army's aware how closings affect communities and has been trying to make them less traumatic. A fort closed in Maryland a few years back has been turned into a high tech center, with the Army's cooperation."

"High tech? I don't know if there'd be call for that around here."

"Maybe not," Grif acknowledged. "But how about other uses. Like—"

"A college. That would be good." That came from Rufus Trent, who ran the tiny local airport.

"A prison," volunteered a balding man from the other side, "I felt like I was in prison when I was in the Army, anyway."

A flurry of other suggestions followed, including a children's summer camp, a church retreat facility and an equestrian center.

Grif let the ideas flow for nearly half an hour before taking control of the meeting once more. He outlined the phases the closing would follow, as well as a preliminary timetable.

"As the community and your leaders decide which projects to pursue, I will work with you to the best of my ability. I've been assured that barring emergencies, I will remain in command here through this process. And—" Grif's eyes flickered to Ellyn then away before she could read their expression "—when Piney closes, I expect to be retiring from the Army so I'll be in a position to continue to help the transition."

As Grif concluded his comments and ended the meeting Ellyn felt as if her body had become a static shell, left behind while her heart went soaring somewhere up toward the roof.

He was staying. *Staying!*

He'd said over and over that the Army and a family didn't mix, but now he was leaving the Army. He was putting aside the uniform that to him symbolized what separated him from the possibilities of home and family. Oh, John Griffin Junior might think he was doing this only to help the community or even to help her and the kids from a "safe" distance, but she knew better. His certainty that he was not cut out to be a husband and father had developed a major crack. She'd keep working on that crack until it was wide enough to let her in or him out. No matter how long it took.

"Mom?"

The young voice, with the slightest tremble to it, jolted Ellyn out of her daze.

Both her children were staring at her. The three of them were the only ones still seated. The rest of the audience was filing out the library doors, picking up information sheets Grif had provided. Grif himself was putting papers into his briefcase, while a private stowed the charts Grif had used in a carrying case.

Without knowing if she meant to leave or go to Grif, she stood.

"Mom? Grif's staying because of Fort Piney? Forever?"

She looked down at Ben's puzzled face. "I don't know about forever, but certainly for a while."

"But…but why would he stay for the fort, but not for us?"

"Oh, Ben, it's not that he's staying for the fort and not us. It's not a matter of…" She heard Grif close his brief-case. Not even aware of Ben's question. How would he react to it? Would he start to understand what she'd been telling him? "You know, Ben. I can tell you what I think, but if you really want to know, you would need to ask Grif that question."

Ben immediately spun around to face the front of the room. "Grif!"

He paused, then clicked the briefcase's locks before he turned his head. "Yes, Ben."

"I wanna ask you something."

Could Grif hear the anxiety in that young voice?

"Okay, Ben."

"You're staying? Even when Fort Piney isn't a fort any-more?"

"That's right. Because I can help Far Hills."

"But…but you told us you couldn't stay, so…so how come…?"

Meg stood beside her brother. "How come you'd stay for the town, but not for us? You said you loved *us*."

Ellyn was aware of the private beating a strategic retreat out the side door. Absolute silence squeezed the otherwise empty room.

Grif looked from Meg to Ben, then met her gaze.

"Ellyn—"

"You're the only one who can answer, Grif. If you think they deserve an answer."

He stared at her hard, then strode toward them down the

aisle between the seats until he was a yard from Meg and Ben. He crouched down.

"I do love you. Don't either of you ever doubt that." For a second, his eyes flickered to Ellyn, then returned to the faces of her children. "But some men shouldn't have families, or—"

"Why not?" Ben interrupted

"Because they're in prison or they run off all the time, like that puppy of Billy's that keeps digging under the fence," explained his sister, delving into the wisdom of her ten years.

"Oh." Ben considered that, then turned again to the apparently speechless Grif. "But you don't do any of those things."

"No, I don't. But those aren't the only reasons. I would give everything I have to be the kind of man who could settle down in a place like this with you—all of you. But some men aren't meant for that kind of life."

Ben's brows knit. "But we've been like your family. You've been doing everything like a father would, so how come you're worried that you can't do it, when you already have?"

Ellyn bit her lip to keep from whooping. Ah, the ruthless logic of children.

But Grif had been making this argument to himself for a long time, and it would take more than that to knock it apart. "This has only been a short time, Ben. Remember how I told you about my father? He's the only person I had to watch for learning how to be a husband or father, and he was a failure at both, so—"

"Maybe he didn't get enough of a chance," Ellyn protested, and saw in the glance he gave her that the same doubt had opened another large crack in his certainty. "Maybe if your mom had been around things would have been different."

And then another voice blindsided Grif from the other side.

"That doesn't make any sense about your father, Grif," Meg said sternly. "You told us about him, but he didn't ever take you riding, did he?"

"No. But—"

"Did he play baseball with you or take you to soccer sign-ups or talk about when you were feeling sad or make you do your homework or go to school for your class like you did for Ben's? Did he?"

"No, but—"

"So it doesn't matter about him being a role model because you're not like him," Meg declared triumphantly.

Grif looked from Meg to Ben and back, then up at her. "Ellyn—"

"I didn't coach them. They're just smart enough to see what I've been telling you all along. You know, for a man who maintains he's not cut out for this, you've helped each of us—Ben with his loneliness, Meg with her anger and me..." She knew memories of their loving were in her eyes—she knew because she could see them reflected in his. "With my doubts."

"So you could come live with us forever," Ben said, apparently feeling this was all settled. He added in a burst of generosity, "You can stay in my room, but you'd have to get your own bed."

"Don't be stupid, Ben. If he came to live with us, Grif and Mom would have to get married, and he'd stay in *her* room, and they'd have a bed together," Meg concluded in a tone that made the thought flash through Ellyn's otherwise preoccupied mind that she should have a certain talk with her daughter soon. "If they want to—and they'll only want to if they love each other."

Ben immediately looked up at Ellyn. "Do you, Mom? Do you love Grif?"

She parted her lips, intending a speech about how this

was one of those complicated issues that adults should sort out in private. Instead a single, choked word came out. "Yes."

Grif stared up at her, his intense gray eyes seeming to melt. Before she could do any more than commit that look to memory, her son turned his attention on Grif. "Do you love Mom, Grif?"

"I've loved your Mom as long as I've known her, Ben."

"Great! Then—"

"No, stupid, it's not great," Meg declared. "He's known her since they were kids, so that doesn't mean anything."

"It doesn't?" Ben demanded of Grif.

"It means a lot, but Meg's right, Ben. It's not that simple. It's… It's… Look, I'm not very good at words, and—"

"That's okay, Grif," Ben assured him with his usual cut-to-the-chase honesty. "Mom always says actions speak louder than words. But I'll tell you anyhow, I love you, Grif."

Tears filled Ellyn's eyes. This conversation had been an emotional roller coaster unlike any she had ridden, and all she could do was hold on for dear life—and for the dear love of the three people in front of her.

As if by agreement, they all looked at Meg. Her mouth worked, but no words came. Then, a single tear tracked down her smooth cheek, gently caught at her jawline by Grif's thumb.

"I love you, too, Grif."

"Meggie…"

With a sob she threw both arms around his neck. As Ellyn wrapped her arms around Ben's shoulders from behind, her own tears spilled over.

Over the heads of her children, she met the burning gray look of John Griffin Junior, and in that look, she saw her future. A future with this man who knew so little about his own goodness. But was beginning to believe. She and Meg and Ben would show him, reflecting back to him the glow of his heart, until he understood completely.

Ben's squirming brought her back to the present. "You're leaking on my head, Mom!"

Meg, whose sobs had subsided, turned and started to giggle.

Grif stood, still not breaking the look between them.

"Meg, Ben, I'd like you to go out to your car. Your mom and I have something to talk about."

She was aware of the kids looking at her, and she nodded. Even after the door had thudded to silence behind them, she and Grif remained where they stood.

She suddenly felt a little shy under the beam of his intensity, even though she had fought so hard to turn it on.

"Will you marry me, Ellyn?"

"Grif, you don't have to—"

"I do have to, or your kids will want to know the reason why."

He smiled. Then he took two steps toward her, the familiar strength of his face drawing near as he bent closer to her. Desire and love silvered his eyes.

He cupped her face between his large palms, and kissed her. Soft and slow. She wrapped her fingers around his wrist and parted her lips. Under her fingers, she felt the surge in his pulse. They leaned into each other, the kiss became neither soft nor slow, pressing against each other until they both were left gasping for air.

"Yes, yes, I do have to. Ah, Ellyn...marry me. Help me be a hero."

"Yes."

Epilogue

"Ellyn, if you and Grif don't get going, you're going to miss your flight," Kendra warned for the second time.

They had stopped by to say goodbye before they left on their week-long honeymoon in San Francisco, and had discovered a crowd. Not only Meg and Ben, who'd started their stay a day early so the newlyweds could fulfill a wish to spend their wedding night in *their* bed at Ridge House, but Marti, Emily, Fran and Luke.

"I know, I know. It's just... If you think the kids are going to be too much for you, you'd say, wouldn't you?"

"Absolutely. But they won't be. We'll have a fine time."

"Besides," said Daniel, "it'll be good for us having more kids around. A little practice before the real thing."

"I suppose, but— Are you?" Ellyn looked from Kendra to Daniel and back. "You are! Why didn't you tell me? How long? When are you due? What—"

"If we answer all your questions, you really will be late. I didn't tell you because I wasn't sure until the past couple of weeks, and you had enough to keep you occupied with the wedding and the end of school and all. The baby is due in seven months.''

That of course called for hugs all around before Kendra called the group to order. ''Now, you two go have a wonderful time, and think about a little Griffin playmate for this Delligatti-to-be.''

''I like the sound of that,'' approved Marti.

''I thought you would.'' Kendra hugged her aunt.

''The laughter of children at Far Hills.'' Marti looked at Kendra and Daniel, then to Ellyn and Grif. ''Kendra's no longer alone, and Grif has a true home. Maybe—''

''Don't start on that legend stuff, Marti,'' Luke objected. ''Besides, the third part's about being lost, but you've run out of Suslands, and nobody's lost.''

''Don't be so sure.''

Marti refused to say more, and the press to reach Billings on time for their flight took precedence. But on the airplane, settling in after takeoff, Ellyn decided she wasn't ready to discount Marti or the legend.

She glanced over at her husband and saw him smiling— that sweet smile in a face some might otherwise call stern, that showed his heart had been truly rescued.

''What are you smiling about, Grif?'' Though she knew, because she was smiling right back at him.

''You know I'm looking forward to this. This trip. Being alone with you.'' He leaned closer and kissed her softly. With his lips brushing against hers, he added, ''Getting a start on making babies with you. Which better start soon, because I'm having a hard time keeping my hands off you. I should have known I'd used up all my self-control in that regard when I first got to Far Hills. Hell, I couldn't even keep my hands off your clothes.''

''My clothes? You mean—?'' She moved back enough to look into his eyes. They told her the answer, but she still had to ask. ''My jeans? Touching my jeans.''

Deeper color pushed across his tan cheeks, but neither his grin nor his eyes faltered. "You thought that was an accident?"

"I thought I was imagining things!"

"You were. You were imagining just what I was imagining. But we don't have to imagine anymore." He settled back against the seat, looking as contented as she'd ever seen him. "And after we finish having babies and raising them with Meg and Ben, then I'm looking forward to being home at Far Hills, and growing old with you."

She put her hand to his cheek. "Yes, we'll go home and we'll grow old together." She grinned, his answering grin beginning even before she finished. "But first...I *did* bring a pair of jeans along."

* * * * *

*Watch for Luke Chandler's
story in*

HIDDEN IN A HEARTBEAT

*the final book in Patricia McLinn's
exciting miniseries*

A PLACE CALLED HOME.

*On sale in October
from Silhouette Special Edition.*

*And now for a sneak preview of
HIDDEN IN A HEARTBEAT,
please turn the page.*

Chapter One

He'd *have* to pay attention to her now.

Rebecca Dahlgren smoothed her tailored jacket and skirt, then pushed her hair behind her ears again in a futile attempt to control the wind-teased strands.

The man she'd tracked to this field eighteen minutes ago finally stopped the tractor cutting neat stripes in the long brown grass, exposing rusty-looking Wyoming earth. He'd seen her when she arrived, giving her a single, brief survey, from head to toe. He'd shown no inclination to pause his work, but now there did not appear to be a single blade left.

Now she'd have her chance.

He descended from the machine, moving with a smooth, confident stride to where the tractor connected to the even bigger machine that had rolled the grass—hay, she supposed—and deposited it in big rounds.

As she approached, walking on the balls of her feet so the heels of her pumps didn't sink into the clinging dirt, she saw him shifting levers, the movement emphasizing the muscles across his shoulders and back that the thin material of his faded plaid shirt did little to hide. Slightly bent over his task, the worn material of his equally faded jeans stretched taut over hard, rounded—

"Stand back," he barked.

She halted so abruptly that both heels sank into the dirt.

He flipped another lever and the hay rolled out the back of the second machine, raising a cloud of dust. He locked up more levers then strode toward the front of the tractor, where she stood. The front of his jeans were worn nearly white, making the zipper area and what was under it stand out in stark contrast. Her throat was suddenly desperately dry. Must be the wind, she decided. She licked her lips.

She shifted her weight, pulling one heel free from the clinging dirt, only to sink the other one deeper.

"Is it okay now?"

From his movement, she thought he flicked her a look, but she couldn't see his eyes under the brown cowboy hat. What she could see were a narrow nose that might have been perfect before it lost an encounter with a fist or some other immovable object and a jaw too square for strict good looks. A thin scar started just below the left corner of his mouth and hooked under his jaw like a misplaced dimple. Stubble all around it made it stand out in stark relief.

"Yeah." There was something warm and a little rough in that syllable—or in her imagination.

"Thank you. I'm—"

He kept walking, even with her, then past her, toward the gate and the lane where her car stood. To talk to him, she had to pry her heels loose, turn and follow.

And to talk to him was the reason she'd been standing heel-deep in dirt while the wind pelted the area beneath her skirt's dignified below-the-knee hem with grit until she feared her shins would resemble the surface of a golf ball.

The sensation was not conducive to being charming. And

she very much wanted to charm the man in the cowboy hat, jeans, boots and tough work gloves.

Because she wanted something from this Luke Chandler, foreman of Far Hills Ranch.

She needed something from Luke Chandler.

She intended to get it.

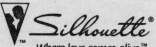

If you enjoyed what you just read,
then we've got an offer you can't resist!

Take 2 bestselling love stories FREE!

Plus get a FREE surprise gift!

Clip this page and mail it to Silhouette Reader Service™

IN U.S.A.
3010 Walden Ave.
P.O. Box 1867
Buffalo, N.Y. 14240-1867

IN CANADA
P.O. Box 609
Fort Erie, Ontario
L2A 5X3

YES! Please send me 2 free Silhouette Special Edition® novels and my free surprise gift. Then send me 6 brand-new novels every month, which I will receive months before they're available in stores. In the U.S.A., bill me at the bargain price of $3.80 plus 25¢ delivery per book and applicable sales tax, if any*. In Canada, bill me at the bargain price of $4.21 plus 25¢ delivery per book and applicable taxes**. That's the complete price and a savings of at least 10% off the cover prices—what a great deal! I understand that accepting the 2 free books and gift places me under no obligation ever to buy any books. I can always return a shipment and cancel at any time. Even if I never buy another book from Silhouette, the 2 free books and gift are mine to keep forever. So why not take us up on our invitation. You'll be glad you did!

235 SEN C224
335 SEN C225

Name	(PLEASE PRINT)	
Address	Apt.#	
City	State/Prov.	Zip/Postal Code

* Terms and prices subject to change without notice. Sales tax applicable in N.Y.
** Canadian residents will be charged applicable provincial taxes and GST.
  All orders subject to approval. Offer limited to one per household.
  ® are registered trademarks of Harlequin Enterprises Limited.

SPED00   ©1998 Harlequin Enterprises Limited

Desire celebrates Silhouette's 20ᵗʰ anniversary in grand style!

Don't miss:

• *The Dakota Man* by Joan Hohl
Another unforgettable MAN OF THE MONTH
On sale October 2000

• *Marriage Prey* by Annette Broadrick
Her special anniversary title!
On sale November 2000

• *Slow Fever* by Cait London
Part of her new miniseries FREEDOM VALLEY
On sale December 2000

Plus:

FORTUNE'S CHILDREN: THE GROOMS
On sale August through December 2000
Exciting new titles from Leanne Banks, Kathryn Jensen,
Shawna Delacorte, Caroline Cross and Peggy Moreland

Every woman wants to be loved…
BODY & SOUL
Desire's highly sensuous new promotion features stories
from Jennifer Greene, Anne Marie Winston
and Dixie Browning!

Available at your favorite retail outlet.

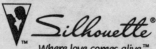

Silhouette®

SPECIAL EDITION®

COMING NEXT MONTH

#1351 BACHELOR'S BABY PROMISE—Barbara McMahon
That's My Baby!
Jared Montgomery wasn't looking for love—until the tall, dark and handsome geologist fell for the blue-eyed beauty he hired to watch his baby girl. Could the winsome ways of nurturing schoolteacher Jenny Stratford transform this most stubborn of bachelors?

#1352 MARRYING A DELACOURT—Sherryl Woods
And Baby Makes Three: The Delacourts of Texas
Strong-willed Grace Foster had left the dashing but difficult Michael Delacourt when she'd realized he was married to his job. Now, to win her back, he was going to have to prove that love was his most important mission of all.

#1353 MILLIONAIRE TAKES A BRIDE—Pamela Toth
Here Come the Brides
When charming rogue Ryan Noble set his mind on taking a bride, he did just that. Trouble was, he claimed Sarah Daniels…the wrong twin! To make matters worse, his *un*intended bride's irresistible allure was stealing *his* heart.

#1354 A BUNDLE OF MIRACLES—Amy Frazier
Rugged police chief Ben Chase built an impenetrable exterior after his beloved Abbie Latham left town without explanation. Only a miracle could reunite these two soul mates separated by a painful secret. Was the bundled-up baby on Abbie's doorstep the sign they'd been waiting for?

#1355 HIDDEN IN A HEARTBEAT—Patricia McLinn
A Place Called Home
Primly proper Rebecca Dahlgren came to Wyoming to learn about her Native American heritage—not to fall for some irksome cattle rancher. But Luke Chandler's powerful presence and passionate kisses were arousing desires she couldn't ignore!

#1356 STRANGER IN A SMALL TOWN—Ann Roth
Single mom Alison O'Hara was struggling to make ends meet when brooding stranger Clint Strong became her new tenant. A few fiery embraces stirred up feelings she'd forgotten existed. But while Alison might have opened the door to her home, would she welome him into her heart?

CMN0900